Tenuous State

Tenuous State

A Tale of Survival in the West

A Novel

William Charland

SUNSTONE PRESS

SANTA FE

NOTES ON PRONUCUATION

Ocotillo: oh-koh-TEE-yo

Florida: flo-REE-da (Spanish for "flowery," re: the Florida Mountains on page 180)

Sunstone books may be purchased for educational, business, or sales promotional use. For information please write: Special Markets Department, Sunstone Press, P.O. Box 2321, Santa Fe, New Mexico 87504-2321.

Book and cover design › Vicki Ahl
Body typeface › California FB
Printed on acid-free paper
∞
eBook 978-1-61139-557-0

Library of Congress Cataloging-in-Publication Data

Names: Charland, William A., 1937- author.
Title: Tenuous state : a tale of survival in the west : a novel / by William
  Charland.
Description: Santa Fe : Sunstone Press, 2018.
Identifiers: LCCN 2018017630 (print) | LCCN 2018019555 (ebook) | ISBN
  9781611395570 () | ISBN 9781632932310 (softcover : alk. paper)
Classification: LCC PS3603.H37638 (ebook) | LCC PS3603.H37638 T46 2018
  (print) | DDC 813/.6--dc23
LC record available at https://lccn.loc.gov/2018017630

WWW.SUNSTONEPRESS.COM
SUNSTONE PRESS / POST OFFICE BOX 2321 / SANTA FE, NM 87504-2321 /USA
(505) 988-4418 / ORDERS ONLY (800) 243-5644 / FAX (505) 988-1025

In
Memory
of
Professor Laurence Cummings
Department of English
Yankton College

Preface

Time passes. Somewhere between the fall semester of 1961 when I took on my first assignment in higher education while still a graduate student, and the spring semester of 2011 when in retirement I finally left, somehow fifty years passed. Today, were you to ask me how the field has changed in that half-century, I might suggest you sit down and listen to a couple of incidents that have always impressed me. In fact, if you don't mind, I'll tell them to you now.

From the early 1960s: In the fall semester of their senior year at a liberal arts college in Wisconsin, two students who had performed as a married couple in a school play evidently got carried away in their connubial roles. Caught in the act by a patrolman one night in a nearby state park, they were suspended from school and not permitted to graduate with their class.

From about 2010: A state legislature decided to revise its funding formula, no longer paying state-supported universities by the numbers of students they enrolled in their courses, but for the numbers who completed them. In response, one of the schools came up with a plan to pay cash bonuses to instructors for the numbers of students they retained in their classes.

If you ask what that means, I'll say while those may sound like two isolated incidents, they feel representative of two eras to me. I imagine few present-day college administrators would feel like enforcing that early 1960s policy, while just as few back then could conceive of taking part in the 2010 gambit. If my experience is any guide, it seems the profession of higher education has undergone a sea change, from a world where colleges were called upon to maintain a stable social order to an environment of survival with no holds barred.

Ask me what has led to this transition and you'll find I'm less interested in any sort of academic analysis, than in trying to capture the texture and flavor of life in this field. What has it been like, working with students, coping with administrative policies, day after day, as the ground beneath the industry has shifted?

That's the thrust of my story. In setting out to tell it, I settled on a place that's become familiar to me toward the end of my career, a half-Hispanic school that I love in southwest New Mexico. That setting will be immediately apparent to those who know it. But the drama itself should be recognizable to anyone who knows anything about colleges or is interested in human relations across the board. For this is a work of fiction, not tied to any current events, and the characters have a life of their own.

One of the issues at stake in this sort of place is uniqueness in an age of uniformity. What does it take for a school that is a little bit different to thrive in that difference and throw off any forces that would compromise its life?

I owe much to a number of people who helped me bring this book to life. Two college friends, Paul Heffron and Dick Graham, both PhDs, served as sounding boards as I crafted this story a fragment at a time, often uncertain where it was going. Their support and criticism were invaluable. I also appreciated three early readers of the manuscript: Sandra Griffin, Howie Morales, and Felipe Ortego—colleagues for whom I have great respect.

—William Charland

"Finally, this is better, that one do his own task as he may—even though he fail—than take tasks not his own, though they seem good. To die performing duty is no ill, but who seeks other roads shall wander still."

—Bhagavad Gita

1

1994

It blew up my world. And, like most explosive moments, it showed up incognito—shrouded in a fog of everydayness. The Clinton era was a quiet time to be a teenager in America, in a suburb of Cincinnati that was equal parts affluent and boring. I grew up there from grade school: stay-at-home mom, dad with a middle-management career in some corporate headquarters. Same commute, year after year. From what I could tell, he kept the same job, something in finance.

An only child, I interacted a lot with adults and heard about his life from an early age. Same talk around the dinner table, night after night, same frustrations. When my parents had friends over, the conversations sounded the same. No one had any complaints about their lifestyle. Everyone had everything. But it was the monotony that got to them, I guess. A pervasive lack of purpose. As a kid, I might have felt a bit sorry for them, experiencing such frustrations. Then, in time, I grew impatient. I was tired of all this complaining. Why couldn't they get their lives together?

Meanwhile, I trekked through high school, though to what end I was never sure. I liked to read, but not the kind of stuff they gave us in classes, so I didn't do particularly well. The school was large and status-driven. A lot of kids I'd known in grade school seemed to disappear in those crowded halls with the bells and buzzers. They seemed to just fall through the cracks.

But I had two resources, and I survived. One was my steady girlfriend, Jenny: "a trim, tailored lass," my mother would say (read: spindly), who liked me well enough to make out—within limits—for hours on end. The operative word was "limits." In the years we were together, whenever I became moderately aroused, she could be counted on to come up for air, push my hand away, and breathe the same word into my ear. That word was "someday."

My other gift came in junior high school when I agreed to start guitar lessons in order to get out of playing the piano. I took to the instrument, playing along to popular music of the day, and found I had a pretty good voice. All of that led to a garage band that performed at dances all over, and a way to be noticed without knocking myself out academically.

So it went, well into my senior year: dates with Jenny, gigs with the band, punctuated by occasional visits to class, enough to stay on track toward graduation. Until the morning I was standing out in front of our house, waiting for a ride to school, when I noticed that the garage door was down. As he drove off for work, my father always left it up.

I walked in the front door and began to smell the fumes. The garage was a cloud, Dad slumped over the steering wheel, and a message on the briefcase beside him. It was a note of two words and a question mark: "The Point?"

I suppose I never got over the shock, a kid in his teens coming upon a scene like that. Part of it left me with a sense of guilt—why hadn't I listened to him?—and an anxiety disorder: a lifelong case of the jitters. But my other reaction was to try to find a path and a purpose for myself. I made it through my senior year, applied to a church-related college, and resolved to look for some sort of meaning in life, pretty much anywhere I could find it. Sometime in my sophomore year, without knowing much about what it entailed, I decided to enter the ministry.

2002

Fast forward eight years to my first job out of seminary, in a small city in the Midwest. A down-to-earth place with a history of manufacturing that had not yet exited the country. A lot of blue-collar workers—twenty bars on the main street—and white-collar managers, many of whom belonged to the mainstream Protestant church where I signed on as assistant minister.

It's worth noting that Jenny was with me. After an on-again-off-again relationship that had somehow survived our college years and into graduate school, we had tied the knot before setting out into the world at large. Was this a tight bond, long as it had lasted? More to follow.

The ministry on which I embarked was fairly clear in my own mind. Much as I had intended toward the end of high school, I wanted to help people find meaning in their lives. It was as simple as that. But the theology I brought was not. It was the product of seven years' study: three years each of Greek and Hebrew. At the end of all that, although there was little in the Bible that I believed to be literally true, I understood a lot about its cultural moorings. The origins of the Hebrews, for example (hapiru in ancient Egyptian meant simply "a wanderer"). I knew that their deity, Yahweh, had come on the scene as a war god, rallying these lost souls into something like a tribe.

Ask me almost anything about the Bible and I could give you the cultural context. The virgin birth? Why, it was the custom among Palestinians around Jesus' time for a couple to live together in a state of "betrothal" until the woman became pregnant. That was the time for marriage. Mary and Joseph were people of their day.

The problem with all of this theological sophistication, I discovered, was that most folks in my congregation had not much interest in it—nor, indeed, in religious questions of any kind. What they were into was a sense of belonging. For them, the church was a social organization.

Sterling Holmes, the senior minister to whom I reported, understood the business of his profession very well. Sterling was a scholarly sort of man with a somewhat quavering voice who looked like an aging poet. He had a silvery beard and hair that flowed out behind his head and wound around a bald spot on top. He was the son and grandson of Ivy League professors, a vocation he must have considered seriously at one time. But there was something about the immediacy of interacting with people in the ministry, outside a classroom, that appealed to him.

True to his academic origins, Sterling was extremely methodical. He prepared his sermons carefully and always prayed thoughtfully over this event or that. But he was most methodical when it came to the events themselves.

Sterling carried a small black notebook in which he recorded everything in his work life. His pastoral calls, for example: he kept track of them like a box score—not so much the needs he encountered nor the subjects discussed, but the fact that he'd been there. If a parishioner were found lying comatose in the hospital, he marked off the call and left a business card.

He was big on church holidays and once took out his book to show me the attendance figures for Easter the year before. "Now, this year," he told me, "we're going to have the ushers set out ten fewer chairs for each service. That way, if the same number turn up, they'll be scrambling to bring out more chairs. And people will believe that the church is growing."

It didn't take long for me to find I needed to come up with something about the ministry that I could believe in, and I knew it wasn't church management. I gravitated toward the cause of social justice.

Why I took this direction, I don't know. I'd never been much of an activist in college or seminary. But there was something that led me to want to put things right. And, in this little city, I found plenty to attend to. Soon I was teaching a course for migrants on English as a Second Language, picketing a local clothing store on behalf of decent wages for Third World garment workers, lobbying for a municipal recycling program. My days were filled with phone calls, my evenings with meetings. Once a month or so, Sterling asked me to give the sermon and I invariably addressed one of my causes.

For Jenny, my burgeoning career as a social activist was a mixed blessing. She seemed to enjoy my lofty status as a minister, someone professionally committed to decency. True, I wasn't home a lot, and we kept deferring plans to start a family, too busy for that. She was into a career of her own, as a first grade teacher and reading specialist. "Someday," she would whisper in my ear, as in high school, although now it was in the aftermath of protected sex.

Sterling, for his part, supported my endeavors, as long as the events I held were well attended. He did require me to make pastoral calls—as a kind of marketing campaign. I would take a stack of cards that visitors filled out at our services and look these people up during the week. And that was how I met Lisa.

Critical incidents are often innocuous. That's something else I've noted: especially in marriage. Jenny and I were coming home from an evening out. "Well, it's scarcely any wonder that Brian stopped telling his story the minute you walked in the room," she started.

"He thinks I can't take an off-color joke? I'm supposed to be some kind of virgin?"

"Oh, you're worldly enough. No doubt, the way you drink. But what did you talk about all night? Some cause. You always do. Anymore, you're some kind of Puritan in plain clothes."

"That's about what they wore," I offered, wryly. "I'd be right in style."

But tensions had been building "Those sermons! They're like college lectures."

It was not that I minded criticism. In a way, I sought it out, always spoiling for a fight. But not from Jenny. Our relationship went back so far, well into high school. Maybe everyone's teen years are like that. Psychologists write about the "reminiscence bump," the way our memories from adolescence are weighted— more vivid than those from any other time of life. That part was natural.

But mine were exceptional: of a girl who had cared for me, held me while I cried when my father had died and I'd found him that way. That's the kind of bond you never lose, no matter where your paths may take you. And ours had diverged: into the airy realms of speculative theology on the one hand and the rudiments of elementary education on the other.

And yet, here we were, still together. Joined at the hip. More than anything, it was the sermons that got her. "You know, life is not all that complex, Connor. God is love, Jesus is our friend, and the church is a fellowship. Didn't they teach you that in school?"

In weak moments, I'd thought of returning to the mainstream form of ministry I'd been hired for. But it was getting more bizarre. Sterling was into sacraments of everyday living. Not just weddings and funerals, but blessing this or that. The Blessing of the Beasts: not just dogs and cats but chickens and geese that were destined for dinner. A goat was hauled up into the chancel where he was so moved by the ceremony that he soiled the carpet. Next, it was The Blessing of the Backpacks when it was time for school. No way was I having any of that.

And so it was back to pastoral calling. Slowly, I became more invested in the process—not so much as a tool to recruit new church members, but as a simple slice of life, a way to get in touch with the raw material of humanity. It may have been my youth, or the fact that I seemed to be feeling out what I was doing, but something unusual began to happen. People started sharing all sorts of stories— about themselves, but even more about one another.

I visited a young woman who told me about her husband's extramarital affair, with the president of our Ladies' Aide. Another described the unusual relationship a friend of hers was in with the minister of another church in our denomination, how she went all over with him, as president of the congregation— his wife at home—sometimes on overnight conferences.

One day, I responded to a call from a middle-aged parishioner who'd welcomed me in her housecoat, pulled down all the shades, and invited me to join her on the couch. I had enough sense to decline, but the incident stayed in my mind, along with others. Enthralled by this fervid underworld of Sterling's congregation, I slowly realized that I was beginning to give up on my own life and thrive on those of others. I was starting to live vicariously.

"Deformacion professional." The phrase in French would translate directly into English if we ever thought to use it. Professional deformation: the ways our lives can become skewed by the work we do. Nowhere is it more fitting than in the religious professions.

A fellow I knew in seminary was a young Catholic priest. One night he got drunk and shouted down the bar that he'd give up the priesthood, except that it would ruin his sex life. We all roared, thinking he meant losing out on intercourse. But after a couple of years in the ministry, I wasn't so sure. Where else can you find more scintillating sex—assuming you're a voyeur—than in the confessional or on pastoral calls?

Soon I found myself praying a verse from Psalm 51. "Create in me a clean heart, O God, and renew a right spirit within me." The act became almost involuntary—later I would learn to call it a mantra—as I encountered one salacious revelation after another. I began to wonder how long I could keep my head above water in the course of my pristine career in the clergy. As it happened, I didn't have long to find out.

It was another sermon, that's all I recall. Something about Third World wages, all the people living on less than two dollars a day. The number of shirts in our closets produced by those working twelve-hour days; I'd counted twenty-six in mine. I could do this by rote and sometimes seemed to watch myself in the pulpit. As I vaguely remember, the parishioners who filed out after the service were of two minds. Some smiled as they shook my hand, others looked aside.

What I do remember clearly was an attractive woman, about our age, who seemed genuinely enthused about what I'd had to say. She was blond, like Jenny, but with fuller hair and—for this I felt guilty—a fuller figure 'neath her blouse. She handed me her visitor's card and leaned in with a murmured, "Call me."

That night, Jenny muttered, "Like a lecture" as she trundled down the hall to her bedroom. It had been some weeks since we'd slept together. Next morning, I took out the visitor's card I'd kept in my pocket and called up Lisa Nordeen. She was in her office at the local community college when I called on her the following day.

"What a good lecture," she said, and told me how she and her husband, Ned, a chemical engineer, had moved here from Rochester where he'd lost his job at Kodak and come to work in a local paper processing plant. "You go where the jobs are," she said sadly, for she'd had to give up her own at the University of Rochester. Now she was consigned to teaching sociology at the two-year college level.

"But I'd love to have you come in as a guest lecturer," she went on. "It's a course in current social problems."

And that's the way it began. I'd come in every two weeks or so and share my latest insights into whatever ailed the world. In between times, we'd meet for coffee, sometimes lunch.

I recall running into John Trumble, at the restaurant one day, the minister who traveled about with the woman who was president of his congregation. He was ordering hot milk. "I've taken to this at night, when my sins get the better of me," he confided. "Now I drink it all the time." He glanced at Lisa, who was going out the front door, and looked back at me with a cryptic smile.

One day John called in an upbeat mood and asked me to lunch. He handed me a flyer on a new form of worship he'd come upon at one of his conferences—the House Church. It was a way of ministering to disaffected church-goers, he told me, a sort of throwback to the early Church, small groups gathering in members' homes. He said the House Church could take many forms, sometimes opening with a prayer or short talk followed by an open forum. Or, one could go deeper into the interpersonal. He showed me a book that had been recommended at the conference: Enriching Relationships. The author was a pop psychologist.

Jenny was skeptical at first. What was wrong with the church as organized? But I encouraged her to give it a try. I invited a few other couples, including Lisa and Ned Nordeen. I knew their marriage had taken a beating what with the relocation and her demotion to teaching at the community college. Maybe we could all minister to one another. There was little to lose, from what I could see.

The House Church met every couple of weeks, and the first few gatherings were like a cocktail party without the cocktails. John's wife was somewhat sullen, even though he'd had the good sense not to invite the president of his congregation. Jenny was uncharacteristically quiet, as was Ned who seemed lost in one of his chemical calculations.

It was about the third session when John pulled out the psychologist's book and led us in a few exercises. The one I remember was a communal back rub. First, we massaged the shoulders of our partners—Jenny was as pliant as a hardwood floor—and then went around the circle. It was all quite mundane, until when I got to Lisa and something exploded. The energy between us was powerful and mysterious as she rose to meet my touch and I probed her. "Electric" is a word that comes to mind, and it would not be an overstatement.

I'm not sure anyone else recognized what had gone on, as we all said our good nights, but the two of us did, and the following week we began an affair. Not that we met often, only odd afternoons in a motel 30 miles out of town, or occasional sessions on the couch in my office at the church. I recorded them in my calendar as "pastoral therapy," and they certainly worked for me. Gloria in excelsis: glory on high. Sex in excelsis. I'd never felt so high.

After a time, of course, reality intruded. There were her school-aged children. She hadn't moved halfway across the country and given up her academic career to abandon them. And, when it came right down to it, Ned was not so stable. His world was his lab and, outside of that, he struggled. Now and then, "Create in me a clean heart…" would echo in my head.

Still, we might have gone on for quite a while: my lectures in her classes, our private tutorials. Until one night about nine o'clock I got a call from Ned who said he had something he'd like to share with me. He asked me to meet him in an hour on the Elm Street Bridge over the Wolf River. It was an unusual place and time, but just outside his office at the paper mill.

I was halfway across the bridge, two hundred feet above the swirling water, when I saw the door to Ned's office open and he came lumbering out—a big, Nordic guy with a diffident smile. Now he wore a puzzled frown as he walked slowly toward me. When he was right up on me, maybe two feet away, his eyes went wild. He suddenly lunged forward, and I jerked back. Then he pulled away and staggered over to the side of the bridge. For some reason, I followed him.

I watched him lean over the railing, from right behind. Some kind of dark spirit seemed to be rising within me, higher and higher, until, for an instant, everything went black. Then the whole scene started to swirl like the river. I felt myself suspended somewhere above us as I watched him raise his hands, look up once toward the heavens, then suddenly pitch headfirst over the side. I leaned over the railing, saw him crash into the water and disappear. I stifled a mad impulse to dive in after him, but took out my cell phone and called the police instead.

Later, they found a note on his desk, two words and an exclamation mark: MY MINISTER! Fortunately, the police also found Ned, hooked on a branch at a crook in the river, two hundred yards downstream. He was taken to the hospital, where he went in and out of a coma for some time. I went to see him once while he was lying there unconscious and just left my business card. I couldn't think of what to say. I'm told he was released a week later.

In my second brush with suicide, I found release as well. I went home that night and told Jenny of my affair. Perhaps I shouldn't have been surprised that she, too, had a confession—something to do with the principal of her elementary school. I don't remember anything clearly after that. Nor could I piece together what I might have seen on the bridge, exactly how Ned had gone over. But I do recall submitting my resignation the next day, packing up, and moving far away to Atlanta where the following fall I would enroll in graduate school.

I suppose if there was something gained in my two-year ministerial career, it was that I found a kind of comfort in a classroom. I would not change fields, in a way, but pursue my calling on a broader plane, studying other faiths while hoping to find a home for my own spirit.

At least that was the plan.

In the rolling hills of southwest New Mexico, there is a broad valley dotted with trees and laced with streams. Coveted for precious minerals—the first Spanish mine, in Santa Rita, dates from the 1700s—this land was a sacred site for the nomadic Warm Springs Apaches who held tribal meetings and buried their dead there.

For centuries, the Apaches warred for the land with Mexicans and Americans alike, until their legendary chief, Geronimo, surrendered in 1881. Meanwhile, a town sprang up in the valley and became a commercial center for the region. First settled by the Spaniards, it would come to be dominated by wealthy Anglos from the East, while remaining half-Hispanic.

The history of this settlement was marked by violence, not only with the Apaches, but ne'er-do-wells within as well. A gunslinger served as sheriff. Billy the Kid was raised and first arrested there. We shall call the town by its original name: San Vicente.

In 1895, only fourteen years following the defeat of the Apaches and perhaps a decade after the sheriff's last gun battle on the main street, the people of San Vicente saw fit to create a college on the hills west of town. Founded on the frontier, it has teetered on the edge of academe to the present day.

They spent some time wrangling over what to call the new institution. The state had suggested "Normal School," since that's what everyone called colleges to prepare teachers. Well, that didn't fly. "Ain't nothing 'normal' about our situation out here," one and all agreed.

Then they considered naming it for one of their number, and feelings ran so high that for a time it seemed another gunfight might ensue. Finally, Marge Ellis, a stout lady who ran a house of "soiled doves" down at the end of main street, took the floor. Marge stood somewhat apart from the upper class in town but she was known to have acquired a measure of book learning in whatever it was she'd done before.

"Why not name it for a cactus?" she proposed. "Some of them are tougher than any of us and more beautiful when they bloom. Have you ever stopped out west of here to take in the Ocotillo: those long, wiry stems with the blazing red bloom at the end?"

"Ocote," murmured Juan Esteve, an Hispanic rancher. "Ocotillo from 'ocote.' It's Español for flame."

"They were here before we got here," Marge continued. "They'll be here long after we're gone, carrying that flame." And so it was settled. The school was Ocotillo College, to be upgraded in time to Ocotillo University, which was quite a mouthful. So everyone would know it as Ocotillo U.

2

I stumbled out of the admin building and grabbed for my sunglasses. Quarter-to-ten in the Southwest, and the sun was blinding. But I was glad for the walk across campus and a chance to clear my head. From Alice Pendergast, for one thing. My elderly, inherited secretary had barely nodded as I'd told her where I was going: head down, nose to computer screen. Sometimes I wondered if there was something in my genes that nettled her, but maybe it was nothing more than that I was not President Driscoll: that he no longer doubled as dean.

There was more I was glad to be free of, if only for a five-minute trek among the hoary old buildings, the statues, and the trees. It was a break in my calendar on a typical Monday morning. Driscoll had cautioned me about the life of a dean. He said it was not unlike that of a dentist: eight appointments per day, and every one associated with pain.

Clarissa Cox had been first on the slate: head of the residence halls, sparkling blonde, mid-thirties—and a party to what had all the indications of an incipient, bloody divorce. Clarissa had settled back in her chair, a strand of hair sidling across her left eye, and half smiled as she'd asked for a semester's leave. She allowed as how she needed to take her son and get away for a while. But there may have been more to it, she'd hinted, and I'd left it alone. Six months into this job, I was beginning to learn not to ask too many questions. That was another of the ex-prexy's maxims: always leave one question unasked, and therefore unanswered.

Still, the conversation nagged me as I trudged along. Why was she afraid of losing custody of the kid? When she'd left, she was no longer smiling.

The door to the auditorium was open but the lights were off. For once I was early, and as I stepped inside the darkness enfolded me like a blanket. In fifteen minutes, the place would be buzzing with faculty, department chairs, computer techs, even maintenance workers and maybe a few students. All of them craning for a look at the four stalwarts who thought they wanted to become the next president of the university.

I took my usual seat in the center section, way up toward the back. "An academic isolate," Wiley Crane of the history department had called me, one night after a couple of beers. "Far from the madding crowd," he'd snickered.

I sat there in the dark and wondered whether anyone would climb up the stairs and join me. But it was only a fleeting thought. Huddling in their coteries—the fund-raisers and the historians, the physicists and the food service—I knew they'd all burrow in with their buddies. Anxiously eyeing the presidential candidates, any one of whom might bolster their careers or else send them into free fall; in a small town where there were no other jobs as good as these. They'd be peering at the candidates like a clutch of bats at the mouth of Carlsbad Caverns.

No, I would be alone. I was sure of that. I half-listened to the susurration as the lights came on and the others flooded in. And I considered a final question, not for the first time. Am I sitting alone because I'm the dean? Or am I the dean because I'm so separate from the rest?

Manny Moreno stepped up to the microphone and cleared his throat, as the auditorium fell silent. He was a barrel-chested fellow with a bald head and a ready smile. It seemed that Manny had played defensive tackle for the university and, in his mid 50s, he looked as though he might suit up still. But these days he was a banker: vice president for community relations, it was said. He looked like the kind of Hispanic that any non-profit organization in town would kill to have as a board member. But he'd been loyal to his alma mater and to Walter Driscoll, the ex-president, in particular. Now it seemed he was still on board, wherever Doctor Driscoll might be.

Reading from a script in a resonant voice, he introduced the first presidential candidate. Then he stood aside and led a round of polite applause as a tall, graying man stepped forward. According to Moreno's notes, this was Wilmont Slade, educational consultant for a Washington D.C. firm I'd never heard of.

Slade smiled at the audience, and fluttered a wave. He wore a dark blue suit, starched white shirt, and a rep tie striped in purple and gold, the university colors. He began by introducing his wife who was sitting in the front row, along with one of his daughters, and he said there was another. He summarized his career in academe—a few deanships along with a couple of presidencies. The past five years, he'd been flying all around the country as a consultant.

"So why am I here?" He paused and took a moment to survey the audience with a wide-eyed grin. "Well, to me, life's an adventure—fortunately Hannah, here, shares my philosophy—and, frankly, I'm up for something new." He smoothed the front lock of his silvered hair. It was molded and massive, encircling his head in something between a coiffure and a military helmet.

He called for questions and a woman from the admissions office stood up and asked about his position on nepotism. "What would you say about a school where people get away with employing relatives, sometimes in their own department?" she offered in a shaky voice.

Slade paused a moment. "Well," he reflected, "You know, there's my wife and my two daughters to look out for. But after that, why, that's it..."

There was a rumble of laughter from the audience, as the director of admissions and the university registrar slowly got to their feet and walked out.

How long had I been sitting there? After a while, I noticed that the auditorium had cleared. I heard a cacophony out in the hall. Coffee break: now I remembered. There'd be ten minutes or so before the presentation by the second candidate. Still, I stayed in my seat, feeling queasy. What was it? I couldn't tell. Finally, I made my way slowly down the stairs and out into the hallway.

"Well, I'm just glad to have tenure. That's all I can say." It was Edna French from the sociology department. "Who knows what a fellow like that could have up his sleeve?"

A skein of female colleagues snuggled around her, murmuring and nodding. "Imagine how the administrators must feel," said Sarah Joyce from humanities. "That small print in their contracts..." Somebody poked her arm and she spun around, almost butting into me.

I smiled and nodded on my way to the coffee urn. There were pastries on the table, but I didn't feel hungry. "Off the tenure track." "Employed at will." I remembered the rhetoric precisely, and my anxiety snapped into place as outright fear. Damn that Driscoll, and me for signing that contract. I poured a cream and three sugars into my coffee, which I always took black. Back in the corner of the lobby, I stood there and stirred it around and around.

Out of the corner of my eye, I saw Wiley Crane break away from some guys in history. He grabbed me by the arm. "Snap out of it, dude." He leaned in, his back to the covey of women who had fallen silent. He was smiling as he shook his head. "Joe Slick is here for one reason. Can't you tell? He's marketing his consulting practice."

Candidate two was a study in contrast—an elderly Hispanic gentleman who came from a large, urban university in the next state where he served as something like vice president for diversity and community relations. He was well-dressed but not spiffed up like the Washington consultant. This fellow looked more like a well-paid, senior professor. Or somebody's uncle.

He told us how, if he took on this job, he would spend his first six months simply walking around campus and talking with everyone he could find. That had been the secret of his successful career, he suggested. He'd got to know people throughout his institution, so that when the lid blew off some festering grievance and threatened to explode into violence, why, he knew all the major players by name and could calm them down. "Tranquila!" one could hear him advising a mob of firebrand Latinos: blood-red bandanas, greasy locks, brandishing placards. "Paciencia!" Whatever else he might offer in the way of academic credentials, you had to hand it to the man. He was soothing.

So much so that before long I was slumping in my seat, my eyelids closing, in deep repose. I found myself lapsing into a kind of languid reverie, the half-trance where I'd been spending a lot of time. And the scenes that preceded my becoming a dean began to play in my mind: that fateful day in the classroom and the meeting afterward in Doctor Driscoll's office.

Compared to the perplexities of my previous profession, up to this point I had found college teaching a balm to the soul. The role of professor offered a certain amount of structure—something I'd found lacking during my two years as a minister—but it allowed for freedom as well. And teaching religion and philosophy seemed to fit me well, not just because I'd studied the subject matter to death but because it dealt with the same big issues of the ministry. One night over a couple of beers, a classmate in doctoral studies had said it well. "You know, teaching is my way of being social, and teaching philosophy is my way of being religious."

I had been excited to get a job offer from Ocotillo U. It was a job in academe, for one thing; a number of my fellow doctoral grads were driving cabs, laying drywall, or racing up and down a throughway, moonlighting as adjunct faculty at three or four community colleges. But here was a job in my field, as well! I set out to engage my students in the exciting adventure of exploring the Big Picture.

Until I began to realize that most of the students in my classes were there to fulfill a requirement in humanities, and that the word in the dorms was that, based on the reputation of my predecessor, religion and philosophy courses were something of a cruise. So I began experimenting with teaching styles. There I'd be with a slug of football players, slouching in their chairs in the back rows, a mélange of run-of-the-mill students in the middle of the classroom, and a few eager beavers up front. I noticed that some of them looked very young.

I would lecture for twenty minutes or so, pointing out which pearls of my wisdom were likely to appear on the next exam. Then I'd write a quotation related to the subject matter up on the blackboard. "What do you make of this?" I'd ask, and stop talking. The silence could go on for five or ten minutes, but I'd sit there, ensconced in a space of my own.

Until finally one of the students would speak, usually someone in the front row, and sometimes that would start an exchange among some of the rest. This particular day—it was an eight a.m. class on The Bible as Literature—I'd expected a long spate of silence, possibly interspersed by snoring. So I wrote out a quote that I thought might get a rise out of them if they could wake up enough to make it out.

> "God has taken his place in the divine council;
> in the midst of the gods he holds judgment:
> 'How long will you judge unjustly
> and show partiality to the wicked?
>   You are gods, sons of the Most High, all of you;
> but you shall die like men,
> and fall like princes.'"

As expected, it was a long time before anybody spoke. Finally, I chimed in. "Who is speaking here?" I asked. A little girl in the front row raised her hand. My heavens, some of these kids were so polite. And young. This kid had no breasts to speak of, her hair in pigtails, and blotches of acne under a layer of Clearasil. She looked barely pubescent.

"Why, God is speaking," she offered.

"That's right," I responded, enthusiastically. "And who is being addressed? To whom is God speaking?"

The little girl thought for a moment and then slowly began to turn pale. "Why, it seems to be other gods." She looked up and frowned. "If I may ask, where did you get this passage? Is it from the Bible?"

I offered a paternal smile. "Yes, indeed. It's from Psalm eighty-two. Does it surprise you that the Bible sometimes contains references to more than one deity?"

She looked down and shook her head. "Is it saying there's more than one God?" Her ashen face folded into a frown. "And that's in the Bible?"

The bell rang and, with more spirit than they'd shown all hour, my students all rose to their feet and headed for the exit. The little girl seemed to lag behind them for a moment. I thought I might invite her to come by and talk some more. Scanning my seating chart, I searched out her name. But when I looked up again, she was gone.

Later that afternoon the phone rang in my office. It was Alice Pendergast, executive secretary to Walter Driscoll. Her voice was officious, even, and low. "The president asks that you come to his office," she said. "He told me to tell you that he's waiting." She hung up.

I had met Doctor Driscoll only a few times but had often seen him on campus. He was a squat, stocky fellow somewhere in his mid-60s. He had a shock of white hair, a ruddy face, and a ready smile. An unrelenting extravert, he hosted an open house for faculty and staff every Wednesday morning. "Donuts With Driscoll," they all called it. It was a time for everyone to come and share their concerns.

Walking up to the president's office for the first time, I noticed that the gilded sign on the door read "Walter Driscoll, PhD, President and Dean of the Faculty." Now, I hadn't been around many colleges but this was my first look at a man who was both president and dean.

There was a small anteroom inside the front door and there sat little Polly Pringle; I now knew her name. She looked straight ahead as I took the next chair. Her textbook for the religion class was on her lap and, on top of that, a Bible. I could hear a loud conversation in the president's office, then silence as Alice Pendergast knocked on the door and opened it.

The fellow sitting across the desk from Walter Driscoll was a middle-aged, corn-fed sort in a plaid shirt and striped tie who looked like he'd stepped off a farm. He, too, had a Bible and he wielded it like a weapon. If Driscoll's cheeks held a healthy glow, this man's face was flushed the color of cranberries. Driscoll introduced him as "the Reverend Buford Schneuter, Pastor of the Harvest Fellowship."

The cleric grasped my hand like an ax handle and, dispensing with any "Howdies," got right to the point. "Young girl from my congregation—I'm her pastor, you know. She looks to me for spiritual guidance, and it seems she signed up for this here course you're teaching on The Bible as Literature. Whatever that might mean.

"So here she is at my study door, just before lunch, and she's been crying. Little girl like that, barely sixteen—and she tells me what you been teachin' her. Pole-aye-thism in the Bible. 'What's that about?' she's asking me, and now I'm asking you. What are you doing, messing with the heads of youngsters like that?"

I took a chair and caught Driscoll out of the corner of my eye. The president was staring out the window and he looked a bit bemused. If he didn't care to join the Reverend Schneuter in his frontal attack on a member of his faculty, it was clear that he wasn't a part of the defense team, either.

I began to feel a surge of irritation and a sense of being catapulted back in time. In the two years I'd spent in the ministry, I'd become all too familiar with this kind of sanctimonious blowhard. These idiots were all over the map: burning copies of the Koran, buying up copies of pornographic magazines down at the bus station ostensibly to dispose of them, preaching a preposterous doctrine of creationism—the earth little more than a few thousand years old. I had always felt embarrassed to be lumped in the same profession as people like this. Now here I was, a full-fledged college professor, safely ensconced in the Ivory Tower. But here was another textbook ignoramus, pounding at the gate, back to harass me.

I thought for a moment, looked down, and measured my response. "Well, you raise an interesting question, Mr. Schneuter," I began.

"That's 'Reverend Schneuter,'" the pastor advised me.

Helpless, I felt my anger rustle. "Sir, the word 'Reverend' is an adjective. It's like 'Honorable'—as in 'the Honorable Judge Brown.' You wouldn't say 'Honorable Brown,' would you? As a member of a profession, it's always helpful if you know what to call yourself."

I caught a glimpse of Walter Driscoll, still looking out the window, with a sly grin.

"Now, the word is 'polytheism,'" I went on, "and it does indeed occur in the Bible, chiefly in the Old Testament, but some believe there's also an instance of it in the New Testament. Still, that's not what we're really here to discuss, do I have that right?"

"Fancy talk—guess that's what we can expect from a college perfessor. No, sir, you are correct. The reason I'm here is that you upset a young child of sixteen, a member of my congregation, with these here theories you're putting in these kids' heads. Got her all unsettled, and what's the point of that?"

"You mean by causing her to think? I always thought that was the aim of a college education."

"But a child of sixteen?" The minister's complexion had toned down, but it was flaring up again.

"Who is enrolled in a university," I retorted. "I wonder if that's not a good part of our disagreement here." I turned to President Driscoll. "I noticed the letters 'CE' on the class roster, next to this student's name, and a couple of others. Can you tell us what..."

"'Concurrently Enrolled,'" Driscoll muttered, no longer smiling. "It means she's still enrolled in high school, but eligible to take college courses. In time, you'll find it's a mounting trend in higher education these days, a growth sector."

And that was basically the end of the consultation. The Reverend Schneuter left with Polly Pringle in tow and without, to my relief, another crushing handshake. The next day, I received a note from Alice Pendergast, indicating that Polly had withdrawn from The Bible as Literature. She also set another appointment with the president, for the following week.

Only six months ago, I reflected, as I shook my head and came to attention. But it seemed an eternity since that dust-up with the local Billy Graham. I knew it was the last time I had said what I thought or felt on this campus without pulling it up by the roots, turning it over in my mind a dozen times. I shuddered.

I was seated even higher in the banked chairs of the auditorium the next morning, possibly distancing myself even further from the others. Or maybe just to watch them more clearly. It seemed there was something different about the clustering of faculty and staff, and at first I didn't get it. The sociologists were spread all over. So were the professors in English, the historians, the cooks and servers of the dining hall staff.

Then suddenly I saw it. The females and males had segregated into different groups. And the women were seated toward the front.

"Ms. Linda Lucero," announced Manny Moreno, "Our next candidate for president of the university." He gave her name an ethnic pronunciation, "Leenda," and slowly took a seat in the front row as he looked her up and down. I had heard about this woman, a firebrand who headed up a community college in San Carlos, the small city two hours away. That college had been growing like kudzu, and President Lucero was in the papers every Sunday: meeting with alumni, hobnobbing with business leaders, leaning on a shovel at the ground breaking for yet another new facility. She'd been riding the crest of an avalanche in enrollment.

Linda Lucero took a moment to shuffle her notes and adjust the microphone while Manny turned aside slightly from the candidate, as if to expunge some ignoble thoughts. Then suddenly he swung around full circle and raised his head. What was it, a kink in his neck? No, he seemed to be looking at something in the back of the hall. I turned to follow Moreno's gaze, all the way up to the projection booth. That's when I thought I saw a shadow move.

Linda looked up with a bright, Latina smile and beamed at the assembled faculty and staff all across the auditorium, perhaps lingering a bit on her compatriots in the front rows. She was a sleek, shapely woman in a dark pants suit that managed to cling to her form. A large turquoise pin splayed across her left breast. She wore her black hair long and it glistened.

She seemed very poised, until she leaned into the microphone and launched into her prepared remarks. Then, as soon as she spoke, she began to quiver. It wasn't stage fright, I could tell; her voice was plenty strong. It seemed a kind of primal energy, a pent-up force that kept trying to penetrate and race ahead of whatever she had to say.

"And I need to tell you of all the excitement in San Carlos, the gains we've made—the modern, new facilities, the leap in enrollment. Why just last week..." The words spewed out with the force of a fire hose. One triumph after the next, and then more. Linda Lucero was an Energizer Bunny in a business suit. It was as though she had ingested a coiled spring.

Finally, she paused and took a sip of water. She looked up with a wry smile. "I should tell you that I'm like this, night and day," she confided. "We're going to be very busy, you and I." The applause was electric, mostly from the women in the front rows. Some were cheering.

3

lice Pendergast was glued to her monitor as I walked by toward my office. She gave a half-glance in my direction and thrust out a half-dozen pink slips with phone messages along with a typed page with the calendar for my day. As it happened, I kept my calendar on my own computer, but I conformed to her routine. She'd been doing her job this way for twenty years, and if President Driscoll followed the drill, I sensed at this point I'd better do the same. It must have been years since I'd seen those pink phone slips.

Alice was a stolid woman with gray hair and horn-rimmed glasses. She looked like somebody's grandmother but, beyond that, I would have had no idea of her age, if I'd thought about it. While I'd sometimes seen her flushed and animated, talking with friends and colleagues on the phone, it seemed she never spoke to me except when her job required it. Mostly that was to pass on forms she'd filled out that needed nothing more than my signature. Sometimes it seemed that if I and every other administrator at Ocotillo U were to retire, die, or be felled by the flu, Alice would have no difficulty running the school.

I sat and shuffled my messages for a few minutes, considering who had called and why. Then I tried to put them all out of my mind. I shut my eyes and settled into a familiar kind of meditation. Whatever it was called—Samadhi would do—it was a way of turning inward, in absorbed concentration on the reality of the present moment. "A state of cessation, wiping consciousness clean." Those were Buddhist terms I'd learned in graduate school. More and more, they'd taken the space of the Christian concepts that once had filled my life.

Now I found myself fighting to fix my mind on the present, focusing on a certain shaft of light that glistened on my desktop. Grappling with my Tanha, the thirst or cravings of ordinary life: the natural state that Christians call "original sin." "This five-fold mass which is based on grasping...the lust that lingers longingly now here, now there." That's what Buddha said and it spoke to me. I had lusts and cravings that scared the hell out of me, several times a day.

Well, whatever this existential contest was called—Jihad in Islam—I recognized that I was losing it. No way could I pursue anything as abstract as spiritual enlightenment this morning. That Linda Lucero had struck a nerve, suffused me with dread. My God, what if she became president of Ocotillo U! Would she fire me the first week? Even worse, suppose she kept me on.

I had put "Leenda" aside and once again tried to concentrate on the bar of light, when the phone rang. I shook my head and slowly reached for the receiver, although I sensed who it was before I picked it up, and why she was calling. "Yes, of course," I told Manny Moreno's secretary. "I'll clear my calendar this afternoon. Whenever it's convenient, I'll see her."

No sooner had I put the receiver down when a buzzer on my desk went off twice in succession. I sprang to attention like Pavlov's dog, my road to Shambala crumbled to dust. It was a signal from Alice Pendergast: my ten o'clock appointment had arrived.

Nancy McBride was an adjunct faculty member in the English department. I had seen her once or twice but we'd never spoken. She was one of the active retirees, I was told, who turned up in college towns and looked to help out at the college. These people had graduate degrees and often teaching experience. Usually they were pretty easy to work with, the president had observed. They had no career ambitions and generally didn't complain about the low salaries offered to adjuncts. "Hell," Driscoll said, "most of 'em would do this for nothing."

So why was Nancy here?

She was a tall, willowy woman—dark hair streaked with gray. Her outfit was casual, but carefully coordinated: a solid cardigan sweater with matching plaid skirt. Unlike the women on the regular faculty at Ocotillo U who dressed like graduate students in a second-hand store, Nancy might have been dolled up for a club meeting or an afternoon at bridge.

"I thank you for fitting me into your schedule, Dean. It's busy, I'm sure, and I won't take up much of your time. It's just a question I have about some of the students here." She seemed somewhat wide-eyed and ingenuous. There was a kind of innocence about her.

She went on to tell of teaching as an adjunct faculty member at a large, private university back East. It had made use of her master's degree in English and was something she'd always enjoyed: connecting with the students, facilitating discussions. She'd always found them stimulating. When her husband, Ed, had announced he was ready to retire and give up the winters of Rhode Island, she'd suggested they find a small college town in the Southwest. So here they were, and she was back in the classroom.

I smiled and nodded, though wary inside. I knew there was more.

"Well, it's the students here," Nancy McBride went on. "They're..."

I sat in silence.

"It's that they're..."

I nodded again.

"You know, this isn't easy to say—but I sometimes wonder why they're here. I assign them material, but I don't think they read very much. Frankly, I'm not sure some of them can."

"Is this a developmental course you're teaching?"

"Yes, and I wasn't sure what that term meant. I saw there were a lot of them listed in the catalog, so I asked one of the other instructors. It means they're not ready for college—is that right?"

I nodded.

"Well, that's all right. I'd be glad to try to help them. But is that what they want? I do my best to involve them all in discussions. The other day I reached out to an older man who seemed especially separate from the rest. They'd been asked to read something about 'McCarthyism' and the younger students seemed to have no idea what that meant.

"So, I called on him. I said, 'Ralph, perhaps you remember that time in American history.' And, do you know what he said? 'Oh yeah, isn't that when General McCarthy stood up to President Truman over the war in Korea and Truman fired him?'"

I tried my best to keep a straight face, but lost the battle and snorted.

Nancy smiled and shook her head. "I asked him to stay for a moment after class. Being older, I thought he might be easier to talk with, maybe find out why he's here...And it was instructive, I must say."

"What did he tell you?"

"Well," she continued, "Ralph had plenty to say. He went on and on, but not about school. No, it was his ranch and how it was failing. And federal financial aid—how much he was able to get every month, as long as he was enrolled here. Then suddenly a light went on. I asked about the other students: how many of them were getting paid to go to school..."

We sat in silence for a long time, as I struggled with a shock of recognition. I tried to get some distance, thinking of what the Buddhists would call this kind of experience: Satori, the moment of awakening; Bodhi, the realization of enlightenment. Maybe this was it, not so much an intellectual insight as a visceral reaction. Clearly, something had me by the entrails.

As Nancy McBride went out the door, once again the double buzzer sounded. I hadn't realized how long she'd been here. Now it was eleven, time for my next appointment. I checked my calendar. It was someone I'd never met, yet the name seemed to ring a bell: Ernesto Morales, expressive arts department.

I had a modest grasp of Spanish, and a word sprang into my consciousness as Morales walked in: varon—i.e., "male" as in "masculine" with a touch of macho. He was a well-built fellow, about average height, with a full head of slicked-back, black hair. He greeted me with a grip one might expect from a man twice his size. In all, he might have been intimidating, except for a gaping grin that showed off a rack of glistening white teeth.

"Call me 'Ernie,'" he declared, and he fell into a visitors' chair without being invited. "I'm glad to meet you, Dean. Now, what can I do for you?"

I sat down behind my desk with a puzzled frown. In all of my appointments with faculty thus far, I'd yet to meet someone who didn't come in with his own agenda. I shuffled through a stack of papers on my desk and, halfway in, I found it. I took a minute to scan the memo from the dean of students office, and handed it to Morales.

The handsome Hispanic shook his head and grinned. "Aw, Dean...what a way to make our acquaintance, verdad? 'Inappropriate touching.'" He snickered. "Do you know how many of these complaints I have received in the past ten years?"

I shrugged and shook my head slowly. For a minute, we two sat in silence.

"Ah!" Morales burst out in laughter. "You don't know what I teach—of course not. I am the professor of ceramics. I teach students to throw clay on the wheel, a delicate maneuver that one can read about forever, or watch someone do it, without ever mastering the art oneself. We call it 'centering,' and for me there is only one way to learn. As a teacher, you sit behind the student, very close. You place their hands on the mound of clay as the wheel turns, and you gently guide their movements."

He lounged back in his chair. "'Inappropriate touching?' Tell me: who's to say?"

I smiled and nodded. Then I felt my face flush as something else crossed my mind. It was another memo. I turned back to the pile, sifted through it, and came up with the other one. It was also from the dean of students, marked "Privileged and Confidential." This time I didn't share it.

"Ernie, I need to ask a couple of questions that are a bit more personal. Maybe they'll sound unfamiliar, or perhaps they've come up before over your ten years." I knew I was stalling for time, uncertain how to say this. "Um, is it ever the case that students, as you're quite understandably touching them, have, uh, reported that you've become...aroused?"

Morales peered at me for a moment with a blank expression, then burst into laughter. He said nothing more.

I paused, quelling a vague sense of unease. "I'm not sure what else needs to be said...except for this last item. You're acquainted with a Jessica Rios?"

Morales shifted in his chair. He nodded.

"I understand you have an apartment just off campus, and she's been seen there at all hours. Is she one of your majors?" I added, though I wasn't sure why.

"Ah, yes, of course," Morales responded. "A dedicated student, one might say. Perhaps a 'protégé.'"

I thought for a moment: "Leaving your apartment at one in the morning."

Morales leaned forward. "Talk to her, amigo. You are welcome to call her in, and I am sure she is not one who complains of 'inappropriate touching.'

"I'll bet not," I murmured.

Morales went on. "As you gain more experience here, you will come to understand that pottery is a sensual craft. It is very basic, a form of intercourse with nature. And, as we all know, there are other forms of union."

"According to my information," I said, "she has been interviewed by others on campus, and..." I glanced at the memo. "She told them she sees you as a 'second dad.' Does that seem accurate?"

Morales sat silent for a quite a while. Then he rose to his feet and started slowly for the door. He turned to me with a sidelong smile. He said, "Amigo, there are many forms of union."

In the afternoon, my schedule free, I buried myself in minutiae—drafts of contracts, minutes from committee meetings—while waiting for the shock of a buzzer or the phone to ring. Much as I tried to put her out of my mind, I knew I was girding myself against Linda Lucero, stopping my senses, trying not to imagine her until she arrived.

Finally, when I'd gone through my entire pile of administrivia, I glanced at the clock. It was after five and the university had shut down. I opened my door and looked up and down the hall. Linda Lucero was nowhere in sight.

As I straightened my desk and turned out the light to go home for the day, there was a knock on the door. My heart fell as I walked that way: so I hadn't missed her after all. But there, filling the aperture—obliterating it, to be accurate—was the dark, looming presence of Wiley Crane, all six-foot-eight of him, topped by a modest Afro. I breathed a sigh of relief.

Wiley was an alum of Ocotillo U, a standout in basketball who'd played enough minor league ball to determine that he wasn't going far in that direction. So he'd followed his passion as an undergrad and got a master's degree in history, taught and coached a few years at the high school level, and gone on for his doctorate. He'd been back at his alma mater for six or eight years and knew the place inside and out, as student and professor.

He and I used to go out with a couple of other profs to the Hanover Outpost, twenty miles out of town in the mining district, for a few beers on Thursday afternoons, missing the crowds that packed the place on weekends. "Thank God It's Thursday," we'd called our gatherings, and I sometimes wondered what had happened to them in the six months since I became an administrator.

"TGIT," Crane announced in his booming voice. It echoed down the hallway. "Come on, Connor. Saw your light on. Thursday! Too late to be into all this shit. Let's go hit the Outpost."

We took his Mustang Classic convertible, top down, and as the road wound into the foothills I couldn't get every word he said. But I caught the drift. It seemed that, following Linda Lucero's show-stopping presentation to the faculty, word had got out that all was not well at her community college in San Carlos. "Big program...occupational therapy...many majors...lotta problems...whistle-blower... fired by Linda...six months before accreditation review... Manny on the line...quick meeting."

He whipped up into the parking lot, killed the engine and turned my way, eyebrows raised. "End of story. Linda Lucero be his-to-ry."

The Hanover Outpost was a big, beat-out ballroom that featured plastic chandeliers, Naugahyde booths in faded red and gold, and a bar at the far end with a Coors sign hanging from the rafters. It was the kind of venue your parents might have picked for their high school prom. Not a place your kids would choose, unless they happened to live in the dusty, decaying, mining town of Hanover.

For the Thursday night crew, the Outpost was an isolated spot for private conversations. Often referred to as the Hungover Outhouse, no one else from the university would think of coming out here. For me, given the news I'd just been handed, no uptown cocktail lounge had ever looked better.

"Grab us a booth," Wiley hollered as he headed for the bar. "Been so long, this round's on me."

I surveyed the sparse crowd of patrons, old Hispanic miners by the look of them, swigging one last cerveza before trudging home for supper. A few sat alone in booths, staring into space. There was a cluster of guys at the bar and I heard Wiley swap greetings in Spanish with a couple of them.

I found a booth off in a corner and watched Wiley as he strode across the dance floor, glasses clamped in his armpits, a Dos Equis in each fist. He had the slow, rolling gait of a natural athlete—a stroll I couldn't master if I took a course in it. How well did I know this guy? I wondered. Well enough to have got past his race and height, the most obvious traits that distinguished the two of us. Wiley had a quick mind and an effervescent spirit. In the darkest of times at OCU, I had never seen him down. Maybe that was why I was still learning to trust him.

"So..." He lowered himself into the booth by stages and slid a bottle my way. "Glass?"

I nodded.

"Good beer like this lager here, you wanta let it breathe."

I poured my beer and took a long draught.

"So, here's to His Deanship!"

I set my glass on the table, and looked up slowly. "Is that supposed to be humorous?"

Wiley gave a sad grin and shook his head. "Remind me to ask you sometime: what the fuck has got into you, ever since you got promoted?"

"What do you mean by that, Doctor Crane?"

"Just trying to have a little fun with you. But that ain't easy these days, no sir." He shook his head.

I sat in silence, took another swig of the Dos Equis. "Okay, Wiley. I know you were just trying to break the ice... Look, this is a difficult time for me."

"I saw that—sitting up there all alone by you'self in the auditorium. Come on down to drink that coffee, you looked pale, man. Even more pale than usual." He snorted. "No offense."

At that, I cracked a smile.

"See, you still got some juice in ya."

I shook my head and drained my glass. "You ready for another?"

As I walked back with the beers, I saw him watching me quizzically.

I tried to say something, stopped, and poured my second beer slowly down the side of the glass. Finally, I looked up at him. "You really believe that? You think I was promoted?"

Wiley gave me a blank look and said nothing.

"Okay," I said. "I'm going to tell you some things I haven't shared with anyone. So if any of this gets out..."

He shook his head and shrugged: an apparent vow of silence.

"There was this girl in my Bible as Literature class. Polly Pringle, dually enrolled high school student..."

"Everyone knows 'bout that," Wiley interrupted. "Matter of fact, lots of folks have had the same experience with those little kids. 'Dual enrolled'? Shit. Why don't they just admit this place ain't much more than a high school?

"Only thing unique 'bout your case was that you stood your ground, which is what makes what happened after that so mysterious. Why does a guy with guts withdraw, once he gets promoted? Presidential candidates come to call, you go white as a sheet—no offense..."

"Do you want to hear the story, or are you just going to sit here and kick me?"

"My bad."

"So I was called in for another audience with the distinguished President Driscoll."

Wiley gave a snort. "'Distinguished' might be overstating it, Homie. Dunno how well you've got to know him, but the man is no academician. Doctorate in some sort of applied psychology and a consulting practice on finding ro-mance. Three or four books: 'How to Find the Love You Been Missing.' Blah blah blah. Landed here as a place to keep his bags packed, flying around giving workshops, lectures."

Once into his street lingo—which tended to be when he was feeling very relaxed or really angry—it always came as a shock to hear Wiley break out his multisyllabic vocabulary. "Academician." But I knew he was every inch a scholar. With a PhD from Northwestern, he might have taught at any number of good schools. I took it that he'd chosen Ocotillo U out of loyalty.

"One question, Wiley, and I'll get to my story. Why would a university hire someone like that as president?"

"People skills. Guess that's the best way to put it. University had pretty good governance policies in place, but some folks on the faculty had been at each others' throats for aeons. When the current prexy couldn't take it anymore and retired, the trustees figured they needed a good mediator. Enter the love-doctah."

"Okay, last question," I added. "How did he get to be dean of the faculty as well as president?"

"This could be a long story, but I'll make it short," Wiley responded. "Not long after Hizzoner turned up on campus, he had to fire the dean. Dude was totally incompetent: good move to can him. But, comes time to hire another one, the faculty couldn't agree on anything, much less on who they were going to report to. So, after three failed searches, he gave it up. 'What the hell,' he decided. 'I'll appoint myself dean.' Trustees went along with him."

"And how long did that last?"

"Three, four years, till it wore on him, cut into his consulting practice. Hey, Bro, you lookin' pretty thoughtful. Could it be that something is beginning to make sense?"

Driscoll had kept me waiting twenty minutes in an anteroom with Alice Pendergast, who wouldn't give me the time of day. Finally, his door swung open and the president came ambling out with his arm around the shoulders of an elderly fellow who was leaning on a cane.

"Everett, how generous!" I heard him swoon as he escorted the donor out to the hall.

When Driscoll ushered me into his office, I noticed for the first time how expansive it was. There was a conference table with a dozen chairs, and a conversation area with a divan and a rocker. His desk sat at the far end and he led me to one of the chairs that sat in front. He stationed himself in a big, executive chair behind it.

Driscoll was still smiling broadly as he looked around his big room, basking in the glow of his profitable appointment. Then I watched his expression slowly darken as he regarded me and remembered why I was there. And I noticed one other facet of the man: his eyes didn't change as his countenance altered. In the months I was to spend with him, I would see that again and again. With all his frequent grins and hearty laughter, Walter Driscoll's eyes remained focused and narrow. He never stopped scrutinizing the person with whom he was meeting.

The agenda of our meeting would leave me in shock, but it didn't take long to accomplish. I was listening to Walter Driscoll go on about his dual life as president and dean, while wondering why he was telling me all this. And then, very slowly, my eyes went wide as my jaw began to fall.

"Con-nor Ran-som." Driscoll seemed to savor all the syllables of my name as he broke into a broad smile. "Connor Ransom, a minister trained in the ways of reconciliation. And a relatively new member of the faculty. How long have you been teaching here?"

I mumbled, "This is my second semester."

"Well, a good foundation. Time enough to learn the ropes, eh?"

The rest of the story was quickly told. "If you don't have many friends here," Driscoll reflected, "you haven't made many enemies, either." Then he promised he would train me in the rudiments of the position, teach me what I'd always wanted to know about being a dean.

And did I have a choice? Not really, he suggested. The religion and philosophy department, in which I was the only current instructor, was on thin ice. It hadn't graduated a major in the ten years he'd been here. Beyond that, there was the issue of Polly Pringle. The Reverend Buford Schneuter might not look like much, but he got around town. If I moved from the classroom into administration, the matter could be made to go away.

"So, end of story, Wiley. Not much more to tell. Six months into my new job, the man who put me in it has decided to retire. And now, two weeks into the process of selecting his successor, there's no sign of Walter Driscoll. It seems he's disappeared."

Wiley said nothing for a long time. Then he drained his beer as he slid to the end of the booth. He looked down and slowly shook his head. He said, "And someone pulled the plug on Linda Lucero."

The drive back from the Outpost was placid and relaxing. As we wended through the dark, wooded foothills back toward campus, it seemed neither of us felt like more talking. The evening air had a chill of early fall, but Wiley kept the top down and the breeze was bracing.

For the first time in six months, I felt a sense of connection. What a relief to tell my story—at least as far as I had. Because, of course, there was more.

But for now I kept my head down, out of the presidential political line of fire. Put me on camera, and you'd see much the same, bland, dutiful dean going through my administrative motions. But inside I was not quite the same. For, slowly, some juices started flowing and my spirit began to break free.

4

I paid more attention to the faculty and staff who came in to see me, for one thing. Clarissa Cox was back the next morning. Same bright, flaxen hair and sparkling smile. But as she settled into a chair, I noticed a certain tightness in her smile. And her bottle-blonde hair looked due for a transfusion, several shades darker a quarter inch from the roots.

She seemed a bit more apprehensive in this second go-round, skipped the small talk and got right to the point. "You'll remember that I asked for a leave spring semester. Well, it turns out I need to leave with Jimmy right away. In fact, next week."

"That soon," I said.

"Well, if you remember, I've made preparations. Sally Barstow is well equipped to handle the housing office, and there's a graduate student she can hire as an assistant. It's not like I'm running away or anything."

On the surface, it was a fairly simple affair, a routine request for leave by a mid-level administrator. She had the form in hand; all I needed to do was sign off on it. But I sensed that something else was going on.

"There's always a question in a job like this," Walter Driscoll had said. "What are they really here for? People walk in with something like a sack slung over their shoulder. You can't see it, of course, but you can tell it weighs them down. Now, do you want to see what's in there? If so, what can you do about it? How much you want to get into that gunny sack?"

I sat and thought for a minute. "I wasn't aware you were running away," I said.

There was a story and she told it fairly quickly. Her husband, Stan Cox—defensive line coach for the football team. Married for five years. "Jimmy is four," she added quickly, as though to legitimize the little fellow. Then, as she put it, the marriage had come under strain. In fact, there were divorce proceedings underway, a custody hearing coming up in two weeks.

"Now, you may have heard something about my being with somebody," she

went on. "But I want you to know it is purely a friendship, a professional association that has nothing whatsoever…"

Back to Driscoll. "Everyone has anchor points," he'd told me. "If you want to
know whether somebody's lying, watch their arms and legs. See if they shift their
weight. And don't assume a liar will avoid eye contact. The bigger their fibs, the
more they'll look at you directly."

Clarissa stared into my eyes as she shifted her weight, one side to the other.

"I appreciate your openness, Clarissa," I responded, not without feeling.
Even under stress, she was a good-looking woman. "I guess it feels important to
get this off your chest," I added, immediately regretting the metaphor.

She looked me up and down with a slight, winsome smile. I blushed involuntarily. Then she drew herself back in her chair. She said, "I knew I could trust
you. Someone told me you'd been a minister."

So that was it. I was safe. And my heart sank. Was there a clerical collar
imprinted on my neck? Did I come across as some kind of eunuch?

When she'd left, signed document in hand, I found a message on my door.
Alice, it seemed, would be back after lunch. She had gone to the dentist. There
was a big carton full of files parked next to her desk with a couple of notes taped
on it. "For ScanPro," read one. The other was in caps. It said, "PRIVILEGED AND
CONFIDENTIAL."

If "ScanPro" wasn't a name I knew—it sounded like something comput-
er-driven—neither did the fellow who appeared a half-hour later look familiar.
He was not a textbook geek, I could see right away. A nice-looking young guy,
medium height with rimless glasses, fresh haircut, clean shaven. He wore a dark
green shirt with the company logo on one side of his chest and a brass name badge
on the other. It read "Aaron Fell," and that led me to look at him twice. Somewhere,
it rang a bell.

It turned out that Walter Driscoll had signed a contract to have the con-
tents of a couple of dozen file cabinets that lined Alice Pendergast's office scanned
electronically, then shredded. I could imagine the confab when Driscoll told her
of the plan and was glad I'd missed it. She'd have gone ballistic at the thought of
giving up control of her data.

Aaron showed me a copy of the contract and I pointed to the box. He
laughed at the sign that said "Privileged and Confidential."

"What's so funny?" I asked, and he told me how the scanning process works.
"We hire low-wage workers, sometimes students at OCU, and the entry-level job

is preparing the files. They'll go through and separate pages, remove all the paper clips and staples. A box like this—maybe three dozen files—it'll take two of 'em maybe half a day. The main thing is to find all the staples, as those will jam the scanner and you'll have to start over.

"Then comes the real business, running sheets through the scanner maybe 30 at a time. Each run becomes a stack that goes in a certain file, maybe ten or a dozen in each. And you have to keep them all separate, clean the memory of one set before opening a new file. There are keywords involved, so that the files can be sorted by name, date, subject matter."

I said, "That sounds complicated."

"It is," he acknowledged, "but after a while you get the hang of it and then, like everything else with computers, it gets boring. The reason I laughed is the idea of privacy. Sure, the electronic files can be locked behind passwords, user names, and whatever—once they're loaded in the computer. But in the meantime, every mother's son who's involved in the scanning can see anything they want, if they care to."

"Do you make them sign some sort of confidentiality agreement?" I asked.

He said, "We used to, but that just made 'em curious and they'd waste time looking for DUIs in personnel files and all. So now, we don't say anything and most of them get so zoned by the tedium they don't pay any attention to what's in there. Of course, there's language like that in our contract with the university."

"You know, your name sounds familiar," I said. "Is there some reason I should know about you?"

"Well, I did go to school here," said Aaron. "Majored in religion and philosophy my first two years..."

I said, "That's it—the field where I was teaching before they made me do this."

He laughed again. "I'm not sure you would have had many students. I enjoyed the courses my first two years. But then I found I was their only major and they couldn't offer the ones at upper level. So I switched majors to computer science."

"How's it worked out for you?"

"Well, talk about a growth industry. Can you imagine the number of organizations that are buried in these damn filing cabinets, need to have their data scanned? In fact, I'm thinking about starting up my own company, mostly just to give myself something more interesting to do. That's what I miss about that religion and philosophy major. I mean, it's hard to make a living from something like that, but it feeds your mind in a way these damn machines never will. Sometimes I just wish I had a reading list, so I could keep up on my own."

Something clicked in the back of my mind, and it wasn't a purely altruistic connection.

"Well, Aaron, you know I'm not teaching now, and obviously I enjoy religion and philosophy myself. What if I were to make up a list of readings in subjects that interest you? We could even talk about some of the books once in a while."

His eyes got wide. "Super. Could I pay you?"

I said, "No, that's not necessary. But, suppose I had access to whatever you scan from these files. It would be helpful in my work, as you can imagine. I mean, it's not something we would need to publicize. You know how some people are with their data. And, of course, as you said, once the scanning starts, it's not like anything is really privileged and confidential."

His eyes grew narrow and he thought for a moment. "There is that contract." He drew a sheet of paper from his briefcase and looked it over. "It says the data belong to the office of the dean."

"And how's it signed? By Doctor Driscoll, as dean?"

He nodded.

"Aaron, did you notice the title on my door?"

He thought for a minute. He said, "I think we can work something out."

Three weeks into my undercover alliance with ScanPro, I was sitting at my desk late on a weekday morning, a couple of meetings with faculty members under my belt and an hour free to pursue my own "research." That's how I put it to myself, although with others I didn't call it anything. No one knew how I was spending a good part of my time.

Aaron Fell had come over the evening after our meeting, with a somewhat unkempt former classmate who now worked in computer services. In twenty minutes, the two of them had set up a mechanism to scarf up every bit of data from Alice Pendergast's files. The scanning was to begin the following day and would go on for as long as Alice kept running off her emails and stuffing them in manila folders. Aaron's buddy showed me a couple of ways to organize the data so I could search and not drown in it.

Now, stacks of paper covered the credenza alongside my desk, with Post-Its on top. "Admissions," "Appointments, Promotions, and Tenure," "Human

Resources." The labels looked innocuous enough, titles of faculty committees. But underneath was a molten core of data, everything I'd run off from her Privileged and Confidential files.

Some of it was noteworthy. A quick scan of Alice's recent correspondence turned up from a sender identified only as the Source, which confirmed what Wiley had reported on Linda Lucero. It seemed she was on thin ice in her presidency of the community college, the object of a lawsuit by an adjunct faculty member who claimed to have been ousted from his teaching assignment as payback for blowing the whistle on the school's accreditation problems.

At times, I'd found myself scurrilously scavenging the raw data, like some pubescent with a new telescope, checking out the neighborhood bedrooms by night. I thought of Aaron's comment and nosed around for DUIs in the personnel files. But I stopped short when I came upon a certain multiple offender. It was Wiley Crane.

It was about then that I turned off the computer and sat for a moment with my head in my hands. A passage from the Bible began to play, somewhere in the back of my mind.

"Have mercy on me, O God, according to thy steadfast love.

Wash me thoroughly from my iniquities

And cleanse me from my sins."

Psalm 51 came up almost involuntarily. Whatever my fascination with the Buddhist tradition, no one had ever probed the dark side of the human psyche better than the ancient Hebrews. What was I doing in Wiley's private affairs? I knew that I wasn't looking at anybody else's dirty laundry as much as my own.

I was flagellating myself in rhythm to the cadence of the Psalmist when a commotion erupted in the outer office.

"Doctor Crane!"

"I know I don't have a scheduled appointment, Ms. Pen-der-gast. But there's no damn reason I can't stick my head in and see him."

As the door swung open, I smiled and nodded for her to shut it. Wiley grabbed a visitor's chair and fixed me with a grin. "Linda Lucero!" he blurted out. "Want to know the latest?"

I might have responded with a "What's the point?" or "You're a little late." But instead, I encouraged him to go ahead and tell me.

"For I know my guilt

And my sins are ever before me."

I tried hard to hear him over the mantra in my brain.

5

eanwhile, of course, there were plenty of things I did want to know about Ocotillo U. How long did students stay here? What was the attrition rate? What happened to the graduates? Why was there no alumni association? And why was Albert McNulty always named Professor of the Year? My mounds of data suggested some answers to these questions. But I needed to hear more firsthand if I were ever to understand this place. The problem was not to let slip how much I already knew.

As it happened, Wiley reminded me, tomorrow night was Thank God It's Thursday. I told him I'd drive myself out to the Outpost. Safer that way.

As I was walking in from the parking lot, I saw a notice posted on the door. "Hey, did you see that?" I asked Wiley, inside. "Closed Next Month for Renovation." He was in a back booth, with several of the faculty and, by the looks of it, had a good head start on Happy Hour.

"Might be they misspelled 'Demolition,'" he hollered, drawing a dark look from the owner who was tending bar. "Hey, y'all recall Connor from when he was one of us?"

It seemed they all did, and some said they'd missed me at these outings. For a moment I felt flushed with warmth, and then a premonition of guilt for the part I was about to play. I got myself a Coors and spent some time schmoozing. "So, how's it going?" "Well, I'm a bit like a ball player still trying to learn a new position, when he finds himself traded to a new team."

It was clumsy, but all I could think of to say. Sometimes in my parish ministry days I'd wondered why theological seminaries didn't offer courses in small talk. It would ease the strain of constantly pondering the Big Picture. But we were only trained to be serious all the time.

Today, there were some sympathetic grunts and nods, and I realized this was the first time that I'd dared to let my hair down here with anyone but Wiley. These faculty members were, after all, still my colleagues. Was I beginning to recover a bit of self-confidence, aiming for something beyond survival?

The range of topics at this TGIT confab was broad. I was amazed at how many hobbies were represented in this small crowd: everything from fantasy baseball to gourmet cooking. They seemed to take a lively interest in one another's after-hours pastimes. But I can't recall any discussion of the university or their jobs.

After about a half-hour, the crowd thinned out and I found myself with a few vaguely familiar faces. There was Wiley, along with three other profs. Bob Clifford was a paunchy forty-something from biology; Jack Lofton, a thin man in his fifties who taught anthropology. The two seemed pleasantly lubricated, laughed a lot, and appeared to be buddies. Finally, there was a gray-haired accounting professor who'd put in a few decades at OCU, Peter Entwhistle. I'd been talking with him when I turned toward the group, raised my voice, and decided to stick my first toe in the water.

"Could I ask a couple of questions?"

They nodded.

"You fellows have been here for a while, and you know that I'm still trying to get this scene in focus." I paused to consider my next step, when Wiley interjected:

"Like they always say, 'Every time I find out where it's at, somebody moves it!'"

That loosened the group up some more, and I ventured on. "So, here's one: who's the head of your alumni association?"

There was silence, till Wiley spoke up, instantly serious. "We don't have one."

"Oh, all right. And, in the same vein, I've been wanting to hear some stories of your most memorable students—you know, the kind you tend to keep up with after they're gone. A few years out of OCU, what sorts of things do you find them doing?"

There was a pause that went on for a few beats, and then a couple of measures.

Entwhistle, the accountant, spoke up. "To be honest, Dean..."

"It's 'Connor,' please."

"Connor, to be honest, most of the best don't stay here all that long."

Another pause. I waited it out, starting to squirm a bit inside.

When a melodic voice with a slightly Hispanic accent piped up behind me. It was an inviting voice, but firm, with a hint of an edge to it. "You know, I've asked the same question," she said, "in the months I've been here. 'What happens to these students?' 'Where do they go?' Oh, and I'm Teresa Ramirez. I teach journalism in the English department."

The others scrunched in the booth to make room for her, introductions all around. I relaxed for a moment as I sat back and took her in. An ally? She was a striking woman, maybe in her late 20s with a beautiful blend of Native American and Spanish features, and black hair that fell to her shoulders. She was dressed casually, but carefully, in a turquoise blouse that set off her hair. She might have stepped out of a J. Crew catalog, like Wiley.

"Well," I continued, "what about the attrition rate at OCU? I'm just trying to get an overview. I know that, nationally, something like fifty percent of students who enter as freshmen wind up graduating from a different school when they're done. Does anybody have a sense of how that compares..."

Bob Clifford butted in. "If you're talking about facts and figures, institutional research, you're probably in the wrong crowd. We're just faculty."

His buddy, Lofton, snorted. "That's right. We're paid to look like we're teaching."

"What you want to do is ask an administrator," Clifford went on. He played his small crowd and paused for effect. "Oh, wait, you are an administrator!"

At that, the other two men drained their beers and started for the door. But I stood up, egg on my face, with nothing to lose. "Just one more question. Who's this Albert McNulty—the perennial Professor of the Year? Can anyone tell me anything about..."

"McNulty," snapped Lofton. "Are you using that as a verb?"

With that, Clifford, Lofton, and Entwhistle were out the door. Joining in the laughter, Wiley trod along behind them.

I wiped my brow and turned to Teresa with a puzzled frown.

"Well, that went well," she said. She gave a sardonic laugh and laid a warm hand on my shoulder. "You were asking good questions, though—appropriate."

"But they weren't having much of it," I responded. I saw Wiley coming back through the front entrance, from the corner of my eye.

"In my profession," Teresa commented, "when we see people behaving like that, there's only one explanation."

"And that is?"

"They got something to hide," Wiley intruded, as she was about to speak. He had covered the distance to the booth in three strides.

"You stole my line," Teresa said with a smile. "And what's there to hide? That's the next question, and it sounds intriguing. But you'll have to excuse me. I have a pile of papers to be graded en la casa." As she got up to leave, she brushed the back of my neck.

My gaze followed her out the door.

Wiley wedged into the booth and I turned to him with a puzzled frown. "I'm glad you found those one-liners so funny. Abbott and Costello must appreciate a receptive audience."

He turned to the bar and put up a peace sign for two more beers. "One thing you learn here and, if you were me, you would learn it well. You go along."

I took a swig of the fresh Coors and thought about his life here among the white-washed masses. "So, does no one really know the rate of attrition?"

Wiley shrugged.

I said, "Well, I do. It's higher than the national average, I can tell you that. In fact, from what I gather, about half these students leave after their freshman year. That's fifty percent attrition, all right. But not in four years: in one. Did you know that?"

He cocked his head.

"And there used to be an alumni association," I went on, "but Driscoll let it die. Why?"

He looked down and began slowly making circles with his beer bottle on the table top. "Y'all quite the Whiz Kid all of a sudden. Step up to the head of the class." He paused. "But you best beware. Next step is a big one, over the edge and gone. I seen it."

I realized that I'd better back off before he began to question how I was accessing this information. But I had one more question of my own.

"McNulty," I said. "Is there some reason that name is so funny?"

He sat silent for a moment. "Connor, you ever heard of 'TWI?'"

"You mean Driving While Intoxicated?" I looked at him uneasily. "DWI."

"That's not what I said."

I gave him a frown. "'TWI,' is that what you said?"

He said, "'Teaching While Intoxicated.' It's a dirty little secret in higher education—subjects like foreign languages, mathematics it gets worse. Can you imagine what it's like to spend your life going over the same formulations to problems you can solve in your sleep? Or teaching first-year Spanish five times in a calendar year?"

"Drinking as a reaction to boredom—is that it?"

He took a swig of his beer and shook his head. "What do you think the life of a prof is like in a school like this? You start out with maybe sixty students in a freshman course, Intro to This or That. And you know, goin' in, that by the end of the semester, you will have lost half of them. Same time, most of the upper division courses in the catalog—subjects that might hold your interest, if not theirs—never taught. Not enough upper division students to take them."

"And not just drinking after hours."

"You know it, Ace. It's the only way to make repetition entertaining. Lemee see if I can remember these dates, solve this math problem, conjugate that verb, when I'm loaded. Ever hear that story about Mickey Mantle—comes back in the dugout after he's hit a home run. Teammate says, 'Listen to the fans cheering!' Mantle says, 'They oughtta cheer. It isn't easy to hit a home run when you're drunk.'"

"I get the point—so what about McNulty."

"Man was here for some time when one year he hits on an idea. Instead of waiting to see how many students are going to drop out of your intro course, why not take the matter in your own hands, and help 'em out the door?"

"How so?"

"Well, he came up with this strategy. First three weeks of class—he was teaching Intro to Literature—he piles on work like you wouldn't believe. Vo-lu-min-ous assignments. Come the second week, as you would expect, students begin dropping like flies. By mid-term, he's cleaned the slate and the fifteen or so he has left are genuine students. So he modifies the syllabus, slows the work load, and gets 'em into some avant garde, cool stuff."

"Interesting. But how did he happen to win all those Professor of the Year awards?"

"It seems Driscoll, who was making the choice, wasn't so invested in social research, nor even what used to be known as common sense. So, by the time he calls in student evaluations, mid-term, Bert McNulty's classes have been flushed of all his malcontents. The students who remain love what he's doing—rate him over the moon. Driscoll has Alice Pendergast tally up the evaluations and neither of 'em thinks to ask about the students who are no longer in those classes. And the winner is..."

"What about that lame joke of Lofton's, 'McNulty as a verb'?"

"Well, let's construct a hypothetical scenario. Say, someone is teaching an intro course on African American history. Early on, this instructor notices that a small enclave of his students are asking good questions, might be ready for some more serious course work. So, again in theory, suppose he spends the next two weeks piling on assignments till he's culled the class."

"And?"

"Course becomes more stimulating—instead of focusing just on African American slaves, you get to explore the broader topic of servitude. Enslavement of Native Americans—in New Mexico, in Massachusetts—only a half-century after the Pilgrims arrived. English selling Indians to slave traders in the Caribbean. Or, the indentured servants settling Australia, almost as many guards as servants, and all of 'em economically enslaved."

"That almost sounds like an upper division history course."

"Check it out, it's in the catalog."

"So, you McNultyed…" Wiley glanced at his watch, stood up, and started for the door.

I trailed him out to the parking lot. "And what about the other forty-five students, three-quarters of the class, who don't get more than two or three weeks of the course?" I shouted, as he started up his car.

"Can't hear you," he hollered. Then, "Where'd you come up with all those data on attrition? And how'd you find out about McNulty?"

I cupped my ear and shook my head. It was hard to hear him, also.

I woke with a start and glanced at the clock, luminous in the night. It was a little after two. Somewhere, it seemed I'd heard voices, and I thought about that. It was one voice, in two tones, and I knew it had come from inside my head. I recognized the voice; it was my own.

"Knock it off!" one said, gruffly. Then, "Aren't you forgetting something?" in a softer tone.

Slowly, I got out of bed, put a robe on, went out to the kitchen and poured myself a drink. Then I turned out the lights and sat on an easy chair in the living room.

Inner voices were nothing new to me, and I knew I was not alone. As early as the nineteenth century, psychologists had found that ten percent of the general populace had heard voices within their heads at one time or another. Recent studies of Parkinson's Disease patients being treated with L-dopa showed three times that number.

I'd done some reading in this field. Up until the mid-eighteenth century, internal voices were regarded as almost de rigueur for any sort of creative work.

A writer might hear stanzas of poetry, lines of dialogue, before putting anything down. Reaching further back in history, as one anthropological theory has it, the human brain was not sub-divided into two hemispheres, but functioned as a bicameral whole. Voices and visions came bounding out of the right side into the left, and there was no neurological mechanism to subject them to critical analysis.

The evolutionary change occurred about 1000 B.C., a couple of centuries past the time of Moses, with his voice from the burning bush. People back then had all kinds of those experiences. In some individuals, of course, the change never quite took hold. William Blake witnessed the visions he wrote about and painted. Kahlil Gibran saw the figures in his sketches.

And what about me? Was I a visionary of sorts, or just some kind of clinical aberration? I replenished my drink, sat back down, waiting for some sort of revelation. What did the voices mean? But, in fact, I registered not a thing till the dawn awoke me slumped over in my chair.

6

There's a trail ten miles outside town that runs along the Continental Divide. Sometimes, out hiking, I've wondered what it must be like for a raindrop that comes down directly on the precipice. The moment would be brief, as moments are, before an inexorable force sends it sliding forward toward the Pacific or back to the Atlantic, one way or another.

That was the essence of my morning. It began with a couple of messages from Alice Pendergast's inbox—the Source again—that had to do with a re-opening of the presidential search (only one candidate this time) as well as a note that the funding formula for institutions such as Ocotillo U was up for re-evaluation in the legislature. I might have seen the second as ominous had I understood it better, but the first was plainly threatening to me.

I tried meditating a bit as I went about my administrative tasks, but was so wasted from the night before that I couldn't concentrate. And so, between appointments, I reached into my grab bag of spiritual practices from grad school and tried the Tai Chi: 96 movements, 24 in a 15-minute span, to quiet the mind, balance the body, and even serve in a pinch as a martial art.

Half-way through the mini-routine, about the seven-minute mark, there was a rap on the door. I unfurled myself from a Strum the Pei Pa and scrambled back behind my desk just as Ms. Pendergast came in with a couple of pink-slipped phone messages. She had a way of doing this when calls came in that she considered important.

One was from Albert McNulty and it read, "Heard you've been asking about me. Would you like to talk?" The other was marked "Teresa." It said, simply, "Lunch?"

Her message sent me up and down the scale, from tingling warmth at one end to a cold sweat at the other. It had been a long time since anyone had touched me that way, and I felt myself slide back to Jenny and then Lisa. And remembered where it all had led, to Ned.

I sat down for a second and took a breather when something remarkable happened. Suddenly, in an instant of grace, all the voices formed a chorus and I understood what they were saying. It seemed that, as people in my new life were becoming more real, some of them were echoing my past. I couldn't argue with that, but it raised a fascinating question. Did I already know too much about Ocotillo U?

That night I slept like a rock.

The next morning, I flicked on the computer and watched my schedule take shape on the monitor. Somehow, I was not surprised to see Albert McNulty first in line, but he caught my attention as he came in the door.

He was a tall, angular man, older than I'd expected—maybe seventy. He had ruddy cheeks and a healthy glow about him, like a retired mountain climber. His academic credentials were solid; I'd looked him up. Undergrad and master's degrees from Brown, doctorate from Harvard.

As he settled into a visitor's chair, he handed me a weathered business card. It read: SOCO, and identified him as president of what seemed to be an organization.

"S..O..C..O.." I sounded out the acronym. "Sounds like a menu item from a Japanese restaurant."

He regarded me soberly for a moment, then broke into a lopsided grin. "That's a good one," he chuckled. "I'll tell you what it stands for: "Save Our Ocotillo U.""

McNulty took me back a dozen years, to the days before Walter Driscoll. "Faculty was terribly divided," he said, "and I was leader of the one side. It was all about a funding formula."

"That sounds familiar," I remarked, then watched as he gave a start. His eyes bore in on me and immediately I wished I hadn't responded.

"Would you be speaking of something current?" he asked, intensely. "How would you know about that?"

I shrugged. "Maybe something in the air."

"Well, I hope it's nothing like before. You see, OCU was half the size it is today, and it was a school with standards. Look around the academic landscape and you'll find places like that. State University of New York in Geneseo, Fort Lewis College in Colorado, New Mexico Tech. There are a few state schools that keep themselves at a certain level and develop centers of excellence, a few good programs. We were that way."

"And what happened?"

"Well, the state legislature in its wisdom decided to scrap the funding formula they'd had for years—basically, dividing up the pie equally among several institutions. No, some idiot came up with the idea of distributing funds based solely on enrollment."

"And I can guess what happened next."

"You bet. Half the faculty, of course, wanted to maintain our present size and quality. The others, well—you see us now. Open enrollment, constant turn-over, terrible morale. Walk through the classroom halls, you'll hear instructors hoarse from lecturing, never a question, nothing like a dialogue.

"Sometimes you'll hear one other voice—a good student who's basically employed to do the reading, sit there and ask a question, maybe disagree with something that's been said. They'll hire honors students on work-study just to relieve the tedium of those damned monologues."

It didn't take long to ask how he'd come up with his technique for winnowing his classes, the method that bore his name. I shook his hand as he got up to leave and genuinely thanked him. Something about his vitality stayed with me the remainder of the day, when I shut down the computer and turned out the lights.

And glanced at the pink slip still lying on my desk. "Lunch?" it said.

There is a certain mystique about San Vicente, the half-Hispanic town that is home to Ocotillo U. And, like many aspects of my life here, I was just beginning to absorb it. The old plaza accounts for a good part of the aura—a dozen small stores and as many shuttered ones surrounding a small park with a gazebo. It's right behind campus.

At the head of the zocalo—which is what I've heard it's called in Spanish—there is a hoary old hotel that draws people from all over via the visitor's guides. El Grande is a sleepy, once-proud, red brick structure with three stories and maybe two dozen habitable rooms, half of which are occupied on a good night. But the main floor is a knockout. A restaurant and bar with a half-dozen beers on tap, "Serena's" is always humming. They serve a humongous buffet brunch on Saturdays and Sundays.

That's where I sat, in a booth bathed in sunlight that streamed through stained glass on the Victorian front window. I'd been gazing out across the park until I caught sight of her. Now I watched with some wonder as Teresa Ramirez came my way, balancing a multi-layered plate.

"Why are you smiling?" she asked as she maneuvered the plate and settled into the seat opposite me.

I shook my head. "I guess I'm astonished that someone who looks like you could eat like that," I said. "But you were smiling, too."

"To your first point," Teresa said. "You may have heard of Zumba—forty-five excruciating minutes, three or four times a week. They offer it here in phys ed."

"And the smile?"

"Well, I wasn't going to tell you this. But I was thinking, 'Damn, this only took two weeks.' So...tell me about yourself."

"That could be a long story. I've been through quite a lot."

"So, I understand. 'A minister, trained in the ways of reconciliation.'"

"Where'd you get that?"

"From a friend of yours: I believe he goes by 'Wiley.'"

"Not a friend who excels at keeping confidences, I'd say. I suppose he shared the whole story of how I got my job."

"Yes, and you'd better be grateful—or, I hope you will be. If he hadn't cast some light on you, I'd have cut out after the first couple of days."

"Well, I've been through a lot."

"You said that. So, tell me one good thing that happened to you this week. I'll bet there's something."

I thought for a moment. "Well, a couple. First of all, I had a very good talk with Albert McNulty. Remember him? 'McNulty as a verb'?"

She nodded.

"Turns out he's quite an impressive fellow. That was Thursday. And then, yesterday, Alice Pendergast, the secretary I inherited who has never given me the time of day, knocked on my door, actually smiled, and asked how I liked my coffee. I could have fallen off my chair."

Teresa thought a moment. "Post hoc, ergo propter hoc?"

"Whoa, that's a first. Latin at OCU. You must've taken logic. 'After this, therefore because of this.' Right? Well, I dunno. But I'm hooked. How about a little personal history?"

For a moment, she was silent. Then, "I'm an anomaly. Hispanic only child. Progeny of a damn-near infertile pair of Beaners. All my friends came from these huge broods. So, growing up alone—in Albuquerque, by the way—I took to books at an early age.

"Studied hard, liked school. Family income in the tank, so I responded to scholarship offers. And not just for academics. Race-based; it didn't take me long to figure that out. All sorts of schools needed some natives in class when they took up Bless Me Ultima, The House on Mango Street. That sort of thing. So I ended up at Mount Holyoke, of all places. South Hadley, Massachusetts. Middle of nowhere, but an incredible school."

"What was it like?"

"Well, the day I got there, I had the impression it was full of nursing majors. All these girls walking around in long, white stockings. By the end of the day, of course, I realized those stockings were…"

I laughed. "Their legs, right?"

She smiled. "Then they gave me this roommate from a place called Greenwich Village. A small town, I assumed. She was, to put it kindly, grungy. That night, I was going to sleep when, across the room, her bed began to quiver. Then I heard some grunts and moans that sounded for all the world like…" I saw her staring at me intently.

"A term I've heard is 'Jilling Off,'" I offered.

"Well, how 'bout that. So I guess it's not sex that scares you, ministerial history and all. Yet, for two weeks, you didn't return my call. Which means there's gotta be an explanation…"

I looked down demurely. "Don't press it. I only go so far on a first date."

Teresa choked on her coffee. "Okay, then, back to me. Next morning, I packed my bags and headed for the housing office. Told my now ex-roommate, 'I think I need to be among my own kind.' And I remember hollering as I went out the door, 'You might improve your social life if you shaved your legs.' My new roommate was Latina, and a high achiever. Someone you might…but, I'll stay on script.

"Long story short, I stayed all four years. Great education. Found a program called 'Nexus' that got me into journalism and out of South Hadley, a semester at a time. Internships at the Boston Globe, Christian Science Monitor. Master's at Columbia, ready for the world."

I noted, "Just in time for the collapse of the newspaper industry. So, what did you do?"

"By this time, I was lonesome for the Southwest, y la raza—my tribe. Do you have any idea what passes for Mexican cuisine on the East Coast? So a job turned up in a little town in southern New Mexico. Alamogordo. Have you heard of it?"

I shook my head.

"Well, you're not alone. Not a lot goes on over there, besides ranching. Small town paper, no one to get involved with socially, as they say. Just shit kickers. I lasted two years till my reporting got a bit too aggressive for some of the businesses that advertised in the paper. High stress, for a small town. Did an exposé on the big Native American casino down the road and that was it. Let go over a weekend. Good excuse to ditch the rancher who seemed queer for his cattle, or at least more interested in them than in me. And the next week, I was gone."

"To Ocotillo U?"

"No, home to parents for a few months. Tried waitressing, pondering what comes next, when this job came up. I'd never really thought about teaching, but..."

"Here you are, trying to figure out this place just as I am."

"Right on. And that's really why I called you. You know, Wiley said something that seemed to fit my first impression of you."

"I guess I should ask what that was."

"That you're a person who spends a lot of time up inside his head. 'Ruminator,' that's what Wiley called you. And, you know, I'm very much the opposite. I've been trained to go after facts and I'm pretty good at it. But sometimes I miss currents that are just beneath the surface. That's what I think you might be good at, and Wiley agreed. He said you're always taking soundings: that's the way he put it. So I think we should be friends, that's all I'm asking—just get together now and then and trade our oddball impressions of this place."

"How about a hike in the forest next Saturday? Meet here, say nine, walk it off after."

She thought for a few seconds. Then she said, "I thought you'd never ask."

7

The next day, I left my car at home and took a half-mile walk to campus on a quiet Sunday afternoon. In early November, fall was still in full sway with trees decked out in the muted hues of New Mexico. Better than the vivid colors and biting cold I remembered from those seasons in the Upper Midwest.

My thoughts drifted back five years or so, and it didn't take me long to get deeper than the weather. It was that cluster of relationships, so much more intense than anything I'd known since then. Not that I'd been in cold storage.

Sex in graduate school was readily at hand (I cringed at the pun), especially in a field as far out as Eastern Religious Studies. Most of my fellow students were females and I knew quite a few of them, in the Biblical sense, quite well. But none had touched my heart, nor I theirs from what I could tell. Sex was a release. I remember one of my partners turning to me in the afterglow and tenderly opining, "You know this is basically like going to the bathroom."

But Teresa would engage me in a different way; I was sure of that. So, was I ready for something more? Would it turn out anything like before? I shook my head to clear out the clutter. This was a beautiful day, well worth my attention, and I invested myself in the present. Just look at those Victorian houses with their high gables and commodious porches, a legacy from the salad days of silver mining. So what if the mines had given out. Thank God the architecture hadn't.

But as I came to the outskirts of campus, I was shocked by a sharp change in style. It was in the dorms and gym and science buildings from the sixties and then the eighties, the eras when enrollment had soared. There were a dozen of these structures—all cubes and squares and rectangles with sharp edges and slick surfaces, a triumph of linearity—cream-colored and in the tan of bathroom tile. Nothing in this ring of new construction complemented the dark red brick buildings at the heart of the campus.

Suddenly, I thought I saw it all in context, as I went spinning off in space. This had been a new wave of architecture, self-involved, a school without a sense of history or place. The thought stayed with me as I approached the administration building that housed my office. For the first time, I stopped and gazed at the mellow dimensions of the place: sandstone base capped by a finished molding, upper walls of stuccoed brick, a sloped roof with clay tiles.

I walked up and, again for the first time, read the bronze plaque by the front door. "Designed by John Gaw Meem, a leading New Mexican architect of his day—responsible for many of the traditional buildings in Santa Fe. Murals on the stairwell by Lloyd Moylan, a leading local artist. Completed in 1937, constructed by the WPA."

Once inside my office, I settled into the stillness of this building and listened to the silence, the decades of human drama that must have been played out in here. In time, I switched on my computer, clicked on the secret G drive, and began to sift through Alice Pendergast's email correspondence.

It didn't take long to come across a heads-up from the Source. We were to expect a confab next Thursday morning for top administrators (I hoped to be included) at which two appointments would be announced. First, the next president of Ocotillo U, a unanimous selection by the board of regents (read: no more convocations, case closed). And also, the incumbent of a newly-created position: provost of OCU.

I had to look up what that meant, and found it signified a chief administrator of internal affairs. (So, assuming I kept my position, I would have not one but two new superiors to satisfy. Yikes, two bosses.) I sat back for a long time and let all that sink in. Finally, I got back on task and finished sifting through the emails. I found only one other item of interest. It was an acronym, an entity I'd learned never to ignore. GOCO it read.

The next morning, Alice knocked gently on my door and entered with a steaming cup of coffee. I thanked her warmly and asked her to stay a moment. She looked at me quizzically.

"Alice," I asked, "I've heard a strange acronym recently, and you know there's still plenty around here that I don't understand. Can you tell me what GOCO means?"

I was surprised to see her give a slight shudder, and even more so as she took half a minute to survey every corner of my office—first around the ceiling, then the floor. Was she taken by the architecture? Perhaps we had a common interest. For a moment I thought I might have found a way to break the ice.

But then she picked up a yellow legal pad from my desk and a black marker. She wrote something very slowly and handed it to me. GOCO, it read. "Grow Our Ocotillo U." Then she turned around quickly and left.

I sat for a moment, chin in my hand. Then I stood up and looked over the corners of my office as she had. Was it possible it was wired?

Later that morning, Alice brought in a registered letter on the stationery of Manny Moreno's bank and signed by his nibs as chairman of the board of trustees. It was an invitation to a meeting in the Presidential Conference Room of Ocotillo U, 10:00 a.m. Thursday. Somehow, it sounded like a confab I didn't want to miss.

For the rest of the morning, I went through my administrative motions more or less on autopilot, worrying about the meeting while wondering what was up with Alice and, not incidentally, whether my office was bugged. But now and then something interesting happened. I seemed to experience a kind of breakthrough to a place where I enjoyed the elements of mystery in my life, just having things to ponder. Was it Teresa? Maybe something she'd said about my gift for coping with the unknown. I wondered.

At any rate, I was glad to have a break from my environs: lunch with Aaron Fell, the fellow from ScanPro with whom I'd agreed to do some sort of independent study. God knows I could use a distraction. We'd agreed to meet at Edmundo's, a place in Hispanic Old Town on the other end of the zocalo from El Grande. I'd never eaten at this Mexican bistro, though I'd heard pretty good reviews from Hispanics on the staff.

As I glanced at the motto above the restaurant, I was grateful once again for my couple of years of college Spanish, which enabled me at least to understand most of the signs in town. This one read: Cuidado! I vowed to order cautiously.

I took a booth toward the front window and watched for Aaron while quaffing a cold Mexican beer. I did a double take as he pulled up in a black Lexus. He waved as he saw me through the window and came over to the booth.

"What are you drinking? Modelo Especial!" He ordered one for himself. "We get spoiled here," he noted. "It's my favorite lager and damned hard to find in this country. Did you know that most of the breweries in Mexico were founded by German immigrants?" He was talking rapid fire and I noticed a periodic tic in his right eyelid.

"So, what's good here?" I asked, perusing the menu. "You grew up in these parts, didn't you?"

"Right. It depends on your fortitude. Did you notice the sign? The green sauce is big time picante. You know, it varies by restaurant; sometimes it's red, sometimes the green." His eyelid kept flicking.

I opted for the red sauce on chicken enchiladas and he got another cerveza for each of us. After some more frenetic small talk, he settled back in the booth and fell into silence.

"Well, I've been thinking about religion some," he finally commented. "Over the weekend. With this new business, I haven't had time to be very reflective."

"It must be going well," I said. "I noticed your car."

"Yeah, it is—and maybe that's part of why I wanted to talk. Sunday morning, I was thinking: I'm consumed by consumption, you know what I mean? I mean, all this energy invested and for what? So I can get more things." He waved his hand around the restaurant, out to the square. "There must be something more to all of this than that."

So he had the bug. We began talking about some books he might read, if I could pin down some of his interests. But his thoughts were racing, scattered all over the map. Now and then I could hear his phone buzz in his pocket. He'd react and start to reach for it like a lab rat, but stop himself and then his eyelid would twitch some more.

"You know, one way to think about the ways our lives can become scattered—and it happens to all of us," I said, "is to consider our human capacity for self-transcendence."

He winced and said, "I'm afraid you lost me there."

"Basically, the idea that we can become disengaged from ourselves because our minds know no limits, our thoughts can take us so many directions."

"I get that," he said, as our food arrived. The red sauce was plenty picante for me.

"So, here's one theme you might find interesting: tell me if it is or not. All religions address the problem of how to corral the infinite possibilities in us in some sort of concreteness that might be called an 'incarnation.' The word means, literally, 'in the flesh.'"

He set his fork down and looked up from his chile relleno with a glimmer of interest. "The infinite and the incarnation, is that it? Sounds pretty abstract, in the world I'm living in."

I said, "Quakers have a concept of 'centering down.' Suppose, in order to head that way, I asked you to look at a few founders of major religions, in order to see how they were able to crystallize their lives and set out in some direction."

"Such as?"

"Well, how about Buddha, Jesus, and Mohammed. We have texts written by or about each of them that could give us a good start. The question would be: how did these guys choose the path that they would follow? What were the circumstances of their lives? How did they get their start?" I took out a napkin and wrote down: The Teachings of the Buddha, the four Gospels of the New Testament and the Gospel of Thomas, and the Koran.

Aaron dug into his chile relleno and gave it some thought. His face had settled down. Finally he pronounced, "I'm up for it. I can get all that on Amazon or interlibrary loan. But just don't give me a deadline." He signaled for the check.

Outside, he shook my hand and said, "You know, I think it's too bad I couldn't have studied with you, held onto that religion major and picked up the computer stuff on the side. Those would have been good courses."

"But who else would have enrolled?" I responded. "Not here. It would take a Mount Holyoke, someplace like that."

He slipped on his Izods and took out his car keys. "Why not here?" he wondered.

There are times in life so momentous that they almost seem to penetrate our DNA. The ancient Greeks had a term for such events; they called them kairos. Not the tick-tock time that merely goes by; that was kronos. Moments of kairos were indelible and defining.

Everyone has those moments. Some of mine were life-threatening: my father's suicide, Ned on the bridge. Others were affirming, expanding my existence: say, Lisa in the House Church. Maybe someday I would look back on meeting Teresa as a moment of kairos.

But meeting the new president was an occasion I that knew at the outset I would never forget. So I dressed for it. While fashion is a convention I tend to ignore, on this day I pulled out my best business-casual attire: patterned shirt, complementary sweater, fresh khakis, matching socks and loafers. Basically, I tried to imagine what Wiley would wear.

As I stepped into the Presidential Conference Room—a low-ceilinged historically restored space with walls that matched the earth tones in the murals on the stairwell—whatever cool confidence I'd gained in recent months dissolved. I was back to the sweaty-palmed days of listening to those speeches in the auditorium, on tenterhooks to find out what kind of figure would hold my fate in a pair of omnipotent hands.

There were a dozen or so administrators seated around a huge conference table, mid-level people I'd come to know slightly, along with Manny Moreno and a few vacant chairs. Manny nodded at me solemnly—no sign of his customary conviviality—which did nothing to bolster my confidence. But I noticed the whole room was silent; everyone seemed subdued.

As the bells on the campus carillon struck ten, Manny cleared his throat and picked up a few pages of prepared text. "This is a memorandum from the trustees of Ocotillo U to the faculty and staff. In the four months since our last president, Walter Driscoll, decided to retire, we have had multiple meetings with your designated representatives, the faculty and the staff senates, and we have reached out to certain unofficial bodies. By any measure, these ventures have proved almost totally unfruitful. We have done our best..."

Manny Moreno was obviously an intelligent man—officer of a bank, after all. But he was no academic and the memo he was reading sounded purely professorial. I'd never heard Manny talk like that. He went on to describe a vexing process of decision-making that had eventuated in a course of action somewhat similar to one that the trustees of OCU had taken in the past.

"And so we have made two historic decisions. Today we are sharing them with an intimate group of colleagues, and later there will be a convocation with the entire University. Now, first, we have chosen to create a new, senior-level position at Ocotillo U. Our provost will oversee all personnel and on-campus activities. For this vital responsibility, we have chosen a veteran faculty member who is familiar to you all. Ladies and gentlemen, I give you, the provost of Ocotillo U."

A door opened at the far end of the conference room and in walked Doctor Wiley Crane, in a coal black business suit, light blue dress shirt, and a rep tie in the OCU colors of purple and gold. Wiley surveyed the table and smiled all around. He took a seat without speaking.

"And now, it is my pleasure to present (Manny continued reading from his script) the new president of Ocotillo U..." (again the door opened and, suddenly, I sat bolt upright. Wide-eyed and slack-jawed, I blinked several times at the apparition who stepped into the conference room) "Doctor Sterling Holmes-Ortega."

In the two years I'd served in the ministry under the Reverend Sterling Holmes, at times I had wondered how much I'd known of the man beneath his vestments. The answer that now came to me was something like: not much.

8

The Raven's Roost is an historic watering hole and steak house in the semi-ghost town of Pinecroft, fifteen miles up in the foothills. If there are any remnants of the Old West in this region, untainted by development, Pinecroft is absolutely one.

The Roost is a low, adobe structure from the nineteenth century with an old opera house next door. The place is redolent of history: log walls with paintings of famous ladies for hire, displays of Native American artifacts, and a replica of a drunken Indian hunched over his drink at the far end of the bar that seems so real, tourists have been known to engage him in conversation.

I, too, was at the bar contemplating my libation as I waited for Sterling to show up. Mid-way into my second margarita, he was already fifteen minutes late: quite unlike the meticulous man I remembered from my days in the ministry. Of course this was a new era. I couldn't recall ever meeting him in a saloon. Finally, he came bustling in the front door, unmistakable in his blue business suit. I raised a hand and he found me.

He mounted a bar stool with no move to shake my hand. "And you're having?" he began.

I hesitated for a moment, taken aback by his tone, till I remembered him as the East Coast elitist I'd known: patrician, laconic. But I wondered if there was something more. "Margarita on the rocks," I told him. "They're pretty good here."

He thought for a moment, and I wondered how often he had occasion to order a drink. He looked up at the young woman tending bar. In tee shirt and jeans, she seemed fascinated by his suit. He said, "I'm still getting used to tequila. I believe I'll have a Scotch and soda."

We sat in silence for some time. Finally, he said, without looking my way, "I wonder what you thought of my comments yesterday."

I said, "Honestly, I was so shocked at the sight of you, turning up here. I can't remember a thing you said. I never expected to see you again."

"Evidently not," he muttered, "given the manner of your departure."

We sat in silence some more. The young woman brought his drink and shot him a quizzical glance as she turned back to the bar.

Finally, I said, "Look. Do you want me to apologize? When I asked you to join me, I thought we might fill in some gaps, tell a bit about how we both got here. It's an amazing coincidence, after all."

He took a sip of his drink and loosened his tie. I thought I saw him wince. Then he launched into a story that, in retrospect, I might not have found all that amazing. The man for some time had been burning out in his profession, uncomfortable with the mounting roster of sacraments for everyday living, that sort of thing.

"It came to a head in an unexpected way," he reflected. "I have a twin brother, did you know that? I suppose not. I'm not sure how much you ever learned about me. Well, Stanley is a college professor: the family script. And he came to visit on a Sunday when, as it happened, I was blessing the animals. To make the story short, it hadn't gone well. A duck got loose—panicked, flew the length of the sanctuary. The senior usher caught him in the vestibule. Well, the congregation thought it was a riot. They always loved that sort of thing.

"But, sitting around after Sunday dinner, Stan sat back and took a look at me. He said, 'Sterling, do you ever wonder what Dad would have had to say about all of this?'"

The rest of the story followed sequentially. Sterling had decided to follow his bloodline and pursue a career in higher education. He found an online program in higher education administration somewhere in Florida, independent study with intermittent colloquia on campus. He didn't let the church know what he was doing, just adjusted his vacation schedule to accommodate the times away, began recycling old sermons into time for study.

"I can't say anyone noticed the difference," he commented with a wry smile. During the sojourns in Florida, Daniela turned up. "Martha and I had accomplished what we'd set out to," he reflected. "The kids were grown, out on their own."

"So, how did the church take to all of this?" I inquired, somewhere into our third drink.

"Well, they'd had a certain baptism, a preview to this sort of thing," he said sardonically.

And so it was a smooth transition, to hear him tell it, an easy evolution. I thought the term "lethargic" might apply. He'd drifted from Martha to Daniela—a middle-aged educator and single parent with a likewise empty nest. There was a quiet divorce—his ex-wife opted to stay in town—and a remarriage that came with a hyphenated surname. A new life as he looked for a job. Sterling implied that he'd been pleased to find how the Hispanic part of 'Holmes-Ortega' cracked open a few doors professionally.

The trail to Gomez Peak is only twenty minutes out of town, but a transport to another world. It takes you up some rugged hills, then levels out onto a path among the pine trees that gives you glimpses of the verdant mountains all around. To have this wilderness almost at the edge of town is one of the blessings of life in San Vicente—a reason some folks would dig in their heels at a threat to their career at OCU, any suggestion they might have to move away.

There's a resting place halfway up the trail where several paths converge. Teresa and I sat down on a big, flat boulder and took out some water. It was our post-brunch hike on the following Saturday morning. We both had calories to walk off, and a lot to talk about as well. I had recapped my reunion with Sterling, back at the hotel.

"So here he is, among us," she said, shaking her head. "A newly-minted, half-Hispanic who can't take the taste of tequila. That's icky, but intriguing. Well, I have other questions. There are some good-size holes in that story."

"But let's keep going," I responded. "It's a good, long trek if we want to get to the top."

"A good trek" was putting it mildly. The trail turned more and more vertical and narrow, cluttered with rocks that could slip underfoot and pitch you over the edge into a steep ravine. Here and there were piles of scat from one or another form of wildlife. There were foxes, bears, and even mountain lions in various sections of the forest. A native of these parts could likely tell the turd of one animal from another, but that wasn't me and large, fresh scat could scare me.

Finally, we wound around the last clump of boulders and clambered onto the scant, flat promontory of Gomez Peak. The vista was worth it: a stunning panorama of wooded hills and a hardscrabble desert that ran seventy miles due south into Mexico. We set down our backpacks and found a couple of rocks to recline on.

"So, 'holes in the story,' I believe you said."

"It was something about the way you left and the preview of his split from his wife. Did I get that right?"

I said she did and, for the next hour or so, I told her a good part of the story.

"Whew," she remarked at the end. "So, should your child consider the ministry? I had no idea sex was such a big part of it."

We sat in silence for a while, then she scooted over and put her arm around me.

"On that subject," I said, "One thing made me curious, when you had all those questions about my not responding to your phone message, you left out one obvious possibility. Do you know what I mean?"

Teresa looked off over the horizon.

"Okay, I'll answer it myself. Didn't you think I might be gay?"

She sat still for a couple of minutes, then got up and started gathering her things. Under her breath, she muttered something like, "la gente que vive en casas de vidrio." Then she said, "Shadows are falling, amigo. Don't you think it's about time to head back down?"

It was late afternoon when we arrived at her place, a svelte condo unit in a nice part of town. I was wondering how the day would end—how quickly I wanted to get involved in what had all the earmarks of a significant relationship. I decided to follow her lead.

"Connor, muchisimo gracias—thank you so much for a wonderful day, and for all that information. I would invite you in, perhaps, but I have a house guest for a few days. Actually, I think she's someone you might find interesting. Do you remember when I mentioned my Latina roommate at Mount Holyoke?"

As we stepped up to her front door, it opened and an attractive woman came out. She had long, flowing hair the same graphic black as Teresa's. She seemed about the same age and looked vaguely familiar. The two of them stepped into a long embrace. Then Teresa clasped each of us warmly by the shoulder. She said, "Connor Ransom, may I present Linda Lucero."

Back home, I uncorked a beer and flopped down on the couch, exhausted. But I got up and took down my Spanish/English dictionary. Hmm. "People who live in glass houses." I thought that's what she'd said.

9

The auditorium was three-quarters full, about the same as for the speeches by the presidential candidates. I headed for the top rows, some vacant except for a few isolates from the various departmental cliques. On the far, right-hand side, a large, dark figure sat alone.

"So, are we still friends, now that I'm reporting to you?" I peered down at Wiley, while hovering over the seat beside him.

He gave a hearty laugh and flipped the seat down. "I guess if we survived your promotion, we can make it through mine all right." Then he quickly glanced off to the side.

I looked over the crowd, still filing in. It was abuzz, animated. I noted the buttons a number of the faculty members were wearing. All were in school colors, but some were large and purple, others smaller and gold. I could see that each of them had five white, block letters in the center, but they were indistinct from where we sat. Still, I could guess what they read.

Sterling sat center stage, along with Manny Moreno, behind a podium. There were flags of the U.S. and New Mexico on the left, and a two-tiered set of risers on the far side of the stage. About ten minutes after the scheduled time—somewhat standard for New Mexico—the lights dimmed and Manny stepped up to the podium. He welcomed everyone and introduced a vocal group that seemed well-known around OCU, the Harmonics.

Twelve men and women—Hispanic, black, and white—stepped on stage and mounted the risers. They were followed by their conductor, a middle-aged Latina who walked slowly and sedately, balancing her weight which was substantial. She bowed to a burst of applause, then turned and blew a note from a pitch pipe. As the singers started up, she began to rock her hips to Stevie Wonder's "Isn't She Lovely," and the audience loved it. Then an acoustic guitarist came out to accompany the next number, which was more subdued: "Sabor a Mi," a slow, Latin love song.

The crowd roared as the Harmonics left the stage, clearly up for whatever was to follow.

"Alicia Domingo," Wiley leaned in and whispered. "Be-lov-ed; been here forever."

Manny gave Sterling an efficient introduction. He spoke of his advanced degree from an Ivy League university without identifying the grad school as a theological seminary, and his doctorate from a school in Florida where he had been named a Shrub Fellow.

I raised an eyebrow to Wiley and he shrugged with one shoulder.

Sterling rose to a round of restrained applause. He clutched the podium and cleared his throat a few times, a habit I remembered from his days in the pulpit. He wore a gray suit with a white shirt and a vivid purple tie. There was a gold, folded handkerchief in his lapel pocket.

"My friends and colleagues," he began, and cleared his throat again. "I am so pleased to have this opportunity to visit with you, and the first item on my agenda is to introduce my lovely wife who is such an inspiration to me. May I present Daniela Ortega!"

He motioned to the front row and a sleek, fifty-something woman in a bright yellow dress with violet flowers stood up and turned to the audience. She smiled broadly and waved to every corner of the auditorium. I remembered Sterling's staid Martha—a somewhat homespun, textbook minister's wife—and marveled at the public presence of this person. What a contrast.

Sterling took hold of the podium again and launched in. "It is difficult," he began, "to overestimate the importance of the work we do in the field of education. For it impacts all of life. More than a century ago, the noted American educator, Henry Adams, had this to say. 'A parent gives life, but as a parent, gives no more. A murderer takes life, but his deed stops there... A teacher affects eternity; he can never tell where his influence stops.'

"Perhaps you know that quotation, but you may not have heard what he had to say about life devoid of learning. 'The scholar finds himself jostled of a sudden by a crowd of men who seem to him ignorant that there is such a thing called ignorance, who have forgotten how to amuse themselves, who cannot even understand that they are bored.'"

Wiley raised both eyebrows and cocked his head at that. I nodded, then found myself musing about Sterling as he went on with more quotes and good thoughts about education: the unexamined life not worth living, and the rest of it. His intellectual acumen was no surprise to me. We had come, after all, from the same seminary: an Ivy League institution where only half of the graduates were serving churches. The others, non-parish ministers, were to be found all over the place—take the two of us, right here.

As I refocused on Sterling's speech, it seemed that the audience, so fired up a few minutes ago, was beginning to deflate. I saw some professors gazing around the auditorium, some whispering with friends. One was working a Sudoku puzzle.

Then, suddenly, he regained their attention. "There's just one problem with these platitudes, all these promises to promote growth in people. We don't know how to relate what we do." He paused and put his text aside. "You see, I believe this is a new era in education. We must learn to make our work intelligible and convincing to those who furnish our funding, the majority of whom, of course, are not professional educators. We must learn to measure our efforts, to quantify results."

For a moment, I cringed, remembering Sterling in the ministry and his little black book of daily activities. Would he bring the same, nit-picking spirit to his presidency?

But he had more to say. On the subject of academic standards, he cited "Academically Adrift," a book that indicts American higher education for its poor record in test results. He said he had a stack of copies in his office if anyone would like to read it. In the same vein, he quoted someone named Michael Gerson on "the soft bigotry of low expectations."

"George W. Shrub's speechwriter?" I whispered to Wiley. He squinted and nodded.

Then he turned to the subject of access to higher education: a study that found some six million young people between the ages of sixteen and twenty-four (fifteen percent of the age group) were both without work and not in school. He paused again and looked up. "Is this not our dilemma," he asked, "to offer quality education to an ever larger constituency, many of whom may be unprepared to receive what we have to deliver?"

It would have been a wonderful place to quit, with just that question. But he put down his script, took a deep breath, and went on. "Some years ago, at about this season, I found myself with a comfortable life in a familiar profession. And then I had a moment of truth, as Hemingway's toreros would say."

His accent wasn't bad—t's half d's, a big strong trill on the r.

He went on to offer a sanitized version of his career transition, no mention of Martha. Then he commented on the force of lethargy in mid-life, the temptation to stay in the rut, wallow in contentment. "Especially in a profession that offers the security of tenure," he added.

An audible grumble echoed around the auditorium.

"But let us remember the words of the Bible," he went on after a half-step, undaunted. "'Whatsoever thy hand findeth to do, do it with thy might.' 'With the whole heart,' we might say. Or, simply, 'with passion.' You know, walking in just now I noticed that quite a number of you were wearing buttons. I wrote down the slogans, though I don't yet know their meaning.

"'SOCO' and 'GOCO.' Intriguing. Those symbols obviously have deep meaning for those who display them, and so I will say: yes. Do follow your passion, your every acronym, all of your ideals. As the latter-day prophet Henry David Thoreau expressed it so well: 'Go confidently in the direction of your dreams. Live the life you have imagined.'

"Let us be bold to follow our bliss. And, whatever it may be, do it with our might!"

Sterling turned from the podium, to a handshake from Manny Moreno. Then he waved to the crowd. The applause was moderate, which passed for academically enthusiastic.

I turned to Wiley. "Well what's your take on Sterling? Three words or less."

He thought a moment. "Erudite, precipitant, naïve." He shook his head. "You know how long stuff can simmer in a self-contained environment like this?"

That night, across campus, the computers went down.

I'd been in my office that evening, hunched over my computer, thinking about Sterling's speech while scrolling through Alice Pendergast's emails on my G drive. Multi-tasking. Actually, I was considering that contrivance as well, wondering whether I ought to call Aaron and have him disconnect it. I also could have my office scoured for listening devices, something I'd let slip my mind.

My concerns about the G drive were two-fold: the new administration, for one thing. Who knew how Sterling might reconfigure the IT operations at Ocotillo U; he was such a detail-oriented bugger. In the process of which, my secret source of information might be found out. Then, too, there was Alice. I'd been paying more attention to her ever since she'd turned friendly. Who was it that lived inside that nondescript body? Possibly an interesting soul. So, should I find an occasion to get to know her a bit? Ask her to lunch or coffee, at least? And if we did form any sort of relationship, how would I feel about continuing to spy on her?

But I'd put those questions aside when another email came through from the Source: more rumors of changes to the state funding formula. This memo used a term I'd never heard, "incentivizing." My God, the rhetoric of bureaucrats; was that even a word in English? But the concept was important, that changes in the way funds were distributed could alter behavior in educational institutions—and maybe in measurable ways.

I rocked back in my chair, and gave some thought to the vagaries of human motivation. Sterling's Bible quote might have been inappropriate in his new profession, but it raised a basic, existential question. Should we go all in with our every endeavor, doing it with all our might? Or is it better to let the game come to us, as a basketball coach might say, a la the Buddhists. Go with the flow. The Bible is inconsistent on that point. There's "Do it with thy might." And then the words of Jesus: "Consider the lilies, how they grow; they neither toil nor spin." And in Exodus Moses counsels the Hebrews: "Yahweh will fight for you. You need only to be quiet."

Moses sounded like a good Buddhist when it came to spiritual practice. But Yahweh was in there fighting, right? It was a stirring thought, and my last of the night. At that point my computer died and the monitor went black.

The next morning, Alice came in with my coffee, wearing a faint smile. She handed me a phone message from Teresa: "See you Saturday, okay, amigo? Same time, same place. And maybe I'll show you a few other places." I started to ask Alice if we might have lunch, but she spun away to answer the phone and we didn't make contact again.

I soon learned that the outage on campus had been somewhat selective. Only the buildings housing programs in the Division of Humanities had been hit: English, Foreign Languages, Expressive Arts. I filed that away for future reference as I left my office in mid-morning for a meeting of the faculty committee on athletics.

Committee meetings were a part of campus life that I'd tried to avoid in my precarious tenure as dean. I was, after all, only an ex-officio member and if I couldn't vote it seemed wise to steer clear of any rancor. But that silent dialogue of the night before had stayed with me. "Yahweh will fight for you." Wasn't it time to take some risks? How long could I continue to drift in this job?

The general classroom building at OCU was about as exotic as its name, a product of the generic architectural sixties. Like the GCB, the faculty conference room had all the earmarks of a low bid contractor: pale green walls; a large, gray conference table rimmed in rubber edges; and stiff chairs that could make a half-hour meeting feel like an all-day symposium. But Wiley Crane was wise in the ways of campus politicians. He knew this room was home turf for the faculty, far more familiar than the more upscale administration building.

Four members of the athletics committee were present: Bob Clifford and Jack Lofton, the good buddies I'd run into at the Hanover Outpost—from biology and anthropology, respectively—and two others I'd not met. Hilda Bielschmidt, I knew, had taught German in the foreign languages program for some time, and Farley Hartshorne, a younger fellow, was in political science. Wiley was there as convener, along with two guests: Aldo Bruski, athletic director at Ocotillo U and former head football coach; and Berenice Falcón, the senior librarian.

Wiley called the meeting to order, and noted that one member of the committee was absent. The agenda was straightforward. Aldo led off, reading a proposal he had prepared on behalf of the athletic department. He was an immense, former lineman—about the size of a walk-in cooler—with a crew cut and tiny rimless glasses that gave him an oddly academic air. But his speech was loyal to his roots on the industrial, far south side of Chicago.

"My colleagues," he began, as he peered at his text and adjusted his glasses. "Last year, when Ocotillo U got promoted to Division I-AA of the NCAA, der was some concern dat, at dis level, we might be overmatched." However, he went on to note, through judicious—he tried the word a couple of times—recruiting from junior colleges in the region, the outlook for the coming season was bright.

"An' here's da problem," he explained. "By the end of da season, we may be good enough to get in a bowl game. But, early in da schedule, we are facing Allbright University—a powerful, Division 1-A school. Looking ahead to an almost certain defeat, which could knock us outta a bowl bid, I contacted the athletic director at Allbright—sometin' of a buddy o' mine—and asked him ta let us outta da game so we can schedule a weaker opponent. Which he has said he would do—but he wants two hundred fifty thousands dollars.

"Now," he looked up from his text. "If we should make it to a bowl—say, da Plastic Bowl in Youngstown, Ohio—we can make half a mill just in TV rights. So, I am askin' dat OCU agree to pay Allbright da quarter mill to make sure of a successful season. We can use da profit ta bolster our program of athletics." Aldo took off his glasses and put down his text.

"Any comments?" asked Wiley.

"By all means, yes," Berenice said. Like those on the committee, she was a mature academic who, one could sense, had been around the budgetary block a few times. "Coach Bruski's proposal is visionary, and—quite possibly—profitable. But only 'possibly' at best. Surely no sport known to grown men," she glanced coyly at Bruski, "is as unpredictable as football. In the meantime," she went on, "we are facing a serious shortfall in the library budget—in the very maintenance of our collection—with the university's accreditation review a scant two years away.

"And so I am proposing," she concluded, "that the aforementioned two hundred fifty thousand be devoted to the budget of our library."

"Questions or comments?" Wiley asked the committee.

I sat through several minutes of silence as the four members of the faculty committee on athletics stared at their shoes, then I waited some more. Finally, I addressed Wiley who looked up at the ceiling. "I'd like to say that, if Ocotillo U is truly a university [I heard a door open behind me], to ask the question of whether a quarter million dollars should be invested in its library instead of its football program—to ask that question is to answer it."

"Exactly!" boomed a voice behind me, and a somewhat agitated Albert McNulty took a seat at the table.

"Is that all?" Wiley inquired. "Well, then, shall we take a count of hands or vote by ballot?"

"Vote by ballot," several members mumbled. And so they did. The football proposal was defeated, three votes to two. I considered staying around to recap the meeting with Wiley. Why had the others had nothing to say? But he got up quickly and left, with the others not far behind. McNulty took time to knead my shoulder before he walked out as well.

Driving home that afternoon, I passed a van from the local electrical com-pany. There was a sign on the back, cautioning customers not to dig in their yards without asking about buried power lines. The sign had a slogan: Know What's Below. I thought maybe I should pick one up and frame it.

That night, the voices of self-doubt returned: "Knock it off!" and "Aren't you forgetting something?" But they were joined by another, the powerful presence of McNulty.

10

Halfway up the trail to Tadpole Ridge, I was huffing—a couple of car lengths behind Teresa who was in full stride and showing no signs of exertion. The trail is not as strenuous as the one to Gomez Peak. But it's a steep incline, and the Mother of All Brunches at Serena's was trying to resolve itself in my stomach. I needed to ask Teresa about those Zumba classes.

Suddenly, she stopped and spun around, laughing. "Desviado—you deceitful devil, hacking her emails. I didn't think you had it in you. But I'm glad Aaron got you unhooked. And what did he have to say about your office being bugged?"

I held up a hand while I caught my breath and motioned to a rock that looked like a place to rest and continue our brunch-time conversation. "There were some wires that looked suspicious around the edge of the ceiling, but they were frayed and disconnected. Must have come from an earlier chapter in the Byzantine drama of OCU."

We sat and grabbed our canteens, took a long draught of cool water. "Speaking of Aaron, does it ever make you feel nostalgic for teaching, when you have your one-on-ones with him? I have to say, now that I'm in the classroom, I think I might miss it if I had to leave."

"Remember, I didn't have much choice. Sure, I miss the subject matter; I really have a deep interest in religious thought. But, I dunno: sometimes I see possibilities in administration, a chance to make a difference if I could ever get my feet on the ground."

Which is just what we were doing, slipping on our backpacks as we got to our feet. "Well, I see what you mean," Teresa remarked. "At one point, I thought I might be headed for administration."

"When was that?" I asked.

She said quietly, "Not long ago."

I did a double take and stood stock still as she took a few steps forward. "Teresa!" I said, sharply. "Does this have something to do with Linda Lucero?"

She looked at me and said nothing as the tumblers twirled in the back of my mind, and a couple of them clicked. "So you're not here because you lost your job in Alamogordo…"

She stood in place and slowly shook her head.

"You came here because of Linda Lucero, presuming she'd be president." Then my heart sank. "And was it just to work for her, or…" I remembered those people in glass houses.

"Mas tarde," she said. "More later. But first, let's get to the top. Perhaps we can see better from there."

The vista from Tadpole Ridge is impressive, far out over a phalanx of rolling mountains clad in ponderosa pine. We doffed our backpacks once again and settled down on a thick, fallen log. "It's a relationship that goes way back," she began. "Two young girls—still teenagers, really, in a strange environment. The two of us had much in common, sure—both Latinas from the Southwest. I was from Albuquerque, Linda grew up in El Paso. Same basic culture.

"But we are also very different. She was from a large family—eight kids all competing from day one, vying for their parents' attention. Some of them turned to crime to get noticed. She has a couple of brothers locked up. But Linda did it with academics. She worked furiously at Holyoke, went on to grad school and got a PhD—straight through.

"But at times she was very lonely. We both were. Long Christmas vacations, no money to get home. More snow than you could believe. Cold winter nights…"

I was beginning to fill in the blank spaces. So maybe there was no rancher boyfriend, but only trips to see Linda, from Alamogordo. I was ready to question her some more, get all the cards on the table when I saw her stand up and peer over my shoulder.

There, rounding the bend on the trail out of the forest was the largest deer I had ever seen. It was a buck standing, shoulder height, four feet off the ground. His thighs were knotted in massive muscles and his rack of antlers was as wide as he was tall. He saw us at once but didn't flinch, nor did he seem inclined to charge us. He just watched impassively.

"The alpha male," Teresa murmured. "On his turf, pretty much in charge of anything he wants to do." And she shuddered at the spectacle of him. Then she turned away from the massive creature and wrapped her arms around me, burying her head into my chest.

In a few minutes, the buck turned toward the forest and trotted away. But

Teresa and I stayed where we were. She rose up as our lips met and we remained that way a long time.

We took our time descending the trail—it was strewn with rocks that could twist an ankle—but we didn't linger, and the drive went fast. It wasn't long till we were at her front door. "Please," she said, as she touched my arm. "Please come inside." It did not escape my attention that she hadn't said "Come in," but "Come inside."

Two hours later the afternoon sun was fading and we were still in her bed. I know I'd nodded off, and when I wakened I began to remember: her bronzed body, dark nipples, black hair flowing as she lowered herself on me and came to a quivering climax. Then I turned and there she was again, lying at my side with a knowing smile. And, of course, we did it all again.

This time, afterward, the questions that had clamored to be heard came forward again. I asked a few of them and learned enough to feel somewhat reconciled to what we'd just done. No, I was not an experiment. Of course she'd been with men. And, yes, a guy in Alamogordo. When it came to herself and Linda, she implied it was complex, a lot to explain. Maybe later on she'd try. But Linda was back home now, while she was here with me. And hoped to be again.

"I have something to share," Sterling was saying, "a moment of inspiration. It came to me over the weekend." Then: "Connor, are you here?"

Indeed I was, at the first presidential cabinet meeting, another of Sterling's inspirations. So far, it was just he and Wiley and I. He'd served coffee and rolls and it felt like a high-level confab as we gathered around the conference table in his presidential office. But Sterling was right; I was something less than fully present this morning, busy re-living the weekend in my head. I'd been in my office much of Sunday—shredding all my ill-gotten data from the G drive. Plus I was pondering my brief history with Teresa: something else to shred?

Sterling went on. "I was thinking about what to do here, how to begin, when a comment from one of my professors came back to me. It was a course in leadership and he'd told us, in whatever action we take, to always try to solve two problems at the same time.

"That thought stayed with me later in the day, when I was reading a fragment of writing from W.E.B. Du Bois to Daniela. It's a passage I've always loved. Here, I made some copies."

"Herein lies the tragedy of the age:

Not that men are poor, — all men know something of poverty.
Not that men are wicked, — who is good?
Not that men are ignorant, — what is truth?
Nay, but that men know so little of men."

"Adjust the pronoun, of course; today we would say 'people.' But, how profound, how timeless." He gave Wiley a long look, pleased I suppose, to have quoted from his black brother. But Wiley said nothing. He hadn't all morning. I noted how ministerial Sterling seemed: all these inspiring sentiments, how he seemed to miss preaching.

"Well," he went on, "'serendipitous,' 'providential'—call it what you will. Suddenly I saw a connection. Might there be a way to attack some of the isolation, the reticence to share our thoughts and feelings which has been noted on this campus, while at the same time broaching the question of accountability? And, at that, I thought of something we might use."

He gave out a single sheet with twenty-one terms. Looking them over, they seemed random: "absolute zero," "the Alamo," "penis envy," "zeitgeist."

"And this is?"

"A quiz on cultural literacy, Connor. The first step toward a consistent curriculum for higher education. Of course, it's infeasible to consider any sort of Common Core at this level, such as we're seeking for the public schools. But cultural literacy is a start. What is it that a college-educated person in this society ought to know? And this is just a whimsical way of raising the issue, an enjoyable exercise. I came across it in Psychology Today."

"And how do you want to go about it?"

"Good question, Connor, and I'm glad you raised it—because I'm going to ask you to share it with the faculty. Just send out a mass email with a personal note, very appropriate for you as dean, and ask them to take a few minutes to administer it in each of their classes. It just calls for a sentence or two to determine that the students grasp the concepts. The professors can tabulate the results and send them back to you. Maybe we'll give a prize to the class with the best score."

"And how do you think that will be received?"

"Very favorably, Connor, I'm sure. It's not much of an inconvenience and maybe it will inject a little life into some of the less inspiring classes. Also, it will be a good way to publicize your presence, to remind faculty members that we have a dean who's here to assist them."

The rest of Sterling's agenda was anything but inspiring—just routine administrative matters—though it took another half-hour to get through it. Wiley said little and I began to space out again, only to be called back to attention by Sterling, who didn't miss a thing.

When he was through, Wiley left and I asked to speak to Sterling. "I can't say that this project of yours fits my job description. Do you plan to have me do more things of this sort?"

He thought for a moment. Then he said, "Well, I should think you might want to go a bit out of your way to help me."

I asked, "Why is that?"

He was silent for a minute. Then he said, "I had hoped we wouldn't have to discuss it."

"'That' being...?"

"Well, all right—the way you left town, the way you were enabled to."

"You mean the Chief?"

"Of course: Ed Hartwell, the deacon. His generous interpretation of Ned's note—"my minister"—as a call for help."

"Which it might have been."

Sterling scoffed, "We all knew what was going on. Of course, we knew. It was an accusation. You might not have known, but he did do himself in, three years later."

"When I was out of the picture."

"Yes, indeed. You know, his wife, Lisa, came looking for you." He smirked. "And I doubt it was to perform the funeral. But, of course, no one knew where to find you."

"So you helped me..."

"Get away. Indeed. Start all over. I imagine it was one more thing you failed to appreciate or understand about me."

I stood stock still for several moments, a question framed in my mind but not uttered. What did Sterling believe might have happened that night when Ned went off the bridge?

He said, "Any more questions about the project?"

I spent that night mired in quicksand, at the bottom of a long tunnel—clawing at the earth on all sides. Far ahead, I could see a glimmer of light, and at times it seemed I was progressing. But then something had me in its grasp. Was it the quicksand? Not entirely. Now and then a hand rose up from the muck, encircled an ankle. It threatened to draw me under.

I woke in a sweat, got up, and uncapped a beer. The dream was not one that called for a lot of analysis. Sterling had me by the short hairs. What a shock, but I might have seen it coming. The ease with which I'd left town, even as Ned lay comatose in the hospital, the failure to ask me hard questions. Now the past I thought I'd left behind was two doors down the hall. And something else Sterling had said: Lisa had been looking for me. I can't say I ignored that.

11

I slogged into my office the next morning and stumbled over a large, manila envelope someone had slid under the door. It contained a pop quiz, like Sterling's. This one was in a multiple choice format: the Black Intelligence Test of Cultural Homogeneity: acronym, the BITCH Test. The author was one Robert Williams, PhD, Professor Emeritus at Washington University in St. Louis—a black psychologist, a note said. I scanned the questions and got the gist of it.

1. CPT means a standard of
     a) time
     b) tune
     c) tale
     d) twist

4. The eagle flies means
     a) the blahs
     b) a movie
     c) payday
     d) deficit

5. Gospel Bird is a
     a) pheasant
     b) chicken
     c) goose
     d) duck

11. Stone fox means
     a) bitchy
     b) pretty
     c) train of thought
     d) wasting time

It came with another note: "The problem is not that they know so little of one another. It is that they think they know too damn much." It was unsigned, but I was well acquainted with the author.

It was Tuesday and I had most of the week to fill with—what? Well, there was Sterling's project, the email with that idiotic exercise. But, then, too, there were my stacks of tasks: class schedules, room assignments, standard faculty contracts to review. As I sifted through the flotsam of my in box, I calculated how long it might be before I could get around to sending out the email and exercise.

And then, for some reason, I began to reflect on my job in terms of how much I had grown in it. I now had a whole array of administrative skills, certainly none I'd have gone out looking for. But I'd learned to manage all of this material, as I'd watched Alice Pendergast.

Would I ever sit down and try to get to know her? She hadn't yet come by with my coffee, so I pushed my paperwork aside and reached for the phone to call her. But just then there was a knock on my door and Alice burst in, shutting the door behind her. "A teacher from the high school out in the waiting room," she wheezed. "I asked him to make an appointment, but he's in a state. So I said I'd ask if you might see him."

Alice had been around the block a few times at OCU and didn't normally react this way, so my curiosity was aroused. I asked her to show the fellow in.

He was a short man, maybe 5-8, with a stomach that preceded him by several inches. He wore an outfit I'd associate with high school teachers who'd been in the game awhile: chino pants, colored shirt with a half-knotted tie. His hair was blond, but streaked with gray—and long, almost to his collar. I placed him in his mid-fifties, a Baby Boomer showing signs of wear.

"You the dean?" he asked, as he held out his hand.

I took it, nodded, and pointed to a chair. "Connor Ransom. What can I do for you?"

He gave a rueful smile. "Sorry to barge in like this. It's my free period and I have to get back in a short time. Oh, and I'm Kent Kronawitter—'Krony.' I teach history at the high school, and it's about this course some of my students have been taking here at the university. Advanced placement, concurrent enrollment, you know?"

("Too well," I reflected.)

"Hot topic," he went on. "'Sex in History.' As you can imagine, hordes of kids wanted to sign up. Instructor's a Doc..." He pulled out his smart phone and scrolled through some notes. "Doctor Whitehead. Know her?"

I paused for a minute, with no desire to be sucked into the maelstrom of his working life—the bells, the crowded halls, all the classes.

"I believe I remember the name," I said finally. "Doctor Margo Whitehead." I knew that she was a new faculty member in sociology, fresh out of grad school.

"Bring her in, call her in, can you? Wanta clear up some things she's been telling the kids." He looked at his watch. "Not much time before the next period starts."

"Why don't you tell me what you think she's been saying," I said. I recalled my audience with Walter Driscoll and the Reverend Buford Schneuter, and wasn't about to call her in.

"Erroneous information, that's what it is. Now, I have no objection to the fact that the course deals with sex—been around a bit myself, ya know?" He offered a salacious grin. "But what you tell these kids must be accurate. And she's putting out plain misinformation."

"Can you give me an example?"

"Two of 'em," he sputtered, again glancing at his watch. "Okay, one's back in pre-history. She's been telling 'em that Neanderthals interbred with homo sapiens. And then, more recent past, that Thomas Jefferson had sex with one of his slaves, and a child by her."

I thought for a minute. "Well, Mr. Kronawitter. I'm no historian, but from what I've read, my understanding is that those statements have been confirmed by recent research, that both would seem to be accurate."

He stood and frowned.

I said, "Tell me, if you would—where did you study history, and when?"

Now he glowered. "Right here at Ocotillo U, and I graduated thirty-five years ago with a B.A. Majors in secondary education and his-to-ry."

"And your studies since then?"

"Education courses to keep up my certification."

"Well, perhaps that's all that needs to be said."

"That's it?" he demanded.

"Well, not entirely," I commented. "I wonder if there's room for another student in Doctor Whitehead's course. I can look into it for you."

Kronawitter stood and fixed me with a baleful stare. "Sir, I want to know who you report to—the name of your superior."

I sat down and wrote out the names and phone numbers of Drs. Wiley Crane and Sterling Holmes, then handed them to him. I said, "One's an historian, as a matter of fact."

I offered my hand but he stormed to the door and swung it open. He vowed, "You haven't heard the last of this!" and slammed it on his way out.

I thought back to my decision not to involve Margo Whitehead in this mess—to handle it and catch the flack myself. From the gray recesses of my cranium, I pulled up a mantra from grad school, a course in ethics. "To whom or what am I responsible, and in what community of interaction am I myself?" In other words, where was my loyalty? Later, I would remember that encounter, and wonder if that was the time when I began to look at my work that way.

The next morning when Alice brought my coffee, she closed the door behind her. She asked if I had a minute. She said, "Connor, I think it's time we had a talk. I should tell you something about this place: not everything, but enough to help you keep your head together."

I invited her to sit down, and took a visitor's chair across from her. She took a long draught of coffee followed by a deep breath, and began. It turns out she was a student here—major in foreign languages—back in the sixties. "Fluent in three at the time," Alice said, "although Spanish is the only one I've kept up.

"It was a time of idealism, of course; you've heard about that. And I was out to take down the Tower of Babel—unite the human race—with my gift for the various tongues. The only problem was figuring out how to go about making a living, doing that. I knew I couldn't teach, didn't have the personality for it. So I finished my degree, and they hired me into my part-time campus job on a full-time basis."

"Academic affairs," I said, and she nodded.

"I had a pretty good grip on the logistics of the office—a damn sight more than the academic gods who came in here as dean, one after the other."

"About as green as me," I mumbled.

She said, "Worse. You never pretended to know anything about what you were doing, but most of the others weren't having any part of humility. Ever heard the Spanish saying: no sabemos lo que no sabemos? Need some help?"

"A little."

"'We don't know what we don't know.' It loses a little in the translation. But you, amigo, have grown—more than I ever did with computers, that's for damn sure. But I'm losing my train of thought. What I wanted tell you was a little bit of what it was like in this school back then. And I guess one way is to look at the relationships you see around here, and I don't mean academic."

"Love affairs, marriages?"

"Do you have any idea how many people on the faculty used to be married to someone else here? Of course you wouldn't. And I'm not talking about ordinary divorces—people who split up and move away. I mean folks who change partners, and then stay. Serve on the same committees: cocktail parties, potluck suppers, all the rest.

"I suppose because the job market in other institutions wasn't good."

"That's it. Well, to answer my own question, it's maybe ten or a dozen couples I can think of." She paused, went back to her coffee for a minute. "Ever met Peter Entwhistle?"

"Sure, in accounting. I was in a committee meeting with him the other day, before that ran into him one night at the Outpost."

Alice snorted. "About the height of his social life, I reckon. Well, I was married to him."

"You were?"

"For twenty years, four months, and thirteen days—fortunately, no kids. Want to find someone to teach a boring subject like accounting, pick a boring guy. Although my folks thought well of him, stability and all that. To be honest, I was pretty wild... I'm losing my train of thought."

"But you didn't marry someone else here..."

"Not exactly...but the reason I wanted to talk to you was that crazy guy yesterday. I thought you handled him well, by the way. Well, I mean, certainly he's stupid. But all of that emotion!"

I thought for a minute. "You mean unlike..."

"This place," she filled in. "The reticence, that dull patina."

"But once in a while it seems to crack and something breaks loose. Albert McNulty, say."

Alice broke into a warm smile. "Oh, Bert..." She sat back and was silent.

"So you think I ought to look for undercurrents around here, like a subterranean river."

She said, "More like molten lava. When people disagree about some policy, a point of academic order—when they organize—well, just think of us thirty years ago. That crazy guy, that energy? What I wanted you to know is: we were like that."

The rest of the week went quietly. I occupied myself with processing paper work and thought occasionally of my conversation with Alice, some other topics I might broach if the time was right and I had a chance. My old boss, Walter Driscoll, say—what was her take on him? But mostly I ruminated on my new straw boss and the odious task he'd assigned me.

Mid-week, I saw an incoming email from Sterling, and cringed. I still hadn't gotten to his assignment. But it was a social invitation, to a gathering at the president's residence Friday evening—six o'clock for drinks, a light supper, and an informal program. Bring a guest, he added.

I called Teresa and she responded enthusiastically. We'd already made plans for another brunch and hike on Saturday. The Friday soiree could make for an overnight; I'm sure we were both aware of that.

Finally, on Friday afternoon, I sent a broadcast email to the faculty, exercise attached. In my note, I suggested that it had been recommended, though I didn't say by whom. I tried to put a light spin on the cultural literacy test—just a fun thing we can do together. Ha hah. But I asked them to tabulate the results and submit them to me within a week. There'd be a prize for the class with the best score, which sounded serious. It was a mixed message if I ever saw one.

When I picked up Teresa that night, she seemed more reserved than on the phone. But it was a short drive over to Sterling's house and I thought little of it. Sterling's home displayed the Latina touch of Daniela—bright paintings on whitewashed walls, and tropical plants like a greenhouse. It was my first personal contact with the woman and she came on strong, upbeat about everything. Before long I began to wonder if her middle name might not be "caramba!"

"Connor!" she exulted. "So much history con mi esposo." I must have blanched, trying to envision how much of it she knew. "And Teresa! We will surely be amigas—so much that we share." Teresa smiled but seemed to take a half-step back, and from Sterling when she met him a few minutes later.

Wiley was there with his wife, Barbara, a tall brunette. She was attractive and I was not surprised to find she was white, that he lived every day with multiculturalism. She seemed fond of Wiley in an equal footing sort of way and had photos of their three children—nice-looking kids, in shades of café au lait.

Wiley seemed relaxed, unfazed in the home of his titular boss. At one point, Daniela was celebrating Sterling's academic attainments. It seemed she had stayed in the same doctoral program long enough to snare him but hadn't completed the degree. Ah, but Sterling had.

"And I'm so proud whenever I hear him called 'doctor,'" she effused. Wiley framed a smirk and I sensed something was coming. "Reminds me of my days back in the 'hood," he remarked. "Sit down at a table with professional folk, you always had to go 'round and ask: 'Are you a doctor?' 'Are you a doctor?' Man says, 'Yes, I is'—then you know what to call him!"

There was a brief silence as Barbara hit him in the stomach and Teresa stifled a snort.

The informal program consisted of corridos, traditional Mexican ballads as rendered by Daniela at the piano along with Alicia Domingo, the choir director. Both had strong voices and Alicia gave a pelvic twitch to the rhythm which piqued my interest in a perverse sort of way. The only number I recognized was la cucaracha, but Teresa knew most all of them and joined in. I glanced at Sterling as Daniela was belting out a corrido and he seemed somewhat remote, like an anthropologist on a field trip. Teresa, on the other hand, did not appear detached. Ever since I'd picked her up, she'd seemed to be harboring something smoldering.

As we were getting ready to leave, a slight young woman came up and touched my arm. She said, "Hi, I'm Margo Whitehead" and introduced me to her husband who said he also taught at OCU—political science. The two of them were small, about the same size, like a pair of bookends. Just out of Cornell, they said, and fortunate to find entry-level jobs in the same institution. "I want to thank you for attending to that fellow from the high school," she said with some feeling. "I heard he was after me. And, oh, I thought the exercise you emailed me was cute, although as a sociologist I have to say, of course, that there are many different cultures."

Teresa was less forgiving. At first she said nothing on the way home, block after block. But then suddenly she unloaded. "All right, I got it, too. So, someone told you to send out that list of random terms to test our 'cultural literacy,' and I'm supposed to give it as a quiz?"

I couldn't think of what to say.

As we pulled up in front of her place, she wasn't done. "I wonder who 'recommended' that, as you say. But no, I'll bet I can guess."

I had nothing to say.

"Well, I can't imagine what he might recommend next. Get ready to bend over, Connor. Hey, is there something about the two of you that I should understand? Or are you just some sort of creepy, knee-jerk conformist?"

"Teresa, you seem really angry. Is it because you don't want to spend the night with me?"

"Not on your life," she snapped as she opened the door. "And let's test your cultural literacy. 'Tonto util'—got that? Well, I'll save you a trip to the dictionary. You know what you are, Connor? You're nothing but a useful fool!"

The weekend seemed vacant. I took the hike up Tadpole Ridge and felt very much alone. Was I lonely for Teresa or simply alone? I had a good deal of time to reflect on subjects such as that. I spent much of it reading on my Kindle, ordering and perusing and deleting one book after another, as my interest waned. Saturday evening found me at Edmundo's on the zocalo. I had a couple of Dos Equis and tried the chile rellenos.

Sunday, I decided to visit the Quaker Meeting at ten a.m. The local Religious Society of Friends is a small group of a couple dozen mostly elderly folks who spend most of their worship in silent meditation. I turn up once in a while and am always welcomed warmly. When someone breaks the silence, the message can be off the wall. But I like the lack of structure and at times a Friend will stand up and have something inspiring to say.

On this occasion, no one spoke and I was glad to spend an hour in the silence. It seemed to help me gather my thoughts—"center down"—as the Quakers say. I found myself meditating on a passage from Buddhist teaching that once had struck me as so meaningful, I'd memorized it. People who are mindful, Gautama said, "do not repent the past, nor do they brood over the future. They live in the present. Therefore they are radiant. By brooding over the future and repenting the past, fools dry up like green reeds cut down in the sun."

I felt that truth again, as though he'd said it to me, and wondered if I would ever climb out of the past—that incident on the bridge that had shown me more of myself than I'd cared to see. At one point I looked up and around the Meetinghouse. These placid Friends in their latter years: had any of them ever done anything they regretted? And would I ever break free?

Monday morning began with the now-customary meeting of the presidential cabinet, all three of us. Wiley spent some time going over logistics of the academic calendar and I was glad to see that Sterling had put him first on the agenda, maybe open to some mentoring. But then it was his turn and the man was a broken record, still dead set on measuring everything he could get his hands on.

The topic of the day was course evaluation: were we doing enough of it, and how might it be done better. Sterling's latest bright idea was to borrow from the pain model of the medical profession, those six images of faces ranging from a total smile to a full frown. "We could pass those out several times during the semester, rather than waiting till the end," he opined. "Perhaps we might visit the hospital. They should have..."

To my dismay, he was beginning to turn in my direction. But just then there was a rap on the door and his secretary came rushing in. She handed me a pink slip with a message. "Please call Alice, immediately."

I got up, went out to the anteroom, and picked up her phone. "Alice, what is it?"

"It's Bert," she sputtered. "Albert: something's wrong. Humanities building, second floor. Please go over and see what's going on, if you can help him."

I dashed back in the conference room, picked up my jacket and briefcase, and headed out, the others watching in puzzlement. The humanities building was halfway across campus, and I took it at a trot. As I approached, I saw an ambulance parked outside. I ran up the stairs and met two emergency medical technicians coming down, McNulty on a stretcher between them. He looked ashen and wasn't moving. I gestured to one of the EMTs and he simply lowered his eyes. I thought I saw his head shake.

In the classroom, a dozen students sat in shock. Some were crying. A fellow came forward and I asked him what had happened. "It's a course in Medieval English Literature," he told me, haltingly. "Doctor McNulty got into Piers Plowman and he seemed to have some strong feelings about it, the way he gets. But his face began turning redder and he dropped his notes, grabbed his chest, and then he just fell over. Cheryl, here, called in on her cell and it took those guys about five minutes to get here. We had no idea what to do. She just held him with his head in her lap. He wasn't moving, and..." He broke down in tears.

Eventually, the students slowly filed out. I looked at the pile of papers on the desk in the front of the room. There were McNulty's notes, something scribbled on top: "With thy might." And then I saw the cultural literacy exercise, twelve copies.

I gathered up everything and headed back to my office. As I mounted the stairs, I was trying to think of how to break the news to Alice. But when I opened the door to her office, I forgot all that. For it seemed the news had traveled fast. Alice Pendergast lay face down on her desk, splayed out across her keyboard.

Alice was unconscious as they carried her out, but I could see that she was breathing. I put some work in my briefcase, posted a sign on the door and locked it. When I got to the hospital, I checked in at the Intensive Care Unit and inquired about Albert McNulty. DOA, I learned. As I'd expected.

There was a quiet waiting room outside the ICU and I set up shop there, phoning Sterling's secretary to let her know I'd be there for the duration. I asked her to try to find out if Alice had any close relatives. Maybe human resources would know. Or her friends at school would, if she had any.

The nurses in intensive care came out to check in with me every hour or so. I'd explained that I was Alice's boss, although it sounded strange to say that. In the interim, I got something to eat at the cafeteria, which did nothing to dispel popular perceptions of hospital food. Finally, a nurse came out to the waiting room and told me that Alice was awake and had asked to see me.

She looked like a small bird in the hospital bed, clad in one of those blotchy, patterned gowns that make everyone look ill. Her skin was the color of newsprint, her hair pulled straight back as though pasted to her skull. But she fluttered her eyelids and raised a hand a couple of inches from the sheets. I reached out and held it.

Alice drew me close. Her breath was labored, but it was clear that she had some things to say. "Had ten years," she began, and tried to smile. "I was done... with Pete, and Bert's wife...Alzheimer's. In a place for that. Ten years...one love... my life.

She paused for breath and closed her eyes for a couple of minutes. Then she peered at me, trying to focus. "That Teresa...latch on to her...fond of you...can tell." Then she was gone again for five minutes or so. The nurse came in and said I ought to leave.

But Alice rallied as she said that, and drew me close again. "Watch out... Driscoll..."

I said, "What's that, Alice?"

"Cent...cent...cent," and she drifted away.

Alice lingered for a couple of days, but never regained consciousness. A niece appeared the second day, from the other end of the state. A rancher, nice gal about my age, and she took care of some private funeral arrangements. She asked me to attend, and said Alice had spoken of me for some months. Long before she'd spoken to me, I reflected.

A few days later, I was getting in some exercise, trudging around the track at the football field, when I noticed an older fellow across the way. He was going pretty fast and he overtook a woman about his age. As he passed by her, they exchanged a word or two and then he slowed down. They walked together for a while.

And I thought of Albert and Alice: how sometimes we make contact, if only for a while.

12

I was up to my ears in files—all of Alice's—the rest of that week, trying to reconstruct the work she had put in year after year to keep Ocotillo U afloat. I covered her reception job with work-study students and asked them to put off individual appointments for a couple of weeks. When those ridiculous cultural literacy tests arrived, I had them sent directly to Sterling's office and was glad to see he had enough sense not to object.

Gradually, I began to construct a job description for the new administrative assistant I would need to hire—and, in the process, began to give some thought to my own. To be sure, I'd lacked the presence of mind and strength of gut to ask for such a document when I was put here by Walter Driscoll. So I had no job description and was vulnerable to Sterling's de facto "Other Duties As Assigned." But fortune smiled and I found one that Driscoll had made for himself when he took over as academic dean. I stuck it in my files. A shield?

Mid-week, Alice's niece turned up—her name was Liz—and said she'd been looking for a minister to conduct the service. Then she'd found out that I used to be one. Would I consider...? I thought for a moment and said, "Sure. I guess it's something I can do for her."

Then I thought of an unusual format—something for non-conformists such as myself—and she said it would be fine. So the next day, after an announcement went out, we gathered at the funeral parlor about ten in the morning. The mortuary had a parlor like a huge living room. I arranged a dozen chairs at one end in a circle: a format I'd seen Quakers use. As ten rolled around, some women who looked like secretaries at the university came in. And then there was Aaron Fell, my independent study client and co-conspirator in the scanning project.

When everyone had settled in, I introduced myself as Alice's co-worker and said I'd offer a reading in remembrance of her life. Then, I said, anyone who had a particular memory or thought about Alice could simply share it, while allowing time between reflections. At the end, I said, we'd stand and join hands for a few moments of silence, a circle of life to commemorate hers and all that she had meant to us.

I began, with apologies for the male pronoun, with one of my favorite Biblical passages, from a work that hadn't quite made it into the mainstream canon: the Book of Ecclesiasticus.

> "Let us now praise famous men,
> and our fathers in their generations.
>   The Lord apportioned to them great glory,
> his majesty from the beginning.
>   There were those who ruled in their kingdoms,
> and were men renowned for their power...
>   There are some of them who have left a name,
>   so that men declare their praise.
> And there are some who have no memorial,
>   who have perished as though they had not lived;
> they have become as though they had not been born,
>   and so have their children after them.
> But these were men of mercy,
>   whose righteous deeds have not been forgotten;
> their prosperity will remain with their descendants,
>   and their inheritance to their children's children..."

There was some silence before one middle-aged woman stood up to speak. She told of a time when things had been rough in her life—something to do with an addiction—and Alice had reached out to help her when no one else would.

There was more silence, then another person spoke, and another, and another. I believe that everyone but Aaron had something to say, and then I spoke a little myself about getting to know Alice toward the end. I thought of sharing a bit about Albert McNulty, but let it go. I'm sure they all knew anyway.

As the sharing unfolded, something remarkable happened within me. I began to have a growing sense of wholeness in her life, and peace in my own. Here was a unique person, multi-faceted in her integrity and, in celebrating her, I felt more whole as well. After a couple of minutes of silence, we got up, joined hands, and then most stayed to mingle.

Aaron came over. "That was cool," he said. He asked if I were free for lunch and we went to Serena's. "Wouldn't it be great," he continued, over a Bohemia, "if we could simply worship that way, without all the liturgy and shit—just give ourselves time and space to think?"

I told him that was what the Quakers were after. Then I said I'd been surprised to see him and asked why he'd come.

"I only met her once," he said. "And it wasn't fun. I came over with a grade change form and she gave me a hard time. I know I wasn't alone. Students used to try to avoid her. That may have been a reason I went along with you on the scanning scam. I knew that was what it was.

"So, maybe I felt guilty. Was that why I came? I guess I thought there must have been more to her than what I saw, and I needed to acknowledge that."

I told him my experience had been much the same, and about my time with her before she died.

"So, maybe there's a universal something-or-other beneath all of that," he mused, over a chicken-avocado wrap. "A need to feel connected, in spite of all the crap that comes up every day and divides us. Some kind of spiritual ground floor."

I told him I thought that was what Jesus had meant by the Kingdom of God, "'the being of all.' Like every religious sage, I think he experienced a kind of breakthrough of being: a sense that everything is connected, and everyone." Midway through my second beer, I was into it.

We broke up about one thirty and I headed back to Alice's files. I suggested a few books to read on the subject of faith. What a student. Could I clone him?

When I arrived back at the office, my euphoria fizzled. There was a message from Sterling who had taken it upon himself to speak at Albert McNulty's funeral at the Methodist Church the next day. Did I have any anecdotes that might fit into his remarks?

I sent back a note about two items I'd found in Albert's lecture notes the day he died: twelve copies of the cultural literacy test he'd evidently felt compelled to administer, and a line he'd scrawled at the top of the first page, "With thy might." What I didn't say was that all of that might have put him over the edge, a hyper-tense guy like that.

What I muttered to myself was, "Man, maybe you ought to consider that in this job, someone might actually take what you say seriously."

The church service was a classic hymn sandwich with eulogies in the middle. There was talk of Albert's allegiance to the church, but nothing of course about his devotion to Alice. Had the Methodists known of that? Some of his students spoke and then it was Sterling's turn. I tried to hear what he had to say—something about McNulty's commitment to his profession—but a tide of darkness kept rising around me. My God, Sterling, did you kill that guy?

That night, I dreamt of standing on a bridge as someone went over the side. It was remarkable how close I'd been standing, next to him. The waters were swirling and I'd leaned over, extending an arm as though to help. But as his head bobbed up, I believe I might have pushed him down, for I thought I'd seen who was drowning. I knew it wasn't Ned. Who was it?

My first thought as I woke was something I'd said to Aaron: a sense that everything was connected, and everyone. But what about lethal connections?

Friday afternoon, I turned my back on my office and the endless task of re-constructing the work of Alice Pendergast and declared a holiday for the weekend. I needed time to breathe.

That night, I dropped in at Serena's, the bistro in El Grande, the big hotel on the plaza, and thought I'd have a couple of beers at the bar. Already, the weekend was beginning to feel like a void and I thought I might find someone to talk to. But as I stepped inside, I stopped at the door. There was only person sitting at the bar and I knew him. Ernesto Morales, ceramics professor from the expressive arts department and legendary lothario, was hunched over a mug of suds, looking all alone and empty as one of his vessels. I felt a shock of recognition—myself in him—turned around, and walked back out the door.

I suppose it was nostalgia that drew me back to Tadpole Ridge on Saturday morning, maybe for a memory of some kind of connection. The weather was blustery in mid-November, and not your prototypical day for a hike. But, twenty minutes out of town, there I was trudging up the trail, wishing all the while I'd worn another layer.

And then, as I rounded the narrow bend to the top, I felt a sudden surge of warmth. On the rock where we had sat, was a solitary figure bundled up in stocking cap and parka. She turned around with a cautious smile, her face bright red from the cold.

I fairly cried out, "Teresa!"

She said, "I still don't know about you, amigo. Not as much as I should."

"I could say the same."

"But I heard about what happened when Albert died, and Alice; you cared for her. It was all over the English department.

"That wasn't my intention, to be publicized. I was just there at the time."

"You were there for those people. And what else is it all about? So I'd like to see if maybe we could..."

"Start again?"

She took four steps in a half-second and wrapped me in a hug. Then a half-step back. "But we're going to have to do something about all this introspection. One way or another, we've got to get your head up out of your ass."

It didn't take long for us to skid down the rocky trail and into our cars, to Serena's. It was too late for brunch, but we ordered a couple of draft beers and tortilla wraps. In an hour or so, the lunch crowd cleared out and we lingered over coffee. Teresa sat back in a corner of the booth and gave me a long look that seemed both serious and caring.

"Connor, I realize this may be difficult. But do you think you can tell me what it is that Sterling has on you—why he has you so spooked?" She paused for a minute. "Take your time."

"I was afraid you were going to ask that." For a while I sat silent. Then, "Sterling could disclose some things about me. I haven't told you everything about how I took off out of town and left the ministry. You see, that night on the bridge with Ned Nordeen. For a minute, I lost touch with myself—blacked out, maybe that's the best way to say it. I remember following him over to the railing, and then sort of watching us both. He was leaning over the edge...everything went dark...and I think I might have...I mean, it could have been a major, local media event—the whole story. But Sterling called off the chief of police, kept it under wraps."

"Which, of course, served his interest," Teresa observed. "He was your boss, right? It happened on his shift... But, I'm curious. Have you ever had any other experiences like that?"

"That's the thing. It's hard to reconstruct. But when I found my dad in the garage, there was a minute when it seemed like...I wasn't really there. Years later, giving sermons in my fanatic phase—there were times I'd be in the pulpit when it seemed...I wasn't in myself. I was watching myself. It's hard to explain."

"'Dissociative reaction,'" Teresa said. "Did you ever see a shrink, hear that term?"

"Sure I have. And that's fine if you want to treat it as pathology. But there's another side to it. Do you know the derivation of 'ecstatic'? In Greek, it meant 'to stand outside'. Do you get that? In some cultures—times and places—people wanted to stand outside their immediate experience. Maybe when we drink, do drugs, we still do."

"So, you opt for all this meditation, these trances, 'cause you like the way it feels? You get off on the sensation, right? Is that why you're so religious?"

"Not entirely. I also have a sense that...this has to mean something."

"What has to?"

"You know—Albert, Alice, you, me, Sterling—all of it, in the long run."

"Like, 'for all eternity'?"

"Exactly."

Teresa had been leaning toward me. But now she took a sip of her coffee and huddled back in the corner of the booth again. For a minute, she sat still. "Connor," she began. "There's just one thing. While you're up in that eternal whirl, things are happening down here in real time. And I wonder...I wonder if that's one reason you need somebody like me."

I thought a minute. "You said one reason, Teresa."

She pushed her foot against my leg under the table and rubbed it lightly up and down. She said, "Could be there are others."

The rest of the weekend was spent at her place: cooking, eating, bedding—a lot of that last. I learned of her tastes in food and in bed, in both cases eclectic. I marveled at the textures of her body and the earth tones of her skin, the endless inventiveness in her lovemaking. She never puckered up when she kissed, but slowly brushed lips, and I found it arousing. For all the multitude of partners I had had, I was coming to see them as mostly the same. And I wondered if intercourse can be quantified, keeping score like some guys do. As she led me to new places, it seemed that I might have had sex only once in my life, the same act over and over again.

Sunday morning over breakfast, Teresa leaned back again and fixed me with a look that was all business. "Fun's fun, Connor," she announced, "but we need to do some investigating. There's something going on at this school and I think we need to get to the heart of it."

"What do you have in mind?" I asked. "A research project? Can I do this for credit?"

She ignored my weak humor. "Here's a method of interviewing I've always liked—from the days of muckraking journalism, turn of the last century. I'm going to tell you what I know about something, all right? And I'd like you to fill in the rest. Or you can start, either way."

I said, "Why don't you go? I still don't get why we're doing this. Are you just trying to keep in practice?"

"It's more than that, but I'm not sure what...Okay, muy bien. Tomorrow morning at your staff meeting, you're going to acquire a subordinate."

"What? You don't mean a new secretary—I haven't even advertised Alice's position."

She shook her head. "No, a guy named Farley Hartshorne. Know anything about him?"

The name rang a bell, and I placed him at the meeting of the faculty committee on athletics. A wiry young guy from political science. As I recalled, he'd voted against Aldo Bruski, the athletic director, and alongside Albert McNulty. I told her all that.

"Will he be full-time?" I asked. "What will he do?"

She said, "Quarter-time, released from a course that didn't make enrollment. He'll be coordinator of assessment, Sterling's brainchild. I'm not positive, but I think he'll report to you."

I sat for a moment, stunned. I said, "And, if I may ask, how in hell do you know that?"

Teresa gave a wry smile. She said, "It's a holy word where I come from: a source."

I said, "Well, I'm impressed...now, I suppose you want me to tell you something."

She waited expectantly.

"I don't want this to get around, and I mean it. But when Alice was dying, there were several things she tried to say. For one thing, that I should latch onto you. She said she could tell that you cared for me."

Teresa smiled obliquely.

"But there was something else and it had to do with Driscoll. 'Watch out' was part of it. She was trying to get out something like 'cent,' 'cent.' And then she was gone."

Teresa looked way off across the room. She got up to bring us both more coffee and then sat down again at the table. Finally, she said, "I wonder about Driscoll, if he's still part of the equation. Sterling seems like some sort of pawn. I can't think that he's a major player in what's about to happen here."

"And what's that?" I asked, somewhat urgently.

She said, "No se. I have no idea. But I know these undercover groups are meeting: SOCO and GOCO. I believe a lot of it has to do with enrollment, maybe something about new funds to expand the football stadium. And I can feel the pressure of all these people locked in with one another, year after year, with no place else to go in their careers..."

I told her more of what I'd learned from Alice, about the breakups and remarriages.

Teresa said, "I'm sure that's another big part of it. But the rest, I don't know. I just have a feeling that Sterling has walked into something he doesn't understand. He seems like a guy with a cigarette standing next to a gas pump, about to light up. Well, stay tuned, amigo. And watch your ass." She smiled. "It's a nice one."

13

Spruced up in his suit and tie, with an outline set before him, Sterling looked primed to make some sort of formal presentation. But he knew that administrative matters of Ocotillo U had to take precedence at his weekly presidential cabinet meeting, and so he sat still for most of an hour while Wiley ran through the logistics of enrollment, class scheduling, faculty promotions and tenure, and the like. Until, finally, the administrative work was done.

Now it was Sterling's turn, a time to show us the way. "Benchmarking," he began. "I've been going through my notes from my doctoral studies on emerging trends in management, and this concept caught my eye. Does anyone know what it means?"

Zoned out on this Monday morning, I'd been absorbed by the décor of the presidential lair. Something about it was different. Perhaps it was the color of the walls—now a soft, gray green that managed to convey a serious air without being stuffy. Or maybe it was the new art work, a painting by Diego Rivera with bold swatches of bright, Mexican colors. I'd bet my paycheck that Daniela had been in here, redecorating the place.

"Does anyone know?" Since neither Wiley nor I had responded, that seemed to cover the options. But Sterling wasn't done. He turned to me as to a recalcitrant student. "Connor?"

I looked his way with a blank expression.

For a moment, he stared back at me. "Well, 'benchmarking' is the practice of improving organizational performance by measuring oneself against leaders in a given practice, regardless of their industry." Reading from his notes, he managed to expel all of that in one breath.

"For example," he went on, "in health care, an industry to which I have been giving attention, it seems that certain hospitals have been able to reduce the time required to register patients in emergency rooms by measuring themselves not against other hospitals, but hotels. Whereas wait times to see a physician could near two hours, hotel guests were being registered in five minutes. And so, hospital administrators began to ask, 'What can we learn from that?'"

He looked up from his notes and surveyed the two of us expectantly. "Now, suppose we were to look to the medical profession to ask how we can improve our own performance at Ocotillo U. For example, I've been doing some research on what is known as the Wong-Baker system of pain measurement—those six faces, happy to sad, that I mentioned some time ago. And I have found that no college or university as yet has thought to use those images to measure students' satisfaction with their professors. It seems the field is wide open."

I muttered something like, "I'll bet," and Sterling shot me a sharp glance while Wiley cracked a smile.

He passed out a version of the images.

"Now," he said, "I'd like someone to take on this project. What I have in mind is to develop some instructions and distribute the instrument to all the members of our faculty for administration in each of their classes, say, every two weeks. We can compile the data and look for trends. Perhaps there are certain lag times in the course of a semester, for example, and professors can learn to prepare some special activities to carry the students through."

He sat back with a self-satisfied smile. "Now, Connor, what about you? I think there's a publication in here that could be a good addition to your resume."

I felt a shock in the region of my solar plexus, the implication clear. "Sterling, perhaps we could talk about this after the meeting."

The rest of it didn't last long. Wiley slowly shook his head as he got up and walked out.

I took out my copy of Walter Driscoll's dean of the faculty job description and handed it to Sterling. "Quite apart from the question of whether this project makes any sense—obviously the instrument was intended for the assessment of physical pain—this is the job I was hired to do."

Then I gave him a copy of the description I'd worked out for Alice's. "And this is the job I need to fill and train someone in. Does it seem to you that I'd have time to take on another project, not to mention that cultural literacy exercise you assigned me before?"

He read both items, put them aside, and thought for a moment. It was a classic game of cat and mouse, and we both knew it. Perhaps it had begun back when I'd worked for him before. Whatever, I knew that now the stakes were higher and stacked in his favor.

"And that comment about adding to my resume, Sterling. How should I take that?"

"You can take it any way you want. I'm tasked with introducing some kind of innovation around here and obviously I can't do it alone. Given our history," he paused for effect, "of course, I thought it would be in your interest to assist me. However..."

I was glad to have a good idea of what was coming.

"Failing that, I am going to assign you a part-time staff member, a young fellow named Farley Hartshorne, as coordinator of assessment."

"And who's he?" I asked innocently.

"A junior member of the political science department. It's been brought to my attention that one of his courses failed to make the minimum enrollment. So, he'll be released one-quarter time and will report to you. He can handle both of those projects, the cultural literacy instrument and the Wong-Baker student satisfaction assessment. See what you can do to help him. If he publishes something, perhaps you can arrange to list yourself as co-author."

"For my resume," I suggested.

Sterling gathered up his things. "As you will," he said.

I saw Wiley at his desk as I passed by, and stuck my head in his office. "Do you have five minutes?" I asked.

He looked at his watch and grinned. "See if I can fitcha in."

I closed the door and told him about my acquisition of a part-time staff member, though not about having received a heads-up from Teresa. "Do you know anything about this guy, Farley Hartshorne?"

Wiley shook his head sadly. "Bright young fella, his second year. Maybe some political shenanigans, cancelling that course. But the kid has some issues in the classroom. Might wanna swing by, watch him in action."

I told him what Sterling had said about having been "tasked with introducing some kind of innovation here" and asked him what he thought that meant.

Wiley took a deep breath and sat back in his big Naugahyde executive chair. He laid a long leg across a corner of his desk. "The years I spent playing ball here, I learned a few things about the game," he began, "one being that there's two parts to it. Called 'offense' and 'defense.' Good lesson for life.

"Lotta guys get enamored of offense, love to watch that ball go through the hole. But defense counts, if you give it attention. I myself liked to play zone defense—charting the court, segmenting it so you know where you belong. Nothin' like that man-to-man kinda defense where you chase some guy's butt all over the floor. In zone defense, you stay put, play your passing lanes." He fell silent.

"So, I guess somewhere there's a moral here," I finally commented. "Are you saying it's time to go on defense?"

"Zone defense. Let him do his thang. Don' be chasin' a guy like that around. Gonna shoot himself in the ass."

"You mean the foot, don't you?" I laughed. "That's the saying, isn't it? He's going to shoot himself in the foot."

Wiley looked at me solemnly. "You hear what I'm saying? Au contraire. Man like that, gonna shoot himself in the ass!"

When I got back to the office, there was good news waiting. While I'd sent out a broadcast email for Alice's job to offices across campus, I hadn't taken any steps to advertise the opening in the community. I'd been half hoping that someone familiar with OCU might come forward and apply.

Audrey Harper was waiting in the anteroom, email in hand. A trim, well-dressed woman of maybe sixty, she looked vaguely familiar, and then I remembered her from the memorial service. It seemed she'd retired recently as department secretary in English but had found herself at loose ends; she missed all the doings on campus.

It took us twenty minutes to go over what Alice had done, and she was familiar with almost all of it. She seemed congenial and I'd liked what she'd had to say about Alice at the service. Leaving room for the bureaucratic dance of the human resources department, I told her I'd get back to her. But I knew I was ready to hire her on the spot.

Later that day, I scrolled through the class schedule and found that Farley Hartshorne was teaching one on American government in the humanities building. I ambled over 10 minutes after it had begun and found the door to his classroom open.

I took a spot in the hall where he couldn't see me. He was as slender as I'd recalled, and fit—like a younger version of Albert McNulty. He wore a twill shirt and chino pants, like an outdoorsman. His voice had a high-pitched, nasal quality and as he lectured on, there was an intense, almost frenetic quality to his delivery. I tried to see how his students were taking it, but couldn't find any in the front rows. And then I began to hear a susurration from the back of the room, a muted rumble, and I realized that Farley was trying to be heard over it.

"The other thing that struck me was his posture. As he threw himself into the class, he had an odd way of knotting himself up like a pretzel." I was having a beer and burrito after work with Teresa at Serena's. It seemed we were getting together more often at odd times during the week, and not just on weekends.

"How in the world did he get into that?" I went on. "I'm sure it's an affliction, like stuttering, that could be helped by a specialist in communications."

She took a minute and thought about Farley in the classroom. "Well, I guess he's like most college instructors—never had a course in teaching. This profession seems to assume that once you've mastered your subject matter, the teaching of it will follow. What a fantasy."

"So, I need to call him in and break the news about his new assignment," I continued.

"Are you going to comment on his teaching style?"

"Not at this time. He's not meeting me for that. You know, afterwards I was thinking of something else Walter Driscoll taught me. He said that when anyone came in my office, I should ask myself three questions. Why is this person coming? Why is this person coming now? And why is he coming to me? Farley's not coming for counseling. Which reminds me of another Driscollism. 'The best advice is that which is asked for.'"

"Well...if I can offer some advice," she went on, somewhat haltingly, "unsolicited, of course. I think you might want to help Farley figure out why the fuck he was singled out to take on a special assignment just because his class didn't make. Or, why he couldn't carry on with less than the required number of students, which I understand goes on here all the time..."

She looked around and began to seem restless. "Well, I guess I need to get home and do some grading...Oh, and this weekend? Connor, I...I'm afraid I'm going to be tied up."

("With Linda?") The question exploded in my mind. But she leaned over and gave me a warm kiss before I could utter it, swooped up her things, and was gone. I sat there in the booth, stunned with a sense of stifled rage, till a line from the old, countercultural comic Lenny Bruce came back to me. "In the fifties, to get a girl you had to be Jewish. In the sixties, to get a girl you had to be black. To get a girl, you have to be a girl, these days."

I sat there for another few minutes, trying to see if I could make myself laugh.

Farley Hartshorne appeared the next morning, looking apprehensive. He said, "Have I done something wrong?" I closed my door and asked him to take a seat.

"If you're like the rest of us, I guess the answer would be 'probably,'" I told him with a grin. "But, no, that's not why you're here. Has anyone told you?"

"Not at all. I just got a call from the president's office and the woman said to come over and see you."

"Have you looked on the course schedule for next semester? Do you know that your class was cancelled?"

"Well, I'd heard that." He began to twist in his chair.

"Would you like some coffee? I can't vouch for it, but it hasn't killed me yet."

He said he would and I went out and got us each a cup.

I asked him a bit about his background, to try to help him relax. He said he was from Waukegan, a small city in northern Illinois, that when he was growing up it had been run by a political machine not unlike the one in Chicago. "And I just took an interest in local governance," he explained. "Not so much as an activist, but a student of it. How do these machines get started? How are they maintained?"

We ended up talking about his interests for a half-hour. His eyes lit up as he went on and on. This guy had a passion for his field of study.

"So," I said, finally. "Would you like to tell me something about that course?" It was from Driscoll, I recognized. (God, would I ever be free of him?) " If you want to understand a problem, don't ask about the problem. Ask the person to tell you the story."

In Farley's case, the decision to cancel the course had been made by the chair of his division of social sciences, Jack Lofton of anthropology. He said, "We have only three faculty members in political science, so we're slotted under that division." I remembered Lofton from the Outpost and that meeting of the faculty athletics committee, along with his bosom buddy, Bob. I told Farley I remembered the meeting.

"Sometimes I wonder if that's where it all began," he said slowly. "Well, I guess I should say something about a meeting I went to the week before—or, as much as I can. They told me it was all in confidence."

I thought of Teresa's muckraking interviewing technique: tell 'em what you know and see if they'll fill in the story. "Was it SOCO—Save Our Ocotillo U?" I asked.

He nodded, nervously.

"Well, I'll bet Albert McNulty was there," I went on. "And, of course, he's no longer..."

"Well, that's true. So, I guess I could tell you what he had to say. As for the rest of it, well, it was pretty dark in there and nobody used any names."

"How many were at the meeting?" I asked.

He was silent for a minute. "Maybe a dozen, 15."

"And did Bert McNulty tell you how to vote at the committee on athletics?"

"Yes, and that was the gist of the whole affair—the committees coming up, the issues, how we should vote, and... That's about all I can tell you."

"And, let me see if I have this right. You think that was the whole reason your course was cancelled." I sat for a few minutes in silence (thanks to Driscoll) to let him fill in the space.

"That's about all I can say, right now."

"Okay, Farley. So, do you understand what you'll be working on for your quarter time?"

He said he didn't, and I outlined Sterling's two research projects: the cultural literacy test, and the pain assessment faces scale for course evaluation. His eyes got wide as I went on. "I'm supposed to work on something like that?" he sputtered. "I mean, I have a background in social research, but not for..."

"Look, I didn't invent this, Farley. If you have any questions, you can go talk with the president. But I'll tell you one more thing about this project."

He said, "And what's that?"

"I want no part of it."

14

For the next week or so, my days were filled with Arlene's job, getting her into it while trying to decide which parts of the work Alice had done that I wanted to take over myself. I learned there was a candidate pool of academics who had expressed interest in Ocotillo U and in time I began to understand why. For, while those endowed with tenure at OCU tended to graze in place, there was a lot of turnover at the low end of the herd.

I remembered the name of Margo Whitehead when I saw it on my calendar one morning—the young, sociology professor whom I'd rescued from the ignoramus high school history teacher. When she appeared later that day, she had a couple about her age with her. Both had unkempt hair and abundant tattoos.

"I thought perhaps you might help us with our problem," she began on a timorous note, as she and the young woman sat down. Margo introduced her as a student in intro sociology. The woman's boyfriend stood looming behind them. He looked like a bar fight about to happen. The issue, said the student, was that she was failing the course, possibly because she had given birth sometime around mid-semester.

"Can't you drop it?" I asked, and the boyfriend glowered at me. That would jeopardize her financial aid for the coming term, he explained darkly. In the end, it was not a long conversation. I noted that Doctor Margo Whitehead was charged with maintaining standards in her profession like, say, the physician who had delivered their baby. But somehow the analogy didn't take, and the atmosphere in my office darkened progressively to the point that I finally asked them to leave.

"I won't forget this," the boyfriend snarled over his shoulder as he slammed the door behind him.

"Margo, does this sort of thing come up a lot?" I asked when we were alone, and she began to quiver.

"When I got out of grad school, I had no idea this was what I was getting into," she sniffled. I got her some coffee and sat with her a while, trying to say something supportive. When she left, I found myself speculating how long she would stay around.

Farley was another who had me wondering. One day he stuck his head in my office and asked if I had a minute. "This girl came by to ask about her mid-term grade, and it wasn't too good. She sat down on the corner of my desk, raised her eyebrows, and looked down at me. She said, 'Is that the best you can do?'

"So, what do you think she meant by that?" he asked me.

Before long, I was back in Wiley's office.

"People think it's easy to teach in an easy school," he commented, as he set a stack of memos aside and took off his reading glasses. "But, in fact, it takes a mastery of craft."

I cocked my head at that.

"You remember reading about those craft guilds in the Middle Ages. Ever study that?"

"Sure, everyone's been through that."

"Well, it's the kinda movement that sticks in the heads of historians. 'Cause in some ways it never died. Look at higher education in a place like this—the range of skills required. See, that's something that got lost in commercial culture—latter part of the 19th century, age of mass industrialization. That's when the paradigm shifted, in them humongous corporations—climbing up the ladder from blue collar to white collar jobs, from doing the work to supervising the work, climbing that ladder—rewarding folks for specialization."

I said, "Isn't that the way it still works, some schools?"

"Mega-universities, you bet. Work your way up to be a full professor, you don't have to mess with students—undergraduates, at least.

"But not here, you're saying."

"I am, indeed. Pity the fool thinks he can get by on the strength of what's in his head."

"'He' or 'she,'" I reflected.

"You bet. Hang around here, you best have an entire array of skills."

I said, "Interpersonal, for example. That's what I've become aware of—the ability to set limits, or to know when you're being manipulated."

"Right on, Jack. Take that last item. Lotta campus liaisons get started from the bottom up. Not always top down sexploitation. And then you'll see instructors inflating grades, from sheer intimidation. It's possible to become taken in—or terrified—by some of the kinds of students we get 'round here."

"So, how do we teach the craft of teaching?" I wondered out loud. "Is it possible to help people develop, or do we just cycle instructors in and out, and tap into the candidate pool?"

"Good question, that," Wiley responded as he set his reading glasses on his nose and picked up a memo from the top of his pile. "Sounds like a topic for a lubricated consultation."

When we did have such a confab, it occurred in a scenario I could not have imagined. And it followed a sequence of events that, even now, seems borderline bizarre.

It began, of course, with another of Sterling's strange presidential cabinet meetings—he and Wiley and I—in his conference room. This edition had been postponed a couple of days, till Wednesday, so that he could address the San Vicente Chamber of Commerce Monday morning.

The theme of the day was, once again, benchmarking. But first he took time to check out the task he'd assigned me to perform, via Farley. "Any outcomes to report, on my first two initiatives, Connor?" He peered at me and I stared back. Interacting with Sterling had become an exercise in antipathy, my bile rising like a mal-digested meal.

"I've not been closely involved," I responded in a non-committal tone. "But I believe that Farley has received almost no responses. There were a few who got back to him on the cultural literacy exam, and a couple on the Pain Assessment Faces Scale. I have the impression that, except for Albert McNulty, all the others were junior faculty in their first year or so on campus."

He looked down and shuffled some papers. "Well, then..." he began, but I went on.

"Have you considered whether the faculty have any incentives to take time from their teaching to engage in these sorts of exercises?"

Sterling shuddered slightly and looked aside. "Certainly that is an issue," he noted, "and I have taken cognizance of it. But, in the long view, I believe my purpose will be clear. I am trying to introduce some innovation to this institution and thus far have been testing the waters. In the near future, I can assure you, the question of incentives will be addressed.

"Which brings me to my next step. I've been spending some more time at the hospital with Doctor Applegate, the CEO, and have been amazed at the trove of ideas there that could be applied to higher education. Do you know, for example, how they maintain quality control within their staff? Have you ever heard of the medical meaning of 'privileges'?"

He looked past me and glanced at Wiley, whose face was impassive as a stone.

"Well, of course not. I hadn't either. But here is how it works. They keep a catalog of all the procedures that licensed personnel can perform within their institution. It's a long list, I'd say more than two hundred in all—everything from delivering babies to setting fractures to performing colonoscopies, not to mention the surgical procedures.

"Well, every two years each staff member who performs a certain function must attest to his or her competence to do so. Usually, a simple personal declaration will do. But sometimes individuals must submit corroborative evidence—not only their formal training, but personal circumstances that may have changed. A surgeon may have contracted Parkinson's disease. Or, someone may have incurred a string of DUIs. I'm told that's not unheard of around here.

"There is a system of proctors, as the medical professionals train and evaluate one another. Now, how about that for a comprehensive procedure! Of course, it's been impelled in good part by the mounting threat of lawsuits. But, do you see where I'm going with this?"

My stomach responded with a grinding sensation.

"Suppose that Ocotillo U became a leader in this field. How do we know who is qualified to teach a given course, as evidenced by formal studies or subsequent research and publications? Does anyone presently monitor their faculty in this way? Why, we could be the first to do so!"

"And you think this practice is transferable to the culture of higher education?" I asked, in what I hoped sounded like a calm, objective tone.

"I believe there is only one way to find out," Sterling snapped at me, "and I am going to involve you—through your assistant, Farley, of course—in answering that question. I want you to have him construct a schema with the titles of each of our courses and the instructors who teach them. We'll lay the groundwork to assess their qualifications to do so, and a procedure to apply for privileges."

He sat back with a self-satisfied expression and patted the table. Then he turned to Wiley. "Doctor Crane, do you have any thoughts on this matter?"

Wiley looked away and began to gather up his things. He shook his head solemnly. "If it's your bag, blow out of it," he muttered.

Sterling looked a bit perplexed. "Well, I'll take that as an expression of assent," he said.

I sat in my dark office at the end of the day. Farley had put in his hours,

Arlene had gone home for supper with her husband, and I was alone. My desk was cleared of paperwork but my mind was cluttered. With all my other meetings, I could not get over my first one in the morning with Sterling Holmes. My malevolence was mounting: not just my discomfort with the wild ideas that constituted his leadership, but the fact that he held me in his grip. It was entirely within his power to fire me.

In the quiet darkness, I turned to meditation—although in what tradition, I wasn't sure. Should I head Eastward, down a path of disengagement? I got up and took down a copy of the Tao Té Ching from my bookshelf—China in the sixteenth century B.C. I read of "... the insight of eyes unclouded by longing..." and that "the world is won by those who let it go."

But tonight the Tao didn't reach what I needed: not a withdrawal from the world, but some sort of reconciliation within it. And soon, head in my hands, I found myself back in Psalm 51: "Create in me a clean heart, O God, and renew a right..."

"Hey, Connor! Try the decaf." I jerked up with a start and squinted at the svelte figure dimly outlined at my doorway.

"Oh, hi, Teresa—haven't seen you for a while. Yeah, I guess I was pretty deep into it."

"That did look intense, amigo. Well, are you up for a pilgrimage to the Raven's Roost? I seem to be craving the green chile chicken Alfredo."

There was a sparse crowd at the mountain restaurant this week night, with only a few Roosters huddled around the fireplace at the front of the dining room. We sat in the back where we were pretty much alone and, after a couple of margaritas and an entree to the amazing marriage of chicken Alfredo and poblano chiles, I began to unwind. As I listened to Teresa describe her classes, my memories of Sterling started to fade.

"Of course, I tell my students there are no discernible jobs in print media at the moment—so don't sign up for journalism as a career," she explained. "But there are skills there that can benefit them in almost any field."

"S...such as?" I wheezed and swilled some water to quell a chunk of chile I'd ingested.

"Accessing information, both real time and online. Digging for facts. Getting at the story that's not apparent. And telling it in a style that doesn't put your reader to sleep, like the typical Christmas letter. 'We did this, we did that, and then the toilet overflowed.' I show these students how to put the important stuff up front and summarize the rest. And, with strong, active verbs. Basically, I teach them how to write."

"Do they get any practical experience?"

"Sure. I send them out on assignments. One girl just turned in a story on Sterling Holmes' speech to the Chamber of Commerce this week."

My eyes popped. "How did you know he was going to do that? I wasn't aware of it till after the fact, when he postponed our God-awful, weekly cabinet meeting."

"Well, 'I have my sources,' as they say. Remember that?"

"And don't ask any questions. I remember that part well."

We fell into a long silence, until finally Teresa looked at me quizzically. She put down her fork. "You look sort of sullen, babe. Is something wrong?"

I thought for a moment. "It's just the secrecy. Like where you went last weekend: don't ask, don't tell. When it comes down to it, I don't know how much I can count on you, Teresa."

"You mean, like Polly, was that her name?"

"'Jenny,' but you've got the idea."

She said, "Uh oh. Sounds like a serious case of SGS."

I looked puzzled.

"'Steady Girlfriend Syndrome.' Hey, Connor, get over it! You know, I love being with you, and when I'm with you, I am truly there. But it doesn't mean that's all there is to me."

I sat for a minute and let that sink in. There was a certain logic to what Teresa had said, and I wondered if I could learn to digest it. Once again, we sat in silence, until she reached across the table and squeezed my hand. "Come on," she said. "Let's clear out and go back to my place." She flashed an accommodating smile. "I've got some things I'd like to show you."

Teresa liked to be on top, and I guess that shouldn't have surprised me. I'd had some intimations, but this night confirmed it. At first, she drew herself above me and nestled for a long while, touching my face, massaging my chest. Then she leaned down and offered her breasts to my lips before rising and circling slowly, until finally her face began to flush and her breath came in spasms.

Suddenly, she cried out, gasped and gripped my shoulders—awaiting my climax—till, at the end, we rolled into each another's arms and lay still until we felt like talking.

"I have his calendar," she murmured in my ear, then raised herself up on an elbow. Her eyes were intent. "I know where he goes to speak, and I send my students there—a different one every time. They blend into the crowd, take notes for their assignments."

I shook myself awake. "You mean there have been other engagements?"

"Rotary Club, the Lions, the month before the Chamber of Commerce. I can show you the students' write-ups. It varies a little, but basically it's the same talk every time. The man has a message, and he's telling the world—a whole lot that he's not saying on campus."

I got up to use the bathroom and when I came back to bed, Teresa was sitting on the edge, fully dressed. "I've got some things to show you," she said.

"As enticing as those I've just seen?" I asked. Standing before her in my birthday outfit, I seemed up for another round of what we'd just done, part of me swelling and swaying.

She glanced up, then quickly looked away. "You have charms of your own, amigo. Por cierto, yo te quiero. But you need to put your clothes on and look over these students' assignments with me. Tenemos trabajo. We have work to do."

So, we spent the next hour at her computer, scanning their accounts of Sterling's speeches, identifying parts that had eluded the students (they all had missed his data on the economic impact of the university on the community—those "holes in the story"). But we were able to reconstruct the substance of his boilerplate spiel, and it looked like this:

Challenge and Response
By Sterling Holmes-Ortega, PhD

While it is difficult to pin down the annual economic impact of Ocotillo U on the community of San Vicente (we have very little institutional data) it is likely to be in six figures.

But that resource is nothing to rely on. For the entire industry of higher education is in crisis. The cost of college is racing out of control. During the past thirty years, tuition has increased 1,120 percent—faster than the rate of inflation, almost twice the rate of health care, and about three times as fast as housing.

And so it is no surprise that Americans owe more than one trillion dollars in student loans, that the average debt total at graduation is approximately $27,500, and that almost one in five families is currently paying off student loans.

While we all have learned to acknowledge the value of a university degree in the marketplace—that college graduates earn higher salaries, etc.—beyond that, the value of higher education is unclear. For, current research has shown that there are few demonstrable standards of quality in the industry. And those measures we do have suggest that many students in the U.S. show no improvement in critical thinking, complex reasoning, and communication during the course of their tenure in college.

In addition to those facts, there are two other problems. First, while access to higher education has improved steadily over the years, graduation rates have not. Currently, only about one-third of college students complete a degree within four years, and only two-thirds finish within six years.

Finally, when it comes to OCU, the number of new high school students, on whom our enrollment depends, peaked in the year 2011, after seventeen years of growth. And it will not reach that same level again until ten years from now.

And so, what can we do to become more competitive? My answer is that we need to define and develop some distinctive characteristics of our institution. Ocotillo U must establish that it is good at something. And what is that? In the apparent absence of any reputation for academic quality, we need to set clear yardsticks for our endeavors, carefully measure our outcomes, and take the lead in earning credibility.

Ocotillo U must become America's first and foremost Accountable University.

I sat for several minutes, perusing what Sterling had said, then looked up at Teresa with a puzzled frown. "Do you see what I see?"

"Do you mean that he's probably right?"

"That's it. The only problem is the weird way he's pursuing his vision."

She said, "He's not making any connection with the institution, his constituency."

"It's not unlike his career in the ministry," I continued. "He had these cool sermon titles: 'The Sacraments of Everyday Life.' 'Religion: A Vantage for the Long View.' He'd put up catchy phrases on the sign outside the church—'Candlelight and Carols' for Christmas Eve; 'Happy? Joyful!' at New Year's. The church looked swell. But all the while, his parishioners were into their own scene. It was a kind of Peyton Place in pews, carrying on affairs, screwing each other senseless."

"Including you, hombre, from what I gather. But Sterling was..."

"Incognizant," I answered, "in his own time zone. The place I saw was something else."

We ran off a copy for each of us, and agreed that, until we figured out a strategy for what to do with the information, it was for our eyes only.

She kissed me at the door. "Gracias, Connor," she said with a sigh. "It is so good to have a partner. Yo te quiero."

I lay awake for some time that night, going over it all. Not just Sterling's speech. It was the format of my meetings with Teresa. How we always began by straightening out whatever might have come between us, then had sex, and wound up going over some issue or other at the university. Sometimes, it felt like in-service training.

Oh, well. I tried to shelve the evening and go to sleep. But something else got me out of bed, and over to my Spanish phrase book. "Yo te quiero"—I looked it up. "One of the most delightfully ambiguous expressions in the language," it read. "The phrase can mean anything from 'I love you' to 'I want you' to 'I want to use you.' Be sure to pay attention to the context."

15

Farley was sitting in the anteroom at his desk behind Arlene's, grading papers, when I walked in the next morning. I told him about his next assignment, developing a schema of who was teaching what at OCU, and his eyes lit up.

"Wow, that sounds like a spot for a relational database," he exclaimed. If I'd heard that term I'd forgot it, so he explained the rudiments—a kind of three-dimensional spreadsheet that could be searched simultaneously, multiple ways. I saw again how invested he was in research, probably more so than in teaching. Maybe someday he'd find a job in a think tank, or become director of institutional research at Ocotillo U if they could ever afford that kind of position and could bear to see the kind of data it would uncover.

"While you're at it," I said, "maybe you could work on another small project." I called Arlene over and asked her about size of the candidate pool.

She thought a moment. "I'd say we have about a hundred," she said. "But I was browsing it the other day and some of them have been in there for ages."

"I could set up a field for date of inquiry," Farley suggested.

"And discipline," Arlene added, "and advanced degrees."

The two of them seemed genuinely excited by the prospect of something interesting to work on. I thought about that as I closed my door and glanced at my calendar for the day. How much time had I spent getting to know Arlene? Was it any more than I'd devoted to Alice at the outset?

I sat down and stayed focused on that subject. How much had I ever paid attention to people to whom I wasn't assigned, say, on a pastoral call, or needed something from? I thought about staff support people at the university. Sterling's secretary. What was her name? Claire. An attractive, twenty-something redhead in a pixie cut with an enigmatic smile. Now and then she'd handed me something when I'd gone in to see Sterling. But I was always so fried by the prospect of meeting with him, I'd scarcely taken time to speak with her.

But I could change, would have to. Wasn't this one of the side benefits of working in administration, being around people every day? It was high time I began getting to know them.

The day was filled with appointments and a current of emails until, about mid-afternoon, one of them caught my eye. It was from Margo: a notice that she and her husband had found other jobs at a large, private university. After this semester, they were through at OCU. She added a note of gratitude for the support I'd given and that felt good. But I was sad to lose her.

When the database was done, I asked Arlene to search the candidate pool for a sociologist, along with a political scientist for her husband's position. I thought about that consultation with Wiley to talk about helping junior faculty. I called him up.

"Sure, after work," he said. "But I can't stay long. Barbara's got me slated to take care of the kids; she's got a dinner meeting. I'll come by."

As I straightened my desk and turned out the lights at five, I thought about the write-up of Sterling's speeches that I'd done with Teresa. I remembered our saying we would keep it to ourselves, but shrugged it off. What did I have to hide from Wiley? So I pulled it from my files and brought it along.

Wiley drove and I blinked when he drove down Main Street and pulled up in front of the Rawhide Bar. The Hide was a blue-collar saloon, infamous for its bar fights. I had, in fact, never been in the place and, as we walked in, remembered why. Two signs were on the front door.

> No loitering. Colors, logos, & emblems not allowed.
> Keep hands off all employees! All violators will be thrown out.

A couple of old grizzled, Hispanic guys stood smoking outside in the doorway. One of them muttered as we passed by, "Hey, what's with all these Yankees around here?"

"Did that refer to us?" I asked Wiley as we sat down on two metal chairs at one of the narrow tables that lined the left-hand wall. On the right was a bar with stools that ran the length of the room. There were no other decorations or furnishings to speak of, just two pool tables at the back. The place had the ambience of a Walmart warehouse.

"You got that right," he answered. "In this crowd, there is us and there is them, and you and I are lumped into the latter." He headed to the bar for a couple of beers.

I surveyed the crowd—some isolated, older drinkers on bar stools toward the back and a volatile clutch of guys in their twenties at the end toward the street. As I took a second look, I recognized one of the barstool drinkers—Pete Entwhistle, Alice's ex, from accounting. Then I glanced again at the pool tables, and spotted Bob Clifford (biology) and Jack Lofton (anthropology) shooting a game at one of them.

"May I ask how you happened to choose this place?" I asked Wiley as he returned with two bottles.

"Like I said, I'm pressed for time," he said, impatiently. "I can't be driving all the way up to the Raven's Roost, where folks like you like to go." Then he grinned. "Besides, when we gotta split this place, you ain't gonna complain."

I shrugged and sat a minute. "So, I wanted to talk about junior faculty," I told him. "We just lost another pair today. But, first, there's something I'd like to run by you." And I handed him the write-up of Sterling's speeches.

Wiley took a long draught of his beer, set the bottle down, and began to peruse the document. There was hollering at the bar, and the crack of balls from the pool tables behind us, but he gave it the attentiveness of a scholar. Finally, he looked up. "Well, I dunno about the 'accountability university' bullshit. But his data are pretty much true, although he could have gone farther. You know what the graduation rate is here?"

I shook my head.

"It is twenty percent. That's all: you got that? One in five who walk in the door walk out with a diploma. I'm talkin' twenty percent, one in five..."

I looked at him wide-eyed—amazed at the data—until my eyes grew even wider. One of the young guys at the front of the bar had separated from the others and was walking our way. I recognized him when he was about five feet off. It was the boyfriend of the woman who was failing Margo Whitehead's sociology course. If he was big before, it appeared he had grown since our first acquaintance, and he was headed straight for me.

What occurred next is not entirely clear, it happened so fast. But I remember getting up out of my chair and taking a step toward the fellow, putting on my best professional smile. Like a pastor greeting his parishioners, I held out my hand. "I remember you," I said, "from that day in my office. You know, I'm Connor Ransom. And, what is your name?"

He stopped about three feet in front of me. Fixing me with a cold eye, he told me, "Bart Bencomo. They call me 'Black Bart'—and you'll remember that."

Then he glanced at Wiley. "No offense to your buddy. I been looking forward to meeting up with you after what you did to my girlfriend, you little turd."

I looked him up and down and saw Wiley slowly get to his feet behind him. And then I did something unusual. I got myself into a balanced stance for Tai Chi and began the opening salute—right fist into open left hand, followed by weaving my arms, right over left, before me. I then raised them straight up and crooked my elbows as I pressed down, after which I bowed.

Bencomo seemed confounded, but laughed darkly as he readied a round-house right. But as he swung, I launched into "Part the Wild Horse's Mane," the next move in Tai Chi. I blocked his punch with the edge of my left arm and, for an instant, that knocked him off balance.

Looking back, I'd rather not speculate on what he might have done, as he hauled off to clobber me. But, from the corner of my eye, I saw Wiley tap him on the shoulder. As Bencomo turned around, he was greeted with a left hook to the solar plexus that bent him in half. Then Wiley hit him with a right cross to the jaw that lifted him from his feet and sent him flying. He landed flat on his back, and his head cracked as he hit the floor. And then he lay perfectly still.

As a small crowd gathered around Black Bart Bencomo, Wiley jerked his head toward the door. I saw him massaging his right hand as he covered the dozen yards in four steps, and I followed. But, as we left, I remembered the summary of Sterling's speech that I'd vowed to keep confidential. I skirted the gang around the fallen Bart who was twisting his neck as he fumbled to all fours. But the sheet was not on the table, nor anywhere on the floor. It was not a good time to inquire who might have it, so I turned back and lit out for the door.

Wiley was silent for about thirty seconds on our way back to the admin building where I'd left my car. Then he cut loose. "What the fuck you doin' in there, some kind of half-assed martial arts when that guy was gonna pound you?"

"It was Tai Chi," I explained, "an ancient Chinese meditation technique, originally a method of self-defense."

He said simply, "Are you outta your mind?"

"Well, I owe you a lot," I replied. "You saved my neck. But you didn't do me any favors taking me in there in the first place." I filled him in on my history with Black Bart Bencomo.

"At least you stood up to him in your office. Lotta folks don't, and that's where it's at. But, my God, man—what were you thinking?"

"Probably that if I was going down, I wanted it to mean something. I wanted a context, not just random violence."

He snorted. "Only context I could see was mortality. He was gonna kick your ass into next Tuesday."

We were silent for a few blocks. Then I said, "Wiley, why were we in there? It wasn't just because the Outpost was closed and the Raven's Roost was too far, was it?"

There was another long pause. Finally, he said, "You try living as a black man—oh, excuse me, 'African American'—in this society, especially around here. Try it in an interracial marriage. And before long you find yourself looking over your shoulder. Maybe ready to run, if some dude looks at you sideways. So, sometimes you need to insert yourself in an unfriendly environment—just to take stock, check out how you reacting."

"I guess I understand. But you said 'especially around here.' I didn't get that."

We parked outside the administration building and sat there for a minute. Then he said, "Wait a sec," and ran inside. He was gone about five minutes. When he came back in the car he handed me a reprinted article from an academic journal. I looked at the title, "San Vicente: A Legacy of Violence." I didn't recognize the name of the author.

"A.C. Abernathy was a cool dude, professor of history, till he passed on one day in the classroom, a la Albert McNulty. The two were buddies. Best mentor I ever had: turned me on to the serious study of history, changed my life—you know, all that. He did this article on violence in these parts after living here for a long time. Of course, it was a hot topic back in the sixties, maybe not so much today. But check it out, see what you think. And get some boxing lessons."

I once took a graduate course in the physiology of religious experience, and learned enough brain science to understand why I couldn't sleep that night. It was all about the amygdala, an almond-shaped cluster of neurons deep in the midbrain that processes emotions and motivations, especially those involving survival. It was pretty clear that mine was on fire.

I tried to cool it with one beer, then another, but it was no good. I needed to find a way to connect the unsettling experience I'd had with some sort of theory in my pre-frontal cortex, a context of some sort. And so I picked up the article Wiley had given me on violence in the history of San Vicente, and waded in. It began with an arresting quote from the nineteenth century.

"Until I was about ten years old I did not know that people died except by violence. That is because I am an Apache, a Warm Springs Apache."

Abernathy proceeded to summarize the history of the Apaches, a loose group of tribes that migrated into what is now the southwestern United States around 1400 A.D. from an area in today's Canadian provinces of Saskatchewan and Alberta. The Apaches are linguistically and culturally related to the Navajo who came with them and developed a sedentary culture in what is now northern New Mexico and Arizona. But, unlike the Navajo, the Apache were mobile. They wandered around the Southwest with free rein until the Spanish arrived in 1540.

The next three centuries saw intermittent dustups between these Native Americans who were defending their lands and the invading Europeans. Then, in the nineteenth century, the clashes flared into outright warfare as the Anglos, who came to dominate the Hispanics, dug in to pursue farming, ranching, and—above all—the mining of gold, silver, and copper.

To the Europeans, the Apaches posed a terrifying specter as they waylaid wagon trains and swooped into towns such as San Vicente, scalping their victims and sometimes even roasting them alive over open fires. Late into the nineteenth century, the settlers of San Vicente lived in terror of these marauders. A newspaper lamented: "We are dreaming of a golden age—a future empire—and fifty dirty, lousy Indians have us in a state of siege."

"How much of this history was ever lost?" Abernathy concluded. "When we see the kinds of tensions that arise in San Vicente: the political strife, the bar fights. Has this town ever really got on its feet? Or is it always on edge, one eye peeled for the Apaches?"

16

The phone rang about seven the next morning and I fumbled with the receiver. My lesson in local history had been followed by another couple of beers.

"Hey, babe, hope I didn't wake you."

I mumbled, "It's okay, Teresa," and spared her the old saw of having to get up to answer the phone anyway.

"Well, I just wanted you to know that there's a story in the works for tomorrow's San Vicente Herald—something about you and Wiley getting in a fight at the Rawhide Saloon. Can that be true?"

I told her there was more to it and asked how she knew.

"It's a tight world down here when it comes to journalism, and I know the reporter, Jessica Madrid. Anyway, she got an anonymous tip from somewhere in the university—she couldn't tell the extension—and they suggested that she call on the president and spring it on him to get his reaction. The meeting's at nine."

I thanked her profusely and scrambled to get dressed. Then I called Wiley, told him the news, and when to meet me at Sterling's office.

En route to the admin building, I thought about the Herald and its competing fish wrap, the Bugle. San Vicente was too small to support even a single newspaper, but somehow the two of them managed to survive. Both were muckrakers, scrambling for any incipient scandal in the two largest institutions in town, the university and the hospital. As I recalled, Walter Driscoll hadn't given either paper the time of day, which raised a lot of ire. I was sure that Sterling, on the other hand, would jump through hoops to raise or save the image of OCU. He seemed to believe that appearance was reality.

As I got out of the car, I gave a quick thought to Teresa, as well. How had she known the time of Sterling's meeting with the reporter? "Oh, yeah," I remembered. "She has access to his calendar." And I wondered how she managed that.

I arrived at the stroke of nine and looked quizzically at Claire as I came in the anteroom of the president's office. She smiled and shrugged, so I went right in. Sterling looked uptight, his face contorted between a grimace and something like a pastoral smile. He was standing next to a squat young woman clad in journalistic jeans and a sweater, in marked contrast to his pressed, blue suit. She had a camera on a strap slung over one shoulder and held a small notebook and ballpoint pen.

Sterling seemed surprised to see me, and then Wiley as he walked in. "What is this I'm hearing?" he sputtered, and I could see that the strategy of dropping the hammer on him had had its desired effect. "A bar fight, involving my top administrators?" He looked incredulous.

"It was more than that," I responded, looking down at Jessica Madrid. "You see, one of our instructors had been intimidated by the boyfriend of a student, over his girlfriend's grade in a sociology class. The instructor brought the two of them in my office and I supported the teacher's decision that the young woman was failing the course and should consider withdrawing."

Jessica was staring at me, slack-jawed, as she realized there was more to the story, but wasn't taking any notes. I could tell there weren't many Pulitzer Prizes given out in San Vicente.

Wiley looked down at her, towering even higher. He asked, "Are you getting this, ma'am?"

I waited while she caught up with her notes. "When he left my office, he made a veiled threat and then, that night at the bar when I was having a beer with my colleague, Doctor Crane, the young man assaulted me. Doctor Crane came to my defense: end of story."

She wrote some more notes, then looked at each of us, in turn. "Not quite," she said. "Bart Bencomo was admitted to the hospital with symptoms of a concussion. Fortunately, he was released later than night. I've not heard that he's filing any charges."

"I'd like to see him try," said Wiley. "You know, there's a larger story here. It is Doctor Ransom's fortitude in standing up to that man in his office, supporting the professor." (It seemed that, in this setting, he was into the King's English, every syllable distinct.) "As any instructor will attest, grading is one of the most conflict-ridden aspects of teaching, especially in an open-enrollment institution such as this."

He turned to Sterling. "And I'm sure that President Holmes will agree."

Sterling said nothing and I smiled inside, suspecting he'd never taught anything beyond a class in Sunday School.

Jessica took a few more notes. "Well, is there anything else?" she asked. "Doctor Holmes, do you have any comment?"

"Only that this is a sad day for Ocotillo U," he muttered, "and that this single incident does not reflect on the stature of our fine institution."

The reporter turned to leave his office as Wiley and I stood at one end of Sterling's desk and he at the other. Then, as she opened the door, she spun around and hoisted her camera. She got a candid shot of the two sides glaring at one another. I thought, maybe there were journalists with savoir-faire here after all.

Teresa brought the Herald in from her front stoop the next morning, brandishing a grin. "What a shot," she exclaimed. "She caught you with your guard down. I've never seen you scowl like that." Then she scanned the article. "But the story seems balanced and fair."

It was early in the morning and I had to leave soon to get back home and change clothes for work, the inconvenience of a mid-week overnight. The previous evening had begun with beers and smothered burritos at Serena's. I'd invited her out as payback for saving my hide from my night at the Rawhide. She was fascinated by the episode and asked me to show her the Tai Chi move with which I had temporarily deterred Bart Bencomo.

"Later," I told her, and that night I did demonstrate that move among others. It was in the afterglow that I 'fessed up about the summary of Sterling's speeches that had been lost in the mayhem. I was surprised that she didn't seem upset.

"I doubted you could keep that to yourself and was pretty sure you'd share it with Wiley," she said. "But I had no idea it would get lost in a bar fight. Now we'll have to see if there are any repercussions."

As I was nodding off to sleep, she stoked me with one other work-related comment. I should have expected it, our typical cycle of making love followed by making business decisions. "While Farley is doing up that data base," she said, "maybe he should tabulate enrollments for each of the classes. That would be easy to do and it might show some interesting contrasts."

And then, as I was almost asleep, she offered one last news item. "You can expect to see a bombshell from the state education board in about two weeks," she whispered. "I'm sure it's going to throw Sterling for a loop."

In time, her prophecy would be fulfilled, but not before I'd seen some other revelations.

When I got into work that morning, I remembered Teresa's counsel and called Farley into my office. I asked him to compile the enrollment data for each of the classes, along with the name of the instructor, and he was pleased by the additional element of complexity.

As he turned to leave, he stopped at the doorway with a puzzled frown. "Connor," he said, "what does it mean when the phone rings, you pick it up, and no one's there? That happened twice last night."

I had no answer for his question, but I stored it somewhere in the back of my mind.

Sometime later in the week, I went out in the anteroom and asked him how the relational data base for the candidate pool was coming. He said it was almost done and I turned back toward my office. But Arlene put a hand on my arm. "This just came in the morning mail," she told me. "You said you were looking for a sociologist? Well, here's one."

I picked up the vita and took it back to my desk. When I started to look it over, I stopped in shock. I recognized the name. It was my one-time lover, Lisa Nordeen.

The rest of the day passed before me vaguely, like a parade in the rain. I know I saw some people who had appointments and can sort of remember who they were, but have no idea what we talked about. Whenever I had time to think, I tried to find some words for the way I felt. The only ones that came to mind were from high school French: frisson (a cold chill), coup de foudre (a sudden, life-changing event—lit., a lightning strike). Why was it that the only French that had stuck had to do with unsettling emotions?

In any case, I honestly hadn't thought about Lisa Nordeen for some time, and had but a vague recollection of what she looked like. The pictures that came to me were chiefly of Lisa in bed—a busty blond with a healthy glow, especially when she...

I shelved those images. After all, was I not with Teresa these days, and weren't we...? Whoa! Just then, I remembered that she and I were on for dinner tonight at the Raven's Roost; Teresa had a late class and we'd meet there. I had better get my act together.

And so I entertained some rational analysis. My options when it came to Lisa's resume appeared to be three. (1) I could drop it in the candidate pool and let things take their course. (2) I could recommend her to Jack Lofton and/or Sterling Holmes (probably killing her chances). Or, (3) I could send an email and invite her to come down and look the place over (and me?).

By the time I began the drive up to Pinecroft, I sensed that I was headed for number three.

There's an L-shaped pair of dining rooms in a new addition at the Raven's Roost, behind the bar. In the far room, you can be heard but not seen and that place seemed to be humming. I took a small table in the near room and half-listened to some business being conducted in the far one, among the clink of glasses. It sounded like some people were forming an organization, and occasionally I thought I heard Daniela Ortega, Sterling's spouse, give out with a caramba!

I had no idea when Teresa would arrive so ordered a margarita on the rocks, and then another. About twenty minutes later, she swooped in. She dropped her briefcase on the floor as she signaled a waitress for a libation of her own and hit me with a wet kiss, all in one motion.

"Subject-verb agreement!" she sputtered. "These students can't seem to get the hang of it, in English or in Spanish. What were they doing in high school? I don't know—sometimes I wonder what it'd be like to teach in a university where people were actually ready for college."

I looked past her toward the bar where I thought I saw someone I recognized.

"Hey, Connor...did you hear what I said? I could use a little therapy here, amigo."

"Sorry, Teresa. I've got some things on my mind. You were saying something about verbs, right?"

She resumed her critique of the students and signaled for another tequila. It seemed she was drinking it straight. The waitress brought us menus but neither of us was ready to order. I tried to hear Teresa but my head was compacted and the noise from the other dining room was distracting.

I made out Sterling's voice, urgent but quavering. "Mission, vision, values!" he declared. "Ocotillo U is on the march, and an active alumni organization can help move us forward."

There was more discussion in a lower key and then Sterling called for nominations. "Daniela Ortega!" a woman shouted and then in one breath, "All in favor?"

There was a chorus of "Aye's."

"Opposed?" A moment of silence, and Daniela cried, "Caramba!"

I looked back at Teresa and she fixed me with a frown. "I can't compete with whatever is going on—back there, and in you," she muttered. "And I had some news you could use, too. Well, buenos noches, Connor." She put on her coat, took up her satchel, and was gone.

I sat in shock for a minute. Had I deserved that? It didn't take long to conclude that I had. I didn't stay to eat: paid the bill and took off to avoid Sterling and his cohorts. I suppose Daniela was to be congratulated, I thought, driving home. It's not easy to be elected president of an alumni club when you're not an alum. Well, it should give her a role and something to do.

I also thought about where I was with Teresa, and was not. Given the ground rules she had set out for our relationship, there wasn't much I could do that was out of bounds. But spacing out on her was a game-changer. So I went home, zapped a frozen dinner in the microwave, uncorked a beer, and sent off an email to Lisa. I gave her the name of a good motel in San Vicente and invited her to come for a visit.

She wrote back the next morning and asked to come the following weekend. "My mother can come take care of the kids," she said, "and a colleague can take my classes. I'd like to see your school and catch up with you—see what your life is like. Mine is in turmoil; I'll explain. So much distance and so much time since the time we were so close—weren't we? Are you still so religious? Give me your cell number and I'll call you when I arrive, try to fit into your schedule. You must be busy as a dean. See you soon, Lisa."

I wrote her my phone number and sent her a piece I'd been working on to share with Aaron, my sometime independent study guy whom I hadn't seen in a while. I suppose it was a kind of credo, and it went like this:

"If there is a world beyond the world—beneath it or behind it or above— how do we access that aspect of life, get in touch with that dimension? Is it instantaneously with drugs, or deliberately through a discipline of, say, service and prayer? I have come to doubt that it's through rational theology or rabid social action, the way I once did. But what is the way? And is there but one?"

She wrote back: "I still find that side of you enticing, pastor." It was a title she'd used facetiously, in the sack. And I spent a lot of the next week in reverie: remembering, wondering.

But now and then, reality intervened at the office. Farley kept having hang-up calls, still two a night though they came in a half hour later. Finally, at my suggestion, he changed his home phone number. But now they came during the day, in his time slot with me. A couple of times he brought in his phone for me to listen. I could only hear someone breathing. I hung up and dialed *69 to trace the call, but all I got was the central exchange at the university.

Then Wiley came in with an envelope sent to him, no return address, and a single sheet marked "Breaking News: According to data from the U.S. Department of Education, growing numbers of graduates and other former students at Ocotillo U are in default on federal student loans. The figure at OCU is twenty-one percent, up three percent in the past year. Schools whose rates of default exceed forty percent for one year—or twenty-five percent for three consecutive years—can lose the ability to offer federal aid. Nationwide, the highest percentage of defaulters are non-graduates: a group that includes eighty percent of former OCU students."

"What you make of this, Ace?" Wiley inquired, and I thought of Teresa's comment on News I Could Use. The timing seemed more than coincidental, pretty clear she had sent that to Wiley. So, what was her agenda: not merely to bolster my career, evidently, but something more. Did she just want a pipeline to the administration?

"Hey, man, you spacing out on us again? Are you there?"

"Sure, Wiley. Sorry. I guess we should take it up with Sterling, although he must know."

We didn't have long to wait for an audience. For the past two weeks, he had cancelled his presidential cabinet meetings, evidently in response to the bar fight. But Claire called us in the next morning—drop everything and come to his office, he'd said.

Sterling looked shaken and, for once, in a position to seek information instead of just dispensing it. I considered broaching the message Wylie had received, but thought better of it. The man seemed fried like a Big Mac.

"Daniela was out last night at an alumni meeting," he blurted out. "She's been elected chair of the local chapter, and she called me on her cell phone, in tears. As she was driving home on Market Street, someone started following her, and they crowded her off the road!

"You two seem to be more in touch with the underside of things in this town. Do you have any idea of who could have done this, and why?"

I gave it some thought that night. A re-activated alumni club. Ex-students defaulting on loans. Could there be a connection? While I was at it, I also pondered the information being leaked from Sterling's office. Who might be doing that? And then I had a chance encounter.

A couple of nights later, I was alone in a booth at Serena's putting down a beer and a smothered burrito, sensing my isolation and the reality that I was going to have to deal with Lisa before I could interact with Teresa again. Were my feelings unnatural? I wondered if my spiritual and amorous cravings were but two sides of the same, needy nature when I became aware of some whispering in the booth behind me. Nothing unusual about that, except that both voices were female. Well, welcome to the new age. To get a girl you have to...

There was a mirror over the bar and, pretty much out of prurient interest, I glanced up to see if I knew the couple behind me. Immediately, I recognized the red pixy cut of Sterling's secretary, Claire. And then I saw the long, black, flowing hair of her companion and lost my breath. Oh, no—but it was not Teresa. I looked again. It was her college roommate, the ex-presidential candidate at Ocotillo U. It was Linda Lucero with Claire.

17

Farley came into my office with his laptop the next morning to show me the relational database, now completed. I watched his demo for a few minutes, then suggested he come into the presidential cabinet meeting the next morning, Friday, to show Wiley and Sterling as well. I phoned Claire and asked her to put him on.

Fortunately, the agenda was light and Sterling slated Farley first. We all watched in a bit of wonder as he searched the data by course, by instructor, and enrollment. Then he put up a few charts that showed some startling trends. There were classes that had very few students, mostly seminars in the humanities. But others—in anthropology, introductory biology, and intro to accounting—had over a hundred students apiece.

"How could that be, in a school this size?" Sterling wondered.

Wiley said, "Those courses are online."

I had an immediate sense that, like Sterling, I should know more about this than I did.

"And are the instructors compensated for the additional students?" he asked.

"You know it," Wiley responded. "They're essentially making twice the normal rate."

I considered not asking my next question but did. "Have you ever thought of teaching online, Farley?"

He flashed me a pained look but quickly recovered. "It's by invitation only," he said.

"Well, let's look at who's teaching those courses," I suggested, although I suspected I already knew the answer. Farley called up the familiar names: Jack Lofton in anthropology; Bob Clifford, biology; and Pete Entwhistle, accounting. I muttered, "O brave new world that has such people in't."

"And how are the students monitored, evaluated in classes that size?" Sterling wondered.

"That's a point we never got to under Walter Driscoll," Wiley said. "But the numbers have been growing like gangrene."

"So, now, we come to the meat of the matter," Sterling said. "Farley, thank you. I think you may go now." He shook his hand and we paused for a moment while he left.

"This is exactly the kind of issue I want to take on," he continued. "How can we tell who is qualified to teach which courses in this part of the curriculum, or indeed in any other? That's why I want Farley to send out a message to all members of the faculty, directing them to document their credentials for every course they teach."

His statement was followed by a silence that was long and deep. Sterling was looking at us expectantly as Wiley stared at his shoes. Finally, I spoke up. "Have you considered two things: why Farley should send out that sort of message when this is your idea to begin with, and how in the world you could ascertain an instructor's qualifications?"

Regarding me with a somber look, he responded quickly. "In original order: why, because he's coordinator of assessment."

I said, "Let's stop right there. Farley has been receiving hang-up calls already, evidently just because he's garnering enrollment information. It's the only reason I can think of."

Sterling snapped, "I've been getting some myself, and then there was that incident with Daniela."

"Well, you're the president, and this is your plan. Don't you think you need to stand up and take the heat for it? Okay, and besides that, how can you perform that kind of evaluation?"

Sterling said nothing for a minute or so and I had the impression he hadn't given this matter much thought. Finally, "Evidence of formal study, publications in the field."

I turned to Wiley. "Do you think that would cover it? Can you tell if an instructor is qualified that way?"

For once, he spoke up in the presence of Sterling. "Sometimes people will put in weeks, months to prepare to teach a course—become expert in a field—and there's no way to monitor that." I noted his use of the King's English, no argot of the street.

Sterling fell silent again, and then he spoke very slowly. "There is one thing I can say about this and other issues before us. It is this: the status quo is not viable." He went on to cite the kind of data in his off-campus speeches that both of us recognized—the increase in tuition nationwide, upcoming dearth of young adult prospective students, and all the rest.

"So we must develop a positive image," he went on, "and soon. I've been spending time up in the capital and I can tell you what the perception is in Santa Fe, of this school and others like it. We have no credibility. Now, of course, we can calculate grade point averages, pass out degrees, and all the rest. But the simple truth is this. They give us no credence. Almost no one believes in the validity of what we are doing.

"There are rumors of a major change that is impending in the state funding formula, probably because they don't trust us, and it's not something I can talk about just yet. But I can promise you this: it could be serious. Well, perhaps that's enough bad news for this morning. But we must take steps to become more visibly accountable."

And with that, he turned his back on us and went to his computer.

"So, what shall we do with the relational database?" I asked. "Should we compile what we have on who's been teaching what?"

"I suppose that would be a start," he said icily over his shoulder. "And, while you're at it, ask Farley to come and see me. I have a project in mind for the alumni organization. Please close the door on your way out."

I had a sense of having dodged a bullet as we walked through the anteroom. But what would he come up with next?

"I coulda told him what to do with it," Wiley muttered as we passed Claire's desk and, for an instant, I saw her smile.

I stopped for a minute. "You know, I've heard other rumors about the funding formula. I think I may need to call Teresa."

Claire said. "Oh, she's already left for Ala..."

I looked over at her. "Alabama? Alaska?" I wondered out loud. And then I had a disturbing recollection. "Alamogordo?"

She went back to her computer.

My thoughts of Teresa hung on my heart like a shroud as I drove up to the Raven's Roost Saturday evening. So was that where she'd headed off to that other weekend—back to Alamogordo, the rancher who was queer for his cattle? He must have lost his taste for beef. I wondered: would I ever settle down with Teresa? And, after seeing Lisa, would I want to?

I'd given Lisa directions over the phone, preferring that each of us have our own wheels after my episode with Teresa. Who knew how she and I would interact after so many years?

As I walked in the front door, I spotted her at the bar with a glass of red wine. We shared a fleeting hug, and then she grasped me at the elbows and held me at arm's length.

"Well, Connor. 'Dean Ransom,' is that what they call you?"

"Mostly they call me 'Connor,'" I said.

She smiled and her face relaxed. Till then, she'd seemed somewhat tired and drawn, dark circles under her eyes, although nothing could quell her red cheeks and blond hair, the ruddy glow of her Nordic genes.

She got up off her bar stool and put her arm in mine as we followed a hostess to a table in a far corner of the main dining room. It was dimly lit except for the fireplace in front and in a glassed-in cabinet filled with Native American relics toward the back. I watched her take in the whole, enveloping scene, one of the most authentically historical places anywhere in the West.

We ordered drinks. "I thought—sometimes hoped—I'd see you again," Lisa said slowly. "But I never thought I'd meet you in this context."

"If there's one thing I've learned over the past five years," I commented, "it is that none of us can predict where we'll wash up. Sometimes I feel like I'm on an inner tube at sea."

She gave a sad smile. "Perhaps I've tried to orchestrate my life too much."

"So, what's going on? Do you want to tell me about it?"

"Maybe in a bit. I think we have some history to catch up on."

I felt a chill. The cocktail waitress brought me a margarita and I slammed it. I signaled for another.

Lisa looked at me. "Gee, Connor, did you always used to drink like that?"

"So, how are the kids?" I deviated.

She gave me a report on the two, aged ten and twelve. I couldn't say I remembered meeting either of them, and I barely knew their names. My relationship with Lisa had been somewhat specialized.

"A woman's life is segmented," she went on, "especially with a profession. You have to decide which part to concentrate on, maybe stabilize. I opted for my family, as most women would, and I traded stability for boredom."

"You mean teaching at the community college?"

She nodded. "I'll get to that, but also Ned."

I shuddered and had a drink of water. It was either that or keep swilling the margaritas.

"You were my safety valve," she said with a smile. "A spot of adventure to counter the monotony of teaching the same courses over and over, and of sex with Ned. Until, of course, it all got a bit too exciting... You know, you never said good-bye."

I waved for the cocktail waitress, to hell with the water. But I switched to beer. Lisa ordered one, too.

"I've never got over that episode on the bridge," I confessed.

"Was it that he might have died?" she asked. "You know, ultimately, he killed himself."

"It was more about my part in it. I still can't call up a clear memory of what happened."

"Well," she said, "we all have places that it's difficult to explore. I've done a lot of that in therapy, all those nooks and crannies. And I've tried to fathom Ned. He had the temperament of a research scientist if not, perhaps, the smarts. He was enamored of data that could be manipulated, modified. He just couldn't deal with anything immediate and random. I know all that about him now. But I'm still stuck with the life I chose, the decisions I made."

We poured our beers and ordered dinner. She followed my lead and tried the green chile chicken Alfredo.

"I remember that you gave up teaching in a four-year school. So the community college never got any better."

"After a dozen years, it became excruciating," she said. "How many times can you lecture on Durkheim? So I finally started proposing new courses on a one-time basis." She paused and drained half her beer. "And that's why I'm here. It was something I'd read about and thought I would try: a course on deviance."

She related the experience in snippets, all through dinner, till she got down to the pivotal event—an assignment she gave the students to go out and commit an anti-social act.

"I wanted them to experience the full force of social norms. In the Upper Midwest, 'most everybody is so conformist they have no idea what they're conforming to. So there they went, dutifully, some just out of high school. And the following class they came back and shared what they'd done."

"My imagination is smoldering," I said.

She smiled. "It feels a little funny now, but at the time... A couple of them drove down the main street at rush hour, side by side, while going exactly the speed limit. Then there were the kinds of minor transgressions you might expect: picking your nose in public, spitting on the sidewalk, bringing a dog in a restaurant, lighting up a cigarette during the prelude in church, walking along downtown holding hands with a member of the same sex."

"Sounds like an interesting course to me."

"Right, it was pretty entertaining to hear them all, until the spirit of competition set in. Some of the girls started changing clothes out at the lake, on the beach. And then, to make a long story short, there was the couple who had sex at noon in the city park. After that, I was called into the dean's office and the police were there. Well, I guess you can fill in the rest."

"So, you're looking for a job," I offered.

"You might say that. Actually, I'm officially on probation, restricted to my customary round of freshman and sophomore level courses. And there's a possibility of legal action on my part. I've been to see an attorney and he was encouraging, if I want to stay—something about a 'Garcetti reservation.'" But, in any event, I'm looking."

"And how did you hear about Ocotillo U?"

"From Sterling, of course. We'd kept in touch some after he left town. I might have been his sole link to the church. Martha, his ex, probably soured all the other parishioners on him."

"And he told you I was here?"

"He did, although I've thought it strange. After that, he's never said a word about you."

After that there was a caesura in the conversation, and a gourmet course of green chile chicken Alfredo. I asked for the check and we made our way outside. Lisa stopped just outside the front door and looked up at the sky. "So many more stars than I've seen," she exclaimed, "maybe ever. And the air up here. I may have forgot what's it's like to really breathe. Connor, do you ever get used to living here?"

I walked with her to her car, wondering if this was the end of our reunion. I asked, "Do you have any plans for tomorrow?" and she said she thought she'd like to visit the Gila Cliff Dwellings, a prehistoric site out in the national forest that I'd never taken time to see myself.

She wrapped me in a hug and brushed my lips with a kiss, and I wondered if this was good-bye. "Well, I said, maybe there'll be time..." Just then I saw a pair of headlights flick on and off, down at the end of the road.

I said, "Lisa, I'm going to go slow down the mountain, and I want you to follow me closely. She looked puzzled. I said, "Don't ask questions. We'll talk when we get down there."

As I led her down the steep incline, going maybe forty, I thought about our conversation and what had not been said. We'd never got to talk about Ocotillo U or the prospect of her moving here. But if she was so tight with Sterling, I was thinking, maybe all of that...

Some lights appeared around a curve behind me, high and blinding, then a pickup truck swooped past me, swerved in front, and almost came to a dead stop. I slammed on my brakes and crept behind the truck as it ambled along maybe five miles an hour for a hundred yards or so until it rounded the next bend. And then suddenly it sped up and raced down into town.

"What was that about?" Lisa asked, wide-eyed, as we stood outside her motel.

"It was a reminder of some things I haven't told you about this place," I replied, "and about myself as well. Suppose I drive you up to the cliff dwellings. It'll give us a chance to talk, and I believe we need that."

I picked her up at eight and we went out for breakfast at the Drifter, whose sign outside, "Best Breakfast in Town," was not an exaggeration. Lisa tried the huevos rancheros—eggs and chorizo sausage smothered in chile sauce—and cleaned her plate. "Do you ever get used to this amazing cuisine?" she asked.

The drive was long but wondrous, through miles of ponderosa pine that opened out into a spectacular vista of the Gila River valley. "This was the first national forest in the country," I told her, "thanks to Theodore Roosevelt and the environmentalist, Aldo Leopold. The Gila Forest is not well known, and I believe there are a lot of folks down here who like it that way."

We had plenty of time to talk and I told her all about the university and Sterling, trying to be as objective as I could. "He has a great capacity to envision the big picture," I said, "most of us theologians do. But he's never taught and has no grasp of reality here at ground level."

"Probably not so different from his career in the ministry," Lisa reflected. "Maybe that's one reason I took a liking to the two of you, that starry-eyed way of trying to transcend things."

I went on and told her about Teresa. She was quiet for a while. Then she said, "I'm not sure what I expected. It's been five years. But, anyway, she sounds exciting."

"That's one way to describe her," I said, "along with 'volatile' and 'high maintenance.' Sometimes I question what I mean to her."

She said, "Are we ever sure about that part of our lives? Incidentally, I called Sterling last night. I told him about our going out to dinner, and spending today together."

"Did he throw up, or threaten you?" I asked her.

She said, "Actually, he sounded very pleased."

I pondered all of that the rest of the way, until we arrived at the cliff dwellings, an outpost of the National Park Service that featured a remarkable hiking trail not only around but up inside the prehistoric structure carved into the hillside.

We were in a cavernous common room of the ancient inhabitants, looking at an image of a vibrant human being that was painted in red on the far wall when Lisa told me some things she'd learned about this place, researching it. "They're called the Mogollon, which is just the name of a Spanish administrator of this territory," she said. "No one knows anything of their language, nor very much about them. They were here about the time of Columbus and only for a few generations, farming down in the river valley. And then they disappeared, leaving this amazing structure. Was it because of a prolonged drought? We have no idea.

"What we do know," she went on, and she took my hand, "is what a short sojourn we have on this globe. With all of our angst and circumlocutions, what a fleeting time."

I left her at the motel and gave her Margo Whitehead's name and number, for a ground-level view of OCU. And I asked her, at the end of it, to let me know what had transpired and gave her my home phone number.

Would I see her again? I wondered. And did I want to? Somehow, I thought so.

18

I'm not sure what I was expecting from Wiley the next morning when I recapped my Saturday night adventure on the highway. "Should I go to the police?" I posed the obvious question. But he seemed more invested in the story of Lisa and me.

"Man, what I hear, you been havin' a time with just one woman. You think you in a position to handle two?"

I realized that I probably had shared more of my experiences in the parish ministry than I'd intended, and wondered how much anyone else knew. That would include Teresa, even though, as I seemed to keep reminding myself, she was in no position to cast judgments—even less so after her latest assignation in Alamogordo.

"One thing you gotta remember," he advised me, returning to the intended topic of discussion. "The po-lice down here is po-li-ti-cal, with capital P's. They tend to answer calls based on who calls in. I doubt they'd give you the time of day."

"So what do you think we should do, Sherlock?"

"Like I said, call off the dogs. Tell Farley to flesh out that database so we can tell who's been teaching what, and leave it at that. Although I can tell you, you're in for some surprises."

I checked in with Farley, back at my office, and asked if he'd met with Sterling. "The president is into this alumni thing," he told me. "Wants me to look for a local grad for every year beginning with nineteen sixty-five, somebody who could serve as class secretary and help find others."

"The others who graduated with them?" I asked him.

"Well, also the ones who would have graduated at that time, but dropped out. Maybe especially those. He seems to be intent on turning up ex-students... Oh, and on the other project, that relational database? For the most part, I can identify the regular faculty member for each course. But for some of those online courses, I have the names but can't find out anything about them. We have no record of who they are."

That sent me back to Wiley for my second consultation of the morning.

He reclined in his desk chair. "Ah, there you have uncovered a squiggly can of worms, my friend. Return with us now to those thrilling days of yesteryear, you' predecessor in the religion department, back when we had one. Dude named Ryan O'Rourke, some kind of former priest, always looking to bestow an act of charity on anyone or anything, ran them courses like a Caribbean cruise.

"Anyway, one day he decides he'll offer a course online and comes up with an instructor from someplace in California, at a distance, which is where most of the online faculty seem to reside. Man sends in his vita, submits a syllabus, Ryan signs him to a contract, and the online course is underway. Only to find out, when a newspaper does an article on the instructor mid-term, that the man is serving a life sentence for murder, did his own PhD online, and now he's touted as an argument against capital punishment, seeing's how he's made so much of his life behind bars. Well, leastways Ocotillo U got some ink. Hey, we made the news."

Somewhat stunned, I made my way back to my office and shared my news with Farley. He winced and went back to his desk. Then he stopped at the door. "Those hang-up calls? I got another one at home over the weekend. Do you think I should change my phone number?"

I suggested that he do so, and told him about my thrilling experience Saturday night. "Doctor Crane suggests there's no point in going to the police, given the culture here."

Then I had another thought. "You know, suppose you hold off on changing it for a while. We might want to pay attention to how many calls you get in relation to what you're working on—say, this alumni stuff. See if the rate goes up. But in the meantime, Farley, I'd watch where you go at night. The president's wife was already forced off the road, and I'm pretty sure that's why that jerk in the pickup wanted me to pass him, to send me off a cliff."

I returned to my round of appointments for the day. A tall, studly student came in to grouse about a grade he'd received from a faculty member who'd co-starred with him in a play the previous semester. "She knew how much time that production took," he complained, "and I thought we were, like, friends." He gave a faint smile. "But then she turned around and gave me a D in Art History. Is there any way of appealing that?"

I offered some sagacious comments on academic integrity and the ways of women as I ushered him out the door. Then Arlene buzzed me. It was Aaron on the phone, my sometime student. Could I meet him for lunch at Serena's in a half-hour? He sounded stressed. I glanced at my schedule and told him he was on.

Aaron was in a booth up toward the front, staring into a beer. He extended his hand as I walked toward him but didn't get up. I could tell he was in a state. I ordered a draft Negro Modelo, sat down, and waited for him to speak.

"It's my dad," he said finally. "He had symptoms of a heart attack Sunday evening and they still have him in the hospital for observation."

I told him I was sorry.

"It's not just his medical condition. They think he's going to be okay. But it's the way it happened. You see, my mother—I guess I've never told you this, it never came up, but I'm sure it's a reason I get into a lot of this theological stuff—she's hyper religious, and I've had to deal with that my whole life. So has my dad. He's an engineer, not so much into the spiritual."

My beer arrived and I took an empathic swig. "Did something in particular happen on Sunday?"

"It was time for their weekly Bible study over at the Methodist Church. He has never wanted to go, feels like he raises questions the minister can't deal with, gets everybody rattled. But my mother's hot for it and I think he feels an obligation. So, Sunday as they're getting ready, he starts getting these chest pains, she calls nine-one-one, and here we are."

"Boy, that's a concern," I said. "no doubt about it." And we sat for a while in silence.

Finally, Aaron went on. "It just seems that, if I could present him with some rational approach to religious faith, maybe it would help their marriage and keep him out of the hospital—but I dunno. Do you want to order lunch?"

We did, sandwiches this time, nothing as heavy as burritos.

"Well, I'm not sure I can help you, especially in the midst of this crisis, but…" Just then I saw Teresa come through the door. I waved to her. She winked and came over.

"Teresa, have you met Aaron Fell? He's a computer mogul who started out as a religion major at OCU. Sometimes we get together and talk about the field he had the good sense to leave behind. Aaron, this is Teresa Ramirez. She teaches journalism at the university."

They shook hands and she sat down.

"So, I'll go on with what I was going to say. Maybe one of the first places to start is the distinction between faith and belief. Is that something we've ever talked about? You know, faith is a dynamic process that incorporates doubt while I think of belief as…"

Teresa got up and went out the door.

He was curious, of course, about what was going on between us and I told him a little. "I'll bet you guys have great sex," he said, "all that emotion and the freedom to take action."

I'm not sure how well I completed my mini-lecture. My head was into what had just transpired. But I reminded him of some books I'd recommended and encouraged him to tell his dad that religion didn't require an unscrewing of one's head.

"'Faith' is like a verb," I declared. "It's a way of venturing into the future, which is ever unknown. And, of course, doubting is a part of that process, because beliefs come and go. But faith means going forward. The crux of religious faith is to keep going forward."

I liked the sound of those sentiments and, by the time he left, he seemed a bit better. If only I had felt the same.

I sent Teresa an email later that afternoon: "Can we get together? I think we have a few things to discuss."

She wrote back: "Claro. How about brunch on Saturday: same time, same place?"

She was dressed to go hiking and seemed in a considerably brighter frame of mind when we met up at Serena's. We talked about this and that from our week at OCU until I brought up our abortive lunch with Aaron. I asked her why she'd got up and left and, for a moment, she fell silent. Then she exploded with a message that sounded so eloquent, I wondered if she'd rehearsed it.

"It was that conceptualizing," she said, her voice rising, "that pedantry. You're a good guy, Connor, and you mean real well. But I'm sick of this shit–all your concepts and the mind fucking it takes to conceive them." She paused for a breath, some people in the next booth glancing in our direction. "We don't need another way to understand the world. We've forgot how to receive it!"

I told her we should finish up, and go hiking. Winter in southwest New Mexico can be a gamble, with intermittent winds and even snowstorms. But today was a gift—clear sky and temperature in the sixties. We headed up the trail to Signal Peak, a rigorous hike among the tall pines along a trail full of big boulders. Teresa had been up there, but I had not and I worked off the brunch at Serena's and then some, keeping up with her.

When we got to the top, we took out our water bottles and sat on a broad, flat boulder, gazing at the emerald hills beneath the azure sky. For a long while, we were silent. I wondered if she had anything to add to her oratorical outburst over breakfast. And, in time, she did.

"You know, it would be incorrect to assume that I'm not religious, just in case you might have. As a kid, of course, I came up through Catholicism, although, thank God, my folks weren't really into it. But then there was Mount Holyoke. It's not just an elite school; the place is steeped in service. There's a statue of the founder in the middle of campus with her famous quotation: 'Go where no one else will go, do what no one else will do.' So, anyway, it's no accident that I'm at a place like Ocotillo U."

I said, "I can understand that."

"And it's not true that I haven't learned a lot of concepts. The professors at Holyoke buried us in them. But I had an awakening, first day of my first internship in journalism. It was at the Boston Globe where I found myself surrounded by all these old guys in the newsroom who were dressed in all these grungy clothes, more or less like college professors. But they didn't think like college professors."

"How were they different?" I asked, and broke out the water.

"My editor took me aside. He said, 'Whatever you have learned in school, when you go out to cover something, interview somebody—I want you to forget it. I'm going to teach you to see everything for the first time, with no preconceptions. Only as you open yourself to all you see will you be able to think productively about it.'

"Well, he did teach me that, and I never forgot it. So, I know I've been talking a lot. Are you still with me, Connor?"

I gave her some water and told her I was game.

"So, the last chapter follows from all of that and it's about you and me. There are lots of concepts out there that have to do with sexuality: homosexual, heterosexual, bisexual, trisexual (I'm not sure about that one, but it seems to follow). I don't care about any kind of sexual orientation, nor about forms of relationships: monogamy, polygamy, polyandry. I have no use for that either. I just go by what I feel."

She scooted across the boulder. "And right now, here on Signal Peak, I'm pretty clear about my feelings. I want you: yo te quiero." She snuggled closer. "Do you think we should go back down now?"

In a conventional relationship, I suppose it would have made sense to have told her more about Lisa, and maybe ask who Teresa had been with in Alamogordo. But that was not how she'd laid it out. So, was this to be my lifestyle? Right now, that was hard to conceive. But this was here and now. And, in any event, Teresa wasn't big on concepts.

So we went back to her place, and put off lunch. "You must have great sex," Aaron had surmised. I might note that we never had lunch.

Sometime late in the afternoon, we got up and had a few beers before supper. Teresa was in a more placid mood: quieted, I guessed, by some combination of the hike, the speeches she'd got off her chest, and sex. We sat out on her patio—I was still getting used to southern New Mexico in March, by now seventy degrees—and she started musing about affairs at OCU.

For a time, I thought I might try to direct the conversation, for there were some things I wanted to understand—the relationship of Teresa, Linda Lucero, and Claire, for starters. After eavesdropping on the last two players at Serena's, I was pretty sure I knew how Teresa was getting her inside information. But what was the rationale? Was Linda still hankering to become president of Ocotillo U, Teresa riding on her coattails? That made more sense than any other explanation I could think of.

And yet, I chose not to broach the subject. The sagacious voice of Walter Driscoll came back to me. "How much do you want to get into that gunny sack?"

So I let her go on. "Did you hear what I asked you, Connor?"

"Sorry, my mind was wandering."

"Not that again!" she groaned. "I was saying, how well do you know Sterling?"

"Well, I've worked with him twice. You know that."

"Have you ever seen him under stress?"

"Maybe only after the bar fight," I quipped.

"Well, I think you may be in for a new era. How committed is he to the Accountable University. That's what I'm wondering. Because there are a couple of big-time threats to the institution coming down the road."

"You mean the defaults on the student loans?"

"That's one. Do you want another beer?"

She came back with one for each of us, our third. "There's a big event coming up around the time of commencement, a program to attract students who never completed a degree. He's calling it "The Ex-travaganza."

"For ex-students, right?"

She nodded.

"Who may have defaulted on their loans," I thought. "I wonder how he plans to attract them?"

"Then, there's the nesht bombshell," she went on. Her words were beginning to slur. "Are you ready for this? OCU and schools like it will receive funds based not on how many students they enroll in their courses, but on how many complete them."

My mind began racing, and it didn't stop all the way through the pizzas we phoned in for dinner. With an attrition rate like ours, what would happen to the university?

"So, my question is this," said Teresa as I was getting ready to go home. "What is Sterling really like? How much is he committed to his rhetoric? How much of it is bullshit?"

I thought of telling her about his faking the attendance records at Easter, but decided to hold that in abeyance, lest it get out. As we said good-bye, I just shrugged and shook my head.

"Connor, I'm sorry I've been a little hyper lately—I mean at lunch, and at breakfast, and up on the hill." She kissed me. Then she whispered, "I heard about the blond."

I took myself to Quaker Meeting the next morning, to try to clear my head. But, on this day, silent worship didn't work. I couldn't "center down." Teresa's words stayed with me all of Sunday, and I had trouble focusing on the work I'd brought home for the weekend. It wasn't just her diatribes, nor her commentary on our relationship—not even the revelation that she'd heard about Lisa's visit.

It was what she'd had to say about Sterling, the oracular warnings about crises to come. Not that I was impressed by her premonitions. I now knew how and where she was getting her information. But I had a gnawing sense that she might be right, that when OCU encountered a genuine crisis, Sterling's vision of an Accountable University might go up in a puff of rhetoric.

So I began to wonder. How much is any of us is really capable of commitment? Is it a basic human trait? And I thought of Jenny, for the first time in a long while. Why hadn't I cared enough to ask Lisa about her?

Just then, as if on cue, the phone rang and it was Lisa. "Sorry I haven't got back to you before this, Connor. You know, it's taken me a week to get all of this together."

"You mean, to get an offer from Ocotillo U?"

"Oh, no," she said. "That happened on the spot. First, Sterling said he wanted to me to come and then he called up the division chair, Jack Lofton."

I could have made a comment, but squelched it.

"He figured out that they could offer me an appointment as an acting associate professor of sociology without publicizing the position and interviewing candidates."

I asked, "How long is it for?"

"One year, he told me, but it's renewable. And, anyway, by then I'd have an inside track on the job, he said. To be honest, I thought he seemed relieved at not having to go through the hassle of a formal search."

Again, I held my tongue.

"My main concern has been with my kids, talking it through and seeing if they're up for moving to a new place. Larry was fine; he's still in grade school. But Kristi's in junior high and really into her clique. So we sat down and aired our concerns. And finally it all came together."

"When are you coming?"

"Almost right away, the end of this term, in May. They want me for summer school."

"Wow!" I exclaimed, feeling a knot form in my stomach. I was silent for a minute. Then finally I came out with, "Is there anything I can to do help?"

She said, "I'm sure there will be quite a lot, if you're up for it. I know we're still sort of, well, in limbo."

Again, I couldn't think of anything to say.

"Connor, can you find me a good realtor? I'll need to rent a house, and soon."

I remembered one, looked up a phone number, and we made small talk about all the logistics of moving. Then I asked about Jenny, admitting I should have done so before then.

"I can't tell you much," she said. "Basically, the woman has refused to have anything to do with me. But I know she has a child and I believe there's another on the way. She married her principal and settled down in a flash."

"Well, it's interesting just to recall that town," I said, as some wheels began to turn in my head. "It seems so long ago. For example, you said you saw a lawyer, something about a case in higher education. And I tried to think whether I'd ever known any attorneys up there."

"Oh, that was Trevor Cranshaw," she said. "He's been around a while but I don't know if you'd have had occasion to meet him. I think he's Unitarian.

I told her the name didn't ring a bell as I wrote it down on my note pad, next to "the Garcetti reservation." I wished Lisa luck and told her to call if I could help her. "As you have me," I might have added.

Later that week, I got a card in the mail. It was unsigned. "All will evolve," was all it said.

19

Sterling turned up dressed to the nines for his Monday morning presidential cabinet meeting, our weekly managerial rite. He had on the black suit that he'd taken to wearing almost daily—I wondered if he owned more than one—with a pale blue shirt and OCU rep tie in purple and gold.

Wiley was considerably more casual in his chino slacks, maroon shirt, and matching sweater, while I looked even less formal than that. I found myself zoning out during the first part of the meeting, as he covered all kinds of data on the university, everything from admissions to physical plant to student services. (There had been a mild outbreak of influenza in January, but it hadn't required the cancellation of any classes.)

I tried to stay alert, but my mind drifted to Lisa and Teresa, more or less in that order. Then I turned back to the assembled group. I seemed to hear an old, southern hymn from a grad school course on American religious traditions: "Before this time another year, I may be gone. O Lord, how long?" It might have been written for Sterling and me.

Should I have filled Lisa in more on what was going on here? Offhand, it seemed I had, although I hadn't blistered Sterling as badly as I could have, since it appeared he was her friend and sponsor at OCU. But did she realize the kind of scene she was walking into? On the other hand, given the circumstances in which she found herself, did she have the luxury to care?

Sterling brought me back to attention as Wiley completed his weekly report. "Doctor Crane, I must say that I think your progress in your position has been commendable. It's not every professor who can move beyond the confines of his own education and interests to grasp the multitude of factors that influence his institution."

He looked at me somewhat knowingly, then back at him. "You deserve high marks for your performance as provost, sir. Now, then, Connor, let's turn to you. I believe I've come up with a research project that might contribute to your professional development and benefit the university, as well. Are you at all familiar with the term, 'prior learning assessment'?"

I acknowledged that I wasn't and he asked me to look into it. He sifted through some of his class notes and came up with an organization, the Council for Adult & Experiential Learning (CAEL). That group, he said, might be a resource for me.

Looking back, I can see that he'd caught me at a "teachable moment," as I'd heard the educational psychologists say. How much had I developed in the eighteen months that I'd been dean? Surely no one could have been less prepared for any job than I for the one Walter Driscoll had thrown me in, and I'd tried hard to learn it. But, in many ways, I was still a novice. Why hadn't I known until recently about the online courses being offered at OCU, to take one example?

Well, here was a chance to learn something. For several days, I immersed myself in the subject of prior learning assessment. I read during breaks in my schedule throughout the day, I stayed up studying at night. It was an interesting subject, with a philosophy of higher education out of Antioch College in Ohio that seemed very sensible.

One article led to another, and finally to a fascinating book out of the progressive education movement, *The Modern American College*, by Arthur Chickering. The root idea seemed to be that education is a form of human development, rather than just a system of credentialing. It followed that every course and degree should have clear outcomes in terms of performance. This was Sterling's ideal of accountability writ large.

Once those behavioral objectives were in place, and faculty were able to specify the competencies they aspired to see in students, then it was natural to assume that performance objectives could be measured for learning that had taken place outside the formal classroom. There you had it: prior learning assessment.

But this process was not to be undertaken lightly. CAEL had developed certain standards for prior learning assessment. There were about ten of them, but the first three stood out:

> Credit or its equivalent should be awarded only for learning, and not for experience.
> Assessment should be based on standards and criteria for the level of acceptable learning that are both agreed upon and made public.
> Assessment should be treated as an integral part of learning, not separate from it, and should be based on an understanding of learning processes.

It seemed they offered consulting services to help an institution orient itself to this whole process, and I could see that Ocotillo U would need plenty of help to do that. But the idea of it captivated me, and I wrote up a three-page white paper to present it to Sterling.

Was I seeking his approval? I thought about that later. After hearing that he seemed to be pleased I was seeing Lisa, could our relationship turn a corner? I guess all of these matters were rattling around in my brain when I called Claire and asked for an appointment to see him.

Perhaps few ventures in life go off as planned. When I went in to see Sterling Thursday morning, he was occupied with another task. He greeted me abruptly and motioned toward a chair. I sat and waited for five minutes till I had his attention, and handed him my report.

Sterling scanned it in a couple of minutes. Then he looked up and said, "Well, that's a start, perhaps a bit more involved than I'd expected." He went on to tell me about the project he had in mind, much of which I knew, thanks to Teresa.

"Around the time of commencement, I want to invite every former student who failed to graduate—we'll call this our OCU Ex-travaganza—back to campus for a time of reunion and recognition. We want to have them record their accomplishments in life and hold out the prospect of receiving academic credit for what they have learned in the process."

I said, "Can you give me an example?"

"A successful business owner will be eligible to receive credits in business administration. A Little League coach, credits in physical education, a faithful member of a church choir, accreditation in music."

I said, "I don't think that's quite how this process works. We'd need to have competencies outlined for each of our courses, and measure their documented skills against those outcomes."

"Oh, yes," he snapped, "if we had world enough and time. But the idea is to get them here and offer them an incentive for coming."

Suddenly a scenario based on my subterranean fears snapped into place. "And what's in it for us?" I asked. "Why do you want this group to come?"

For a minute, I thought he was about to level with me, come clean about his interest in nabbing the deadbeats who were threatening our federal financial aid by defaulting on their loans. But it was too much to expect.

"I don't think we need to go into that just now," he said, hurriedly. "The point is that I want you to communicate with the faculty, outline the

Ex-travaganza, and alert them that we may be asking them to accredit the accomplishments of our successful ex-students, much as I have described. It's fairly straightforward."

"And suspect," I replied. "Whatever your objective may be—and you haven't stated it—this is a misuse of a carefully conceived academic procedure. And I don't intend to take part in it. Frankly, I'm very disappointed in you."

His face turned red. "And I in you, Connor. To the degree that you may have just sealed your fate in your position and your tenure in this institution."

"Should I take that as a threat?" I cried.

"You can take it any way you want," he shouted, "and out the door!"

We were at the Hanover Outpost late that afternoon, re-opened after a remodeling that appeared to have consisted mainly of painting the walls a new shade of tan. The Naugahyde booths looked scarred by the same cigarette burns, but the floor may have been waxed.

I picked up a couple of Coors from the bar and brought them to Wiley, stretched out in a back booth. He'd said he had about an hour till Barbara was expecting him for dinner, and I thanked him for making time for me.

"Same song, seventh verse," I told him of my latest confrontation with Sterling. "Except this one seemed more serious. It ended with his telling me to get out the door and I wasn't entirely sure what that meant." I described the controversy over prior learning assessment.

Wiley took a swig from his bottle and unlimbered a bit more. "Well, I don't know how much good it does to try to crawl inside his noggin," he responded. "But I'll tell you a basketball story. I don't suppose you follow the NBA much, do you?"

I told him my knowledge of the League pretty much ended with Michael Jordan.

"Hmm. Well, back in the seventies, before you' time and when I was still a kid, there was a couple interesting dudes played for the Denver Nuggets. David Thompson was a phenomenal jock—a forty-four-inch vertical leap. (You stand a yardstick on end and add eight inches to it, you'll see how high that guy could jump.)

"Called him Skywalker, phenomenal dunks, put up seventy-three one night against the Seattle Sonics. Jumping out of the gym, as we say. But then one year he got hurt, and as he rehabbed, he lost an inch or two in his verticality. Of course, he had problems getting high in other ways. That was part of it. But the bottom line is that his career pretty much ended right there."

I asked if that was all there was to the story and if he wanted another beer. When I returned with refills, Wiley went on.

"Part two is about another guy who came on a couple years later. Alex English was a little taller, maybe six-seven, small forward. And he was a totally different player. Dude had but one move, a jumper (if you could call it that, he barely got off the floor) that he shot with his arms extended way up over his head. Quick release, got it off so fast it was hard to guard him. But this guy was anything but spectacular. They called him The Silent Assassin, 'cause a lot of times you never noticed how much he was scoring."

"So, I'll bet there's a moral to this story," I prodded him.

"Yes, indeed, young amigo. When the NBA careers of those two dudes ended, who do you suppose had played twice as long and scored twice as many points as the other?"

"I'm going to guess 'Alex English.'"

"Right on," Wiley replied. "Now, you see a parallel with you and Sterling?"

"Maybe one of us is constantly soaring and the other..."

"Should stick to what he does best," he said. "Sure, you might not be flashy, but you care about the folks you' dealin' with. You' an easy guy to talk to, and all that. So maybe the idea is to play to your strengths, keep your feet on the floor. Let Sterling keep throwin' down them slam dunks, heavin' up jumpers from mid-court. We'll see who wins in the end."

I took that wisdom home that night, and it rang a bell. I leafed through the *Tao Té Ching*, and found the passage I was looking for: "On tiptoe your stance is unsteady; long strides make your progress unsure..."

Was that enough guidance to go by? For certain, it helped me get to sleep. But I awoke with a start to the sound of a stern voice, in the middle of the night. "Out the door!" it hollered, and I shot bolt upright in bed. Of course, no one was there, but it took me a couple of beers to get Sterling out of my system and doze off.

I woke up in a fog, but knew in the first dawning that Wiley's advice to simply play my own game wouldn't do. I had to take some action. And so I turned to a couple of options I'd been mulling over for some time.

Later that morning, I called Farley into my office and closed the door. I asked him about SOCO, the Save Our Ocotillo U cohort. Were they still in operation? He said they were, and that in fact there was a meeting that evening.

"Do you suppose I could join you?" I asked.

He hesitated for a moment, then frowned. "Nothing against you," he assured me, "but to these people, administrators are anathema. You know I don't feel that way, but they've been burned in the past. And, for this bunch, it's strictly us-against-them."

I told him I understood, and that I wished them success in whatever it was they were up to. But later I looked up his home address in the phone book and, about six thirty that night, found myself parked across the street from a small, white bungalow in a modest neighborhood. I was wearing a baseball cap pulled low over my eyes, as well as dark glasses.

I thought I recognized his car out front and knew I had the right place when I saw him through the living room window. He was standing there talking with a young woman who may have been his wife. Yet another case of not knowing my co-workers well enough, I reflected.

About ten till seven, Farley came out the front door and got in his car. It was almost dusk, but as I pulled out and followed him I left my headlights off for a block or two till he turned onto a main drag. He drove for a couple of miles to an upscale part of town, not far from Teresa's place. He parked across the street from a big, Tudor house, rang the bell, and went inside. Fortunately, I was able to find a space just up the street. I pulled in, turned off the ignition, slumped down a bit in my seat, and waited.

So, who belonged to SOCO? Before long, as other members went up to the door, I began to form an impression. Maybe fifteen people arrived and I recognized almost none of them—it was getting dark, for one thing—but the few I did were from humanities. A lot were women, but not all. There were three or four strapping young guys, who appeared to be cut from the same cloth as Albert McNulty. Well, I thought, maybe he'd hired them. Perhaps they'd been drawn to OCU not just by his example, but because of the nearby Gila Wilderness.

The next day, Farley stopped by my desk, mildly smirking. "So, what did you think of the group?" he asked.

I gave a start.

He said, "It might have gone better if you hadn't driven your own car."

Later that afternoon, I made move number two and called Trevor Cranshaw, Lisa's lawyer. I knew instantly I'd never met him when he came on the phone in a gruff, crusty voice I'd have remembered. I asked him how much he charged and he told me: two hundred dollars an hour. "I'm going to give you to my secretary," he graveled on. "She'll get your credit card information. And the next time you hear my voice, the meter's running." He followed that with a cackling laugh.

He asked about my problem and I told him, adding that I assumed anything I said was confidential. He assured me that it was and, with a chuckle, said he hoped I'd treat him the same. Then he asked about the parties involved. When I mentioned Sterling's name, he made a gagging sound.

"Not to be unprofessional," he said, "although at my age, it probably doesn't make a lot of difference. But I remember when he lived up here, served on a couple of civic committees with him."

There was a long pause before he went on. "Pretentious bastard who'd do almost anything goddamn thing as long as it was popular, like blessing people's pets. You know, I heard a good neologism the other day: 'ignoranus.'"

I said, "What's that?"

"An ignorant person who is also an asshole."

Badly in need of some comic relief, I broke up at that. Suddenly, it seemed that, at two hundred dollars an hour or whatever, Trevor Cranshaw might be a pretty good investment.

"So let's hear the story. And I know that, with the clock ticking, you're going to be succinct."

I outlined my formal relationship to Sterling within the university and summarized his series of outlandish administrative decisions, in most of which he'd directed me to participate.

"And how did you respond, based on your best professional judgment?"

I described my refusals to take part.

"And his response to your decisions?"

"Displeased," I said, "sometimes heated, to the point that after our last confrontation, he told me to get out the door."

"Was he threatening the loss of your employment?"

I said, "That's what has me worried. I could take that statement a couple of ways."

He thought for a moment. "Well," he went on, "there is one way to forestall someone like that from taking action. It's an aggressive letter from an attorney, often referred to as an order to 'cease and desist.' The purpose is to threaten him with a lawsuit if he doesn't stop what he's doing—i.e., threatening you with the loss of your job."

"But on what grounds could I sue him?" I asked. "Even if I were rich enough to do so."

Again, he thought for a minute. "I think you may have caught a break," he said. "Not long ago, I took on a case somewhat like yours at our state university. And I did some research that might be right up your alley. I'll summarize it for you, and you can see what you think."

The legal precedent dated from the late eighties in Los Angeles. A deputy district attorney found himself questioning some shoddy investigative work on the prosecutorial side of a pending trial. He ended up siding with the defense. That led to a bitter argument with his boss, who thereupon denied him a promotion, reassigned him to another position, and transferred him to a different courthouse.

The deputy district attorney filed a lawsuit and the case got all the way to the U.S. Supreme Court. He claimed that he was being denied his right to free speech under the first amendment to the constitution. "The justices narrowly decided in favor of the deputy attorney's boss, a district attorney named Gil Garcetti," Cranshaw explained. "In their ruling, they said that freedom of expression does not apply to communications pursuant to one's occupation.

"But, and here's the corker, they made an exception when it came to freedom of speech and thought associated with a university environment. That's called 'the Garcetti reservation.'"

I said, "Whoa!"

"That's right," Cranshaw responded. "Now, there have been legal battles back and forth as to exactly what this ruling means. For example, one court decided that it doesn't apply to teachers in public secondary schools. But—and here's the pertinent point in your case—there is just cause to assume that the Garcetti reservation on academic free speech may apply to an administrator's judgments as well."

He told me what was involved in doing up a cease and desist letter—basically, another hour of his time—which could be dated and sent to Sterling at my discretion. And then he added a word of advice. "You have to be aware that such a letter constitutes a threat of legal action, but it has no legal standing in itself. And, like any threat, it works only once. So, you have to decide when you're down to your last straw, and have me send the letter right then."

I thanked him for his counsel and asked him to draw up a draft that I could fill in with specifics. And I told him how much better he'd made me feel.

But I woke in the night from a very bad dream. I was up on a tightrope over a yawning pit. And as I cleared my head, a question came to me. What if he fires me before I can get the letter off?

Teresa called me at the office the next day while I was documenting my stand-offs with Sterling, for Trevor Cranshaw's cease and desist letter. The tone of it was almost vitriolic, and I sensed that had something to do with whatever had gone on between those two in the past.

I told Arlene I'd call her back, gave the draft a final once-over, and emailed it to Trevor. Then I tried to tell myself I should feel a bit more secure with that arrow in my quiver.

Teresa answered the phone with an exultant, "Chimichanga Night! Hey, are you up for the Raven's Roost? If we get there at five, we'll miss the masses."

I asked her to back up and tell me what a chimichanga was—evidently a fried tortilla, stuffed with whatever was at hand. I said I was always up for an adventure and, later that afternoon, took the gorgeous drive up the hill to Pinecroft. On the way, I found myself feeling emotional, in what some might call "a well of grace." My heart was filled with gratitude for the support of Trevor Cranshaw, and for friends like Wiley and Teresa.

Would I add Lisa to that list? I hoped so, although I still didn't know how that would meld with Teresa. It occurred to me just then that I probably ought to let Lisa know I'd hired the lawyer whose name she'd given me. I was not sure how that had slipped my mind.

Teresa was into her first margarita when I found her at the back of the Raven's Roost's main dining room. As she predicted, almost no one else was there. That was probably a good thing, as she was pretty vociferous about her day of teaching, trying to bring the OCU students up to par. I thought back to the material I'd read from Antioch College, that educators should define the outcomes they expect from their students, the behaviors they want to see. And I sensed, once again, that here was one professor who was able to do that.

She asked how I was doing and I related my latest confrontation with Sterling and my dealings with Trevor Cranshaw. At that, her dark eyes caught fire as she shook her head vigorously. The chimichangas arrived in the wake of a couple of more margaritas, and they were as good as advertised—lightly fried and filled with roast pork, avocados, tomatoes, and fresh lettuce. I found myself thinking what a treat this would be for Lisa.

Teresa passed me a copy of the letter Sterling was preparing to send out to the alumni class secretaries Farley had found, and I thanked Claire, silently, for leaking it out of his office. I was glad not to have seen it till I'd digested the fried burrito, as my stomach churned with each paragraph. He had quoted liberally from the paper I'd written on prior learning assessment: recognizing knowledge attained from a variety of sources and honoring career achievement. But there was no suggestion of how this process would transpire, and I couldn't guess what he proposed to tell the faculty. One way or another, I knew I would not be involved.

For a while Teresa sat in silence as I stewed in my juices. Then, finally, she spoke up.

"There's a question that's been bugging me," she said, "and it's very basic. How did Sterling get into this position in the first place? I mean, you think of a university president as sort of a hunk, right?—some kind of alpha male. But he's nothing like that. I look at him and a phrase from Spanish keeps coming back to me: chivo expiatorio."

"It has a nice ring to it," I commented. "What's it signify?"

"Chivo expiatorio," she repeated, slowly. "A 'sacrificial goat.' I mean, what if this guy's been set up? If so, then who's behind it? No, that's weird...but what is really going on here?"

She shook her head for a moment as if to clear it. Then she said she needed to go. She got up and leaned over me, her breasts brushing against my shoulder. She murmured, "It's the wrong time of the month for fooling around, mi amigo. Tal vez, mas tarde."

I could translate that: "Maybe later."

Then she kissed me and launched a closing line. "This weekend? I'm afraid I'll be away." And, in an instant, she was gone.

I sat for a few minutes and thought about what she'd just said. "What is really going on here?" Up to my ass in anxiety, I knew that I was not the guy to ask.

As I drove back down the mountain, that well of grace that had filled my heart was dissipating by the mile. Damn that Teresa: another weekend alone. It was about then that I decided to get back in touch with Lisa. And so, soon after I got home, I sent her an email, asking if she'd finalized her contract with Ocotillo U. I added that I'd engaged the services of Trevor Cranshaw, told her what I done with him, and thanked her for giving me his name.

About an hour later, the phone rang and I answered. There was silence on the line. Again, I said: "Hello." I waited another half-minute, then blurted out, "Look, if you're one of these damn-fool hang-up callers, why don't you do so right now. All of us have had enough of this, and if you do it again, I'll trace the call and show up on your doorstep with the police."

I was about to set down the receiver when I heard something that sounded like a sob, and then another. "Who's there!" I demanded. And then I heard a choked voice: "Connor, how could you do this to me?"

"Lisa? I could hardly recognize your voice. Do what to you? What on earth is going on?"

After another couple of sobs, her voice came back, and with it, a tirade. "How could you jeopardize a job that I need very badly, taking advantage of my telling you my lawyer's name!"

"Well, you gave it to me!" I hollered. Then I remembered the context—"oh, by the way, I wonder if I knew that guy"—and suddenly felt enveloped in guilt. At some level, I'd surely have known what I was doing. I told her all of that and she calmed down.

"Okay, so I apologize for my subconscious," I said. "But what's the big deal? There's no way Sterling would know I got Trevor Cranshaw's name from you. And, besides, don't you already have your contract with OCU?"

She was quiet for a minute and sniffled again. "The answers to your questions are, in order, yes and no."

"You'd better explain."

"I told Sterling everything about the problem I was having at the community college. I thought he should know the story, and besides he might find out. And I told him which lawyer I'd consulted."

"I'll bet he was pleased. From what I hear, those guys were real buddies."

"He made a comment under his breath."

"And the contract?"

"It's hung up somewhere, I believe with the division chair."

"Ah, Professor Lofton," I reflected. Probably immersed in his cast-of-thousands online courses.

"Well, all right, Lisa. Look, there's no reason for him not to assume I'd known Cranshaw when I lived up there. But, I'll tell you what. I will ask Sterling's secretary to track down the contract and try to make sure it gets in the mail to you."

"Well, thank you for that."

"And remember, that cease and desist letter I wrote you about? Nothing will happen with that unless Sterling tries to fire me."

"After which, he could find a reason to rescind my contract," she sputtered. "I'm 'acting,' remember? You know, I had no idea that relations between you and Sterling had come to this."

"You thought we were having a love fest down here, is that it? You didn't know the university was having problems?"

Now her voice was quiet and she seemed more settled. "I knew and I didn't know. I saw what I wanted to, I guess. There's a condition in the field of social psychology called 'attention blindness.' I've taught the theory and I guess I should apply it to myself." She laughed for a half second.

By the time we hung up, we seemed to be sailing in the same direction, though hardly on a placid sea. Lisa was jumping ship onto what might turn out to be a badly leaking raft.

20

As the weeks rolled by toward the end of spring semester, I didn't hear much from Lisa: only that her signed contract had finally arrived, thanks to the ministrations of Claire. But she was never far from my mind. Sometimes I found myself pondering my motivation in extricating the name of her lawyer, and the extent to which it had been unconscious. I looked up a squib I liked in Ecclesiastes and at times found myself absorbed in it.

"But all this I laid to heart, examining it all, how the righteous and the wise and their deeds are in the hand of God; whether it is love or hate man does not know." It seemed to speak to the obscurity and ambiguity within my own character, and I tried to apply it to that of Sterling. Does any of us really understand our deepest motives, what we are basically about?

Meanwhile, I continued to see Teresa, sometimes a little of her and at other times a lot. But, indefinite as our sex life may have become, she never failed to update me on Sterling's calendar, thanks again to Claire. When I was with him in the presidential cabinet meetings, in which for some reason he continued to include me, I could tell he was feeling upbeat.

Based on his calendar, I thought I knew why. The man was giving talks all over the time zone. One week in Tucson, the next in Albuquerque, then El Paso and Las Cruces. It seemed that OCU alumni clubs were springing up throughout the Southwest and Sterling was on tap for all of them. I could envision our dark-suited, sometimes diffident prexy, along with the ever-effervescent Daniela, making a grand entrance into one venue after another. Caramba!

The secret to his popularity, of course, had been a brainchild of his own making, aided by my ground-tilling research: the promise of academic credit for experiential learning. From time to time, I wondered how the old codger was going about it. Then Teresa came by one day with a message she had siphoned from the president's office.

It was a letter to the multitude of ex-students Daniela's organization was turning up. Beginning with a banner headline—OCU IS PROUD OF YOU—it outlined a path to acquiring academic credit for life experiences. All that was required was to send in a summary of one's accomplishments: say, in business, family life, or community service. The office of the dean, he said, would contact the appropriate departments and they'd do the rest. It seemed a certificate with the seal of Ocotillo U might be in the offing, suitable for framing.

And, by the way, there was an opportunity to make a tax-deductible contribution to the university, and online courses available should one wish to seal the deal on a complete degree.

What a sham! The sages of Antioch College would be turning in their graves. But that wasn't the worst of it. At the mention of the dean, my blood ran cold. Hadn't I made it clear I wanted no part of this boondoggle? I thought of charging into his office, but decided I'd hold my peace till the next presidential cabinet meeting. Was this the time to activate Trevor Cranshaw's letter, to cease and desist? The thought of Lisa stopped me.

As time went by, I began to receive a stream of requests for accrediting non-classroom learning. I just set them in a stack on my credenza and watched my blood pressure rise as the pile mounted. At first, I thought I might carry them into the next cabinet meeting and throw them at Sterling, or perhaps drop them at his feet. Then, for some reason, the letters stopped coming and, as the next meeting came around, I decided to let them be. Perhaps inaction was the best course, at least for the time being. I continued to feel the tug of Lisa.

But Sterling never brought the matter up again and his mood seemed to change in mid-term. Whereas a few weeks ago, I'd seen him walking around campus talking flamboyantly with students, now he seemed subdued and strangely silent. I called up Teresa and asked if she could find out what was going on. We made plans for dinner that night at her place.

As always, I never mentioned Claire and waited for her to share whatever insights she'd come up with. We had a few beers and a pizza and spoke of many things before adjourning to the bedroom for our nightcap. And then, once again, the info flowed in the afterglow.

"He's starting to get some pretty heated letters," Teresa murmured, "irate and even threatening."

"And why's that?" I asked ingenuously, though I could guess what was coming.

"There was a deal with the federal agency that monitors student loans. The idea behind wooing the ex-students, of course, was to turn up some deadbeats."

"So, did that happen?"

"In spades; they found a lot. The plan was to keep that information on ice until the Ex-travaganza, before commencement. But there was a leak within the agency, deliberate or no, and some of these folks began getting dunning letters from the feds maybe a week or so after they'd heard from Sterling."

"Do you think the cat is out of the bag, on a broad scale?"

Teresa thought for a long moment. "Probably not, unless the media gets hold of the story." Then she appeared to doze off to sleep.

I let myself out and drove back home where, like the author of Ecclesiastes, I spent some time examining it all. Was it love or hate inspiring me, and would I ever know? Could I trust myself to take some sort of action, or should I sit back and let events run their course—waiting for Sterling to bring himself down? I laid it all to heart.

"Hey, Wiley!"

As I passed by his office the next morning, the door was open and he was hunched over his computer. "Mind if I interrupt?" I asked, and he waved me in.

I said, "I won't take long."

He shrugged. "Whatever you're here for, it's gotta be more fascinating than these budgets. Whassup?"

I took a second to consider my agenda, which was based on something surreptitious: my access to the calendar of Sterling Holmes. "Oh, I just came across a place I hadn't heard of, and it sounded sort of interesting. What do you know about Columbus, New Mexico?"

To be honest, I might have added what it was I found of interest in the town. It was the site of Sterling's only speaking engagement that wasn't in some sort of city.

"Col-um-bus," he sounded out the syllables. "Not to be confused with Columbus, Ohio or even Columbus, Nebraska—Columbus, New Mexico is a burg of maybe fifteen hundred souls maybe three miles north of the border with Mexico, straight south of here."

"What else do you know about it?" I asked.

"Well, not much about its current status, haven't been there in some time. It's on the way to Palomas, State of Chihuahua—little town about three or four times its size, in Mexico. Columbus is one of those places, it's hard to tell where the two countries begin and end. I've known folks from there who not only spoke

English as a second language, they could barely speak it at all. But you also got Anglos down there, including a colony of aging hippies—built their houses out of concrete and beer bottles. Will that hold you?"

"I suppose so. I'm not sure what else to ask."

"Well, to round out the story, Palomas is known mostly for trafficking in immigrants—call 'em mojados, 'the damp ones,' wetbacks in Spanish—and drugs. Sometimes kidnapping as a sideline. Oh, and one more thing about Columbus. I'd better look up the details..."

He went back to his computer. "Here we go: On March 6, 1916, 4:00 a.m., Pancho Villa busted across the border with five hundred of his rebel band and attacked the town, pissed off because the Americans had switched loyalties to his adversary in that Mexican civil war. Killed eight U.S soldiers and ten townspeople before he hightailed it back. Got a statue of him on horseback down there in Palomas. Villa lost a hundred men—it was an army base he attacked—and then Black Jack Pershing took off after him with ten thousand troops. But they never found him, had to turn around and come back."

I said, "Given what you've told me, I suppose that's what most visitors to Columbus do."

"Right, after about a half-hour in town. But some go on across to Palomas. They got doctors and dentists, pharmacies—all cut rate. A good deal, long as the drug wars are cool."

"So it's dangerous down on the border?"

Wiley stroked his chin. "I always tell folks, Palomas is like Chicago. Gotta know where you are at all times, and don't be walkin' around after dark."

Walking back to my office, I pondered all of that. Sterling in Columbus: what a concept.

Very quickly, the rest of my day took shape. There was an email message from Lisa who was coming to town this weekend, to look for a rental. "Will you go with me on Saturday? Then perhaps we can take a hike, and..."

That hanging clause got my attention, until I remembered I'd already made plans for the weekend with Teresa. I whipped off a note that something had sprung up and she responded immediately: "Well, okay, I've seen it do that. Just be careful where it goes."

I was still considering that advice when Arlene brought in a memo from Sterling. Two doors down the hall, the man might have asked me to stop by for a consultation, but I'm sure we both knew it was safer to keep a slip of paper between us. The message outlined the sea change in the state higher education funding formula, which I'd known was coming. From now on, we'd be rewarded not for the number of students who enrolled in our courses, but for how many completed them. I shook my head. What the hell were those legislators thinking?

But then Sterling went on to share a few thoughts of his own, and the plan he came up with made me shiver. He had appointed a special task force of "senior faculty" to devise a retention strategy for OCU, keeping students enrolled at least until the end of each semester. Well, so far, so good. But then I read the roster. The task force consisted of none other than Jack Lofton, Bob Clifford, and Peter Entwhistle: the guts of Grow Our Ocotillo U—i.e., GOCO. Talk about putting the fox in charge of the chickens. It seemed that Entwhistle, the fabled ex-spouse of my late secretary, Alice Pendergast, would serve as chair.

The task force would report on its recommendations at next Monday's presidential cabinet meeting. Then there was a last item, which qualified as breaking news. It seemed that Sterling's bait-and-switch Ex-travaganza for the former students of OCU had suddenly been cancelled. That had to rank as the best decision I'd seen him make thus far in his reign.

As Arlene stepped out, I rocked back in my desk chair and spun it around a few times, trying to find some fresh perspective on the task force. When that didn't work, I went out in the anteroom, found Farley, and asked him to come back to my office. As I passed by Arlene, she tapped me on the shoulder and showed me my schedule for the rest of the morning. "Here's a half-hour at eleven thirty," she said. "That reporter from the paper, Jessica Madrid, asked if she could see you today. Should I slot her in there?"

I nodded abstractedly as I walked back in my office and closed the door. Farley was sitting in front of my desk. Without comment, I handed him Sterling's memo.

He scanned it and said, simply, "Hmm."

I peered at him and said, "You don't seem surprised."

Farley looked aside for a few moments. Then he said, in a lowered voice, "I don't think I should tell you what I'm about to, but I guess I will. You know, Connor, you would understand a lot more about what's going on around here if they'd let you come to the SOCO meetings."

"But I guess that's not in the cards," I acknowledged.

Again he was silent. Watching him cogitate, I marveled at the transformation of that awkward, geeky instructor I'd first encountered in his classroom. He seemed so much more self-possessed, and I wondered if I might have had something to do with that maturation.

Finally, he spoke, sotto voce. "'Save Our Ocotillo U' is more than a slogan," he said. "Some guys in this group are aging radicals from the sixties. You know, 'by any means necessary.' When it comes to whatever they believe in, not too many options are off the table. And they're into a sort of reverse discrimination. It's like, never trust anyone under forty. Of course, I know you better, but they're afraid you might be some kind of norm-less Yuppy."

"That's about all I need," I sighed. "So, is that all you wanted to tell me?"

"We've got a mole in GOCO," he went on. "I'm sure they've got someone planted in our group as well. So I can tell you about their motivation. It's pretty simple. Aldo Bruski, the football coach, is hot for his upgrade into NCAA, Division 1-AA with all the revenue from regional TV and the rest. To maintain that, he needs numbers: bigger bucks from student activity fees to enlarge the football stadium. And in the end, what with the TV dollars, he should be able to turn a profit, maybe support some other sports."

"Or, in the worst case, the library," I noted. "But this new funding formula should undercut all that."

"Absolutely," Farley responded. "Of course, they can boost enrollment through online courses, clicks versus bricks, but still they can't afford to lose many locals, no matter what condition these students are in when they show up here."

"So what are they going to propose?" I asked.

Again he felt silent. Then he mumbled, "I can't tell you that. If it ever got out, my ass would be grass. So, you'll have to wait and find out for yourself."

"And you think there could be repercussions, once the announcement is made?"

He cocked his head. "These people are serious about not trashing OCU. And, as I said, there aren't many options off the table."

Jessica Madrid had lost no weight nor added to her wardrobe since the last time we met. But she had the same, jaunty sparkle in her eye: a journalist smelling a story. As before, she was equipped with a notepad and pen, but this time I didn't see a camera.

"It's about this Ex-travaganza, coming up weekend after next," she explained. "I called the president to ask what the whole thing was about and he said something about reaching out to the former students who'd never graduated. But then he referred me to you. He told me you were in charge of it."

I blanched at the impudence of that maneuver, then remembered I was off the hook. "The program has been cancelled," I gloated, and watched her face fall.

"We've slotted it for a front page feature next Monday," she said. "And that's a big deal. You know, not much happens in a town like this, and we can't just ditch a story. So tell me something, will you? I mean, what was the Ex-travaganza all about, and why was it cancelled?"

I thought for a moment and my stomach creaked at the thought of recap-ping another of Sterling's insanities. Then I remembered she had a press release or she wouldn't be here, and also something I'd done. I walked over to the end of my credenza where I'd stacked all the letters that had come in, those requesting credit for lifelong learning and the others griping about having been found out by the federal loan officers. I picked up the lot and brought them to Jessica. Then I handed her the list of class representatives that I'd just received from Farley.

"Here's your story, original source material," I told her. "A bit more digging, but it should have a freshness about it. You can talk with these people and find out what the president's program meant in their lives. When you're through with the letters, I'll need them returned."

Somewhat grudgingly, she took the pile and headed out. Relieved to see that she didn't have a camera, I turned back to my desk and scanned my calendar for my next appointment.

"Oh, Dean Ransom, one more thing," she called from the doorway.

I looked up, scratching my armpit, and heard a soft click. She'd caught me with her cell phone.

I remembered the upcoming story now and then over the next few days and wondered if Jessica would really accomplish all those interviews. But mostly I thought about Lisa and her visit. Now that she seemed poised to become a more permanent presence in my life, I considered the feelings I might still have for her.

"All will evolve." That's what she'd said.

As Friday rolled around, I began to wonder if Lisa would make contact for the weekend, or if I should. I phoned the motel where she'd stayed before and found that she was registered again. I was about to call back and leave a message, suggesting dinner, when Arlene buzzed me. It was Aaron on the line.

He was calling from the hospital, and sounded distraught. Could I meet him about five in the Courtyard Café? I recognized the name as nothing but a euphemism for purveyors of hospital cuisine and doubted they'd have a liquor license. But I said I would come.

"Can you tell me what's up?" I asked.

"It's my dad. Those symptoms were no false alarm and he's in bad shape. The docs have offered to operate, but he doesn't want that. I'm just trying to support him. I'll tell you more when I see you."

He said it all in a flurry, but then he gave a dark chuckle. "And you can order anything on the menu. I'll pick up the tab."

Absorbed with Aaron, I forgot about Lisa till Arlene buzzed again, mid-afternoon. I gave a guilty sigh as I picked up the phone. But it wasn't Lisa. It was the reporter, Jessica Madrid.

She, too, sounded agitated. "Dean Ransom, I shouldn't tell you this—it's not very professional. But we've been working on this story all week."

"That's you and your tapeworm, 'we'?" I quipped.

"Teresa's journalism students—they've been calling all those class reps, and following up with the ex-students. It's grown into quite a story. Anyway, what I want to let you know is that the Ex-travaganza, or something like it, is going to happen."

"But, as I told you, the president called it off."

"He may have tried," Jessica responded with a sense of urgency, "but some of these people are so pissed off, they're getting together on their own."

"Here on campus?"

"I'm not sure, but I don't think so. It seems they've got hold of Holmes' speaking schedule, so I think they may try to confront him on one of his gigs. But beyond that, I don't know—except for one thing."

"And what's that?"

"Whatever is to come off, it's slated for next week."

I put the phone on speaker and rummaged around on my desk for Sterling's schedule. Scanning the week, I found it—his only engagement, seven p.m. next Monday at the public library in Columbus, New Mexico. "You Can Count on the Accountable University: OCU."

I said, "Jessica, I want to thank you for all the information. You didn't have to do this."

"I know," she said, "but you were so forthcoming. You gave me all those letters."

"Well," I reflected, "the fellow who hired me for this job was a great one for giving advice. And one of his maxims had to do with media relations."

"What was that?"

"'If you can't think of anything else to say, try telling the truth.'"

It was the first time I'd thought about Walter Driscoll for quite a while, and it gave me pause to wonder what he would do. The answer that came to me was: nothing. I decided not to tell anyone about my conversation with Jessica, not even Wiley. But then I wondered if I should connect with someone who would already know. Maybe I'd call Teresa, eventually.

That reminded me of Lisa, and I finally left a message at her motel. I told her I'd meet her Saturday morning at eight, for breakfast at the Drifter. After tonight's repast of hospital gruel, I was sure to be up for the huevos rancheros.

I got to the hospital cafeteria at five and, by five fifteen, there was no sign of Aaron. I walked around to the front desk and asked for the room number of someone named Fell. An elderly lady in a pink smock surveyed the patient roster. "Oh, Benjamin Fell," she exclaimed as though she knew the man. "Room two fourteen. Just take the elevator up to the second floor."

This was my first visit to the hospital and I found the elevator impressive, the slowest moving vehicle I'd ever ridden: evidently to give people in wheelchairs time to get off and on. After one false start, I figured out the room numbering system and found my way to two fourteen where a honking voice was raised in what sounded like an intercessory prayer. I stayed out in the hall where I couldn't see what was going on. But I caught the gist of the prayer, a few stock supplications for recovery—and eternal life if that didn't work out.

Finally, I stuck my head in the doorway and saw Aaron standing by himself at the foot of a hospital bed. A pudgy, red-faced man in a wrinkled suit stood on one side of the bed, grasping one hand of an elderly fellow hooked up to some tubes. The fat man was doing the praying and he looked vaguely familiar. A well-dressed woman, maybe in her sixties, was holding the other hand and sounding an occasional "Amen." The patient himself had his eyes closed and might have been in a coma. But now and then I thought I saw him grimace, which was pretty much the expression Aaron had.

As a couple of them filed out, I recognized the preacher. It was the Reverend Buford Schneuter who had given me a hard time over the high school student in my religion course, it seemed a lifetime ago. He was walking intently, head down, and took no notice of me.

The woman, whom I took to be Aaron's mother, followed on the heels of her minister. I stepped into the room and found Aaron sitting beside the bed, his hand on his father's shoulder. The old man's eyes were open slightly and it appeared that he could see him. I heard Aaron ask him a question and then I saw that his father was conscious. He nodded slightly.

Twenty minutes later, we'd gone through the cafeteria line and were sitting at a table in what was indeed a courtyard—a graveled area with a couple of big sculptures, surrounded by a quadrangle of two-storied, adobe-colored buildings. If you had to be in a hospital, this was a warm place on a human scale. And, in late April, it was a comfortable time to be outside.

Aaron seemed to relax a little as he dug into a plateful of humdrum, hospital-style, chicken enchiladas. "I just need to talk," he said. "Thanks so much for coming out here."

"I'll be glad to help any way I can," I said. "You'll just have to let me know if I get too theoretical. Remember how Teresa ripped me the other day."

He laughed. "No, actually, that's exactly what I want. I've got to get some distance from this scene with my dad, my mother, and that minister. You see, if he goes into surgery, he could come out disabled—maybe never get out of bed. My dad doesn't want that. He'd rather let this illness take its course."

"But, your mother..."

"And this Reverend Schneuter, they say that turning down the operation amounts to suicide. He could be dead within a couple of weeks without it. And they believe that's wrong."

"So what shall we talk about?"

"I suppose it's 'suicide.' Do you think it's immoral to let your life end?"

"And concepts are okay, correct?"

Aaron said, "Go for it."

"Okay, so here's a class from an ethics course you never got to take. I always like to start with etymology. In this case, let's look at the derivation of the term 'suicide.' It's a compound of two Latin words, a verb that meant to cut or kill and a pronoun meaning oneself. Which brings us to a working definition of 'self.' Are you with me?"

Aaron said, "Right on."

"Now, I see 'selfhood' as a sense of wholeness, of being at one with ourselves in a place where we are free to make choices. Of course, that may sound somewhat rosy, and it certainly isn't the way most people feel when they're flat on their back in a hospital. But I believe it's a good norm, a place to start. Basically, I think that's who we are. The question becomes, when it comes to medical interventions such as surgery, what will the effect be on a person's selfhood?"

Aaron said, "If the outcome is life as a bedridden invalid, it's probably destructive."

I said, "Possibly. What we want to aim for is enhancing a person's selfhood. And that's where a second concept comes in: 'biocide.'"

He said, "I haven't heard that one, but I suppose it means destruction of an organism."

"You get an A. Of course, that's pretty clinical and abstract, compared to the crisis your dad is in. But, when it comes to making a decision about someone's quality of life, clarifying those concepts can be very helpful."

"So, prolonging life could be an act of suicide," Aaron reflected. "And biocide, letting life go..."

"Could be a way to affirm who we are," I said. "Maybe it's an idea worth considering."

He did so for a few minutes, as we sat out in the courtyard in the gathering darkness. Then he got up and wrapped me in a bear hug.

Driving home, I thought of a quote from Soren Kierkegaard, the nineteenth century Danish philosopher: "To be a self and have a world is God's greatest gift to man. At the same time, it is eternity's demand upon him."

And I thought about the crisis I faced in my own life: whatever to do about Sterling. Is this not another form of suicide, to be decimated by indecision? I had to wonder.

21

It may have been a sparkle of sunlight on her golden hair, or perhaps just the lapse in time since I'd been with her, but something about seeing Lisa felt energizing the next morning. She greeted me with a smile as I found her table in a far corner of the Drifter, and took me in her arms. This seemed to be my weekend for hugs. Whatever else it signified, at least she seemed to have got past our conflict over my calling her lawyer.

She was excited about being back in San Vicente and up for looking at houses. "I've got this neat, older guy with Morgan Real Estate," she exclaimed. It was the agency I'd found for her, evidently the best in town.

"We're to meet him at his office at nine, and he said he has a couple of different options for me to consider."

"How are the kids taking to the move?" I asked as I signaled for a waitress, trying to get an order in ahead of the crowd. On a Saturday morning, the Drifter was filling up rapidly with its potpourri of retirees and ranch families. With "The Best Breakfast in Town," as the sign read, all sorts of folk were drawn to the restaurant. If you wanted to see a harmonious blend of Anglos and Hispanics, the Drifter was the most ethnically integrated spot around.

Lisa was looking over the clientele with a faint smile, watching everybody interact, a sociologist in her element. She wore a blue denim shirt over a lime green tee shirt and jeans, a color scheme that highlighted her flaxen hair. She was glowing.

"Did you say something, Connor?"

"No problem. I'm just glad to see you looking so much at home. I was wondering how your kids seem to be feeling about pulling up roots and moving here."

Lisa smiled broadly. "I think they're really into it. I've described all the places to see and things to do down here, and I believe they're ready for an adventure."

As the waitress took my order and brought Lisa her plate of huevos rancheros, I glanced again at the mix in the restaurant crowd. The word I heard was that, some days, race relations were not so placid in the schools, and I wondered what kind of scene her kids were in for. But today all was sunshine in the world of Lisa Nordeen and it was not my place to cloud it.

The fellow we met at the real estate office was short and wiry, maybe in his 70s, and a retired military officer, he said. He looked like he'd never been out of shape in all his life. "Gus Armstrong," he told us, as he shook our hands and took our names.

He paused and looked me up and down. "Weren't you at the hospital last night, visiting Ben Fell?" he asked me.

I blinked. "Maybe so, but how would you know that?"

"Oh, my wife is with the auxiliary, helps out at the front desk. And then I had coffee this morning with our pastor, Reverend Schneuter."

I shuddered, involuntarily. So he had recognized me. "Oh yes, the Rev and I go way back," I muttered.

We got in the car with Gus and he proceeded to show us houses available for rent in a couple of parts of town, first the historic district where Lisa fell in love with a hoary old Victorian place with a wrought iron fence, built in bookshelves, and stained glass windows.

"It's perfect," she exulted, "but there's no yard. I really need some space for the kids."

Option two was a neighborhood on a hilltop overlooking town. "These places went up in the sixties," Gus explained. "They call it 'Chloride Park.' All sorts of professional people settled here—college professors, bank executives, lawyers—and all about the same age. Then, about five years ago, they all began dying, one after the next. I can show you three or four houses where the offspring are dickering over what to do with the properties they inherited. Meanwhile, these places are sitting vacant and up for rental."

It took the rest of the morning to traipse through those sleek, Kennedy-era split-level houses. Sometimes, I half-expected to see Doris Day jump out of one, or maybe Peter Gunn. Lisa settled on an attractive, stucco place with a large yard and an eye-popping view of the environs. Cooke's Peak stood out in the distance, halfway to Mexico.

We went back to Morgan Real Estate and Gus processed all the papers. He handed her a key to the Chloride Park place, for when she returned in a few weeks with her family. Lisa took a number of deep breaths as we drove back to my townhouse where I put together some sandwiches for lunch.

"Oh, my God," she said, as she collapsed on my living room sofa. "You have no idea how free I feel, with this new life in view—opening up right before my eyes."

We were having coffee after lunch when Lisa asked me about what Gus had said. Had I been to the hospital? I told her about my friendship with Aaron and described his dad's case with a broad stroke and few details. Unlike the members of the hospital auxiliary, it seemed, I believed in confidentiality.

Then I told her of my history with Buford Schneuter. "He made me feel ashamed to ever have been in the same profession. But in a way, I suppose, he did me a favor, if that pertains to my present position. I'd probably not have got this job if that episode hadn't happened."

"And I'd not have seen you again," she sighed, "after you went away like that, ever."

We took a hike up Boston Hill in the afternoon. Deeded to the town of San Vicente some years ago, it's a vast expanse of permanently undeveloped land pocked by former silver mines, mostly reclaimed, although in some places you still have to watch your footing. There are trails up and down, and deep ravines from which a coyote now and then emerges. The place has a distinctive beauty, dotted with juniper bushes, cactus, and scrub pines among the dark, old mine tailings. White-wing doves always fill the air with their plaintive, echoing cries.

When we got to the top, we sat on a couple of benches and looked down on Chloride Park. "Look," Lisa exclaimed, "There's my house. Oh, isn't this place magical." Just to the east we could see the entire campus of Ocotillo U.

I found myself inhaling her enthusiasm, celebrating the day. But something about this renewed relationship kept feeling unreal. I knew what it was: Sterling, and the conflict I knew that was bound to ensue when his task force gave its report on Monday. I'd kept looking for an opportunity to open all that up, but didn't want to put a damper on her spirits.

And so, for some time, we sat in silence. Finally, I'd had enough. I blurted out, "Look, Lisa. I'm excited for you and looking forward to your coming down. But you seem to be living in a bubble. Don't you understand that there are serious problems here? Do you really not get the complexity of this situation?"

She was quiet some more 'til she laid a hand on my knee. Then she turned around and reached into her backpack. She pulled out something that looked like a packet of letters.

"You know, Sterling didn't leave Martha all at once," she said quietly. "It was a process, and I had something to do with it."

"You slept with him? Oh, my God!"

She smiled and went on, "Not exactly. You see, after you left town so abruptly, and in the middle of that first crisis with Ned, I felt the need for some kind of deep support—a spiritual need, I suppose you'd say.

"And so you..."

"Turned to Sterling. I made an appointment and went in to see him late one afternoon, after classes. I told him everything that had been going on, most of which he seemed to know. And then I felt better. Until, as I was leaving, he came up and gave me a pastoral hug, I guess you might call it.

"Uh huh."

"Except that, he suddenly slid his hands all the way down my back and, and cupped..."

"I think they'd say he grabbed your ass, in the local parlance."

"Well, yes. And I told him I was not up for that—not here, not now, not ever. I didn't need a surrogate for you."

"And then what?" I was turned toward her on the park bench.

"Well, he called me up the next day and he was feeling terrible: just massive guilt and embarrassment, bordering on humiliation. I tried to calm him down. It seemed to have been the first crack in the shell of his carefully polished, professional persona. And then later I sent him a poem. Would you like to see it?"

She leafed through her packet of material, took out a single sheet, and handed it to me.

Some days our lives look like a tapestry.
We stand and gaze at the order of it all:
marriage, vocation, the entire display.
But there may come a moment when one thread
starts to quiver, slowly separating from the rest.
And the montage of our lives can come undone.
Sexuality is like that single thread:
Elusive, importunate, alive.

"That's really nice," I said. "And certainly apropos. I didn't know you wrote poetry."

She gave a wry smile. "Did we ever have time to get to know one another? Well, after that, he sent me a few letters. Not really as a lover. It was more like I was the only one who'd seen through him, maybe the only friend he had."

"And that's what you have in your hand? You're going to show me his letters? I'm not so sure that's ethical."

She paused for a moment and looked down across the campus and the town. Then she turned to me and said, "Connor, how would you say your relationship is going under present circumstances?"

I felt my stomach go into contortions, not knowing how much of this I was up for. Did I really want to have a look at Sterling and his bare soul? But I told her to go ahead, and maybe just excerpt some segments she thought might do any of us some good.

She leafed through the letters and picked one out. "I'm a religious fraud," she began to read, "a hypocrite of spirit."

Some other squibs fleshed out the crisis that Sterling had been having. He was still in the pulpit, but it was after his twin brother, Stanley, had called him out over the Blessing of the Beasts. He complained about a profession where one is constantly called upon "to say yes to need." Then he shared the dilemma he felt performing funerals. "It's either a rote, pro forma business of reading pre-digested liturgies, or else an exercise in anguish, if one had any feeling for the person who had died."

Sterling reflected on death: "The human race has to be some kind of evolutionary error, a cosmological mistake. How else can we account for the consciousness that we are mortal, and yet the incapacity to do anything about it?"

The man was twisted in knots and, while I suppose he might have had lunch or a couple of drinks with Lisa, there was the matter of impulse control. One summer, he wrote her from Florida about a temptation "to step off the ledge of convention and fall into a swirl of more emotions than one can imagine." I suppose it was when he was getting to know Daniela.

By this time, it was late afternoon and I was beginning to feel I'd had enough. Shadows were falling like an omen from the few trees on Boston Hill. I thought I heard a coyote howl.

"Hey, Lisa," I broke in, "Why don't we head up to the Raven's Roost?"

"Oh, good," she said, "and get something to eat."

"And get hammered," I added.

After a few margaritas and a dinner of chile cheese steaks—another revelation for Lisa—she told me a bit more about Sterling's correspondence from Florida. He'd become acquainted with a group who had a message that made sense to him and offered, as he put it, "a fresh path to vocation." It was something called The Shrub Foundation.

"He didn't say much more about it," Lisa said, "except for a slogan: 'Measuring the good we do, the impact of our ideals.' But he also said they seemed to have an interest in him."

That night, in her motel room, we made love for the first time in eons. She began below, then rose up and lowered herself slowly—swiveling, settling to the place our bodies met. She bent down and kissed my eyelids shut as she once had. And our rhythm rose with the swirl of her hips, 'til it built to a peak and her breath came in gasps, at the same time I erupted. And then I felt her soft contractions grasping me, again and again.

I awoke in the night, not wanting to disturb Lisa who had a plane to catch, three hours away, in Tucson. So I lay there bathed in sweat, in the wake of a most disturbing dream. I was on a bridge, leaning over a railing. My hand was on the back of a man who was almost falling. Would I push him or save him? He turned toward me in fear or anger and I recoiled, for I recognized him. But now it wasn't Ned whose life was in my hands. This time it was Sterling.

There are times in our lives that may prove to be less painful than we fear: a rectal exam, a root canal, a blind date. As I arrived at work Monday morning, I wondered if the presidential cabinet meeting would be anything like that. It was a typically sunny day in New Mexico and I had had a weekend of renewal with Lisa. I found myself asking, "Why not?"

In the twenty paces it took to hike down the hall from my office to that of Sterling Holmes, I tried to clear my head of three competing voices I'd been hearing, without respite, ever since she'd left for Tucson Sunday morning. There was Teresa's "go after him," which was followed by Wiley's "let him take himself out," to Lisa's "open your heart to the poor fellow." I gave a shudder as I walked by Claire's desk and she looked up with a sympathetic smile. I noticed she had a stack of newspapers, and she handed me one: The San Vicente Herald.

Sterling sat at the head of the table with the team of GOCO reps on his right hand and Wiley to his left. At first glance, it looked like a civil rights negotiation. I could have huddled in next to Wiley, but took a seat directly opposite Sterling, at the far end of the table. They were all engaged with the newspaper and I soon saw why.

The flimsy little eight-pager typically carried huge headlines, to compensate for a chronic lack of content. But the lead story this morning was prime news—EX-TRAVAGANZA EXPOSÉ—and well-documented. Jessica and her team of journalism students had interviewed all sorts of dropouts from OCU, many of whom were incensed at Sterling's bait-and-switch promise of academic credit that had resulted in their having been turned over to federal authorities for defaulting on their student loans. In the first paragraph of the story she had identified the principal source of her contacts: Dean Connor Ransom.

As Sterling finished reading the newspaper and folded it, his face was a mild shade of maroon. "Well, Connor, I don't know if we have you to thank for the supply of newspapers this morning." I shook my head and shrugged.

"But, clearly, that reporter is indebted to you for her article. And I must say that, in the full course of my career, I have never seen (his color deepened as his quavering voice was rising) a more graphic example of insubordination!"

I looked him in the eye. "Or, perhaps, 'accountability,'" I said. It seemed my reservoir of empathy had run dry.

I expected some kind of rejoinder from Sterling, but there was only a minute of silence as he got himself collected. Then he called on Wiley, who sat stifling a smirk, for a summary of administrative matters at OCU. Most of them were routine logistics of commencement, now two weeks away, and he was brief.

And so we turned to the time bomb of the day: the report by Jack Lofton, Bob Clifford, and Pete Entwhistle on our institutional response to the change in the state funding formula. Lofton led off and I thought he gave a pretty decent overview of the possible consequences of the legislators' disastrous decision.

"Basically," he said, "we're talking about growth and attrition. How many students enroll here, how long do they stay, and if they don't persist—how can we induce them to stay longer, and how can we get more?"

He addressed these questions in reverse order, pointing out the potential of increasing online enrollment. ("It's a lot like the universe," he indicated. "We don't know the dimensions of this market; no one can tell the outer limits.") He touted the benefits of increasing the enrollment at Ocotillo U, principally so that the school could become more competitive in athletics and garner regional television coverage. ("We're talking about a couple of million dollars a year in revenue," he claimed.)

So far, I found little to quibble, until he got to the matter of retention: how to stem the high tide of students exiting this place and the resulting reduction of state revenues. He said, "We're talking about an incipient disaster."

That's when he passed the ball to Pete Entwhistle, whom I'd never heard speak before. He called up some charts from his laptop and projected them against a wall. All in all, the man seemed well organized and I began to consider that Alice Pendergast, his ex, might have given him a bum rap. But that was before he got to the core of his proposal.

"How do we incentivize faculty to retain students in their courses?" he began by asking. (I thought back to the last time I'd heard that term. Wasn't it from Alice, on her death bed?) He went on: "Speaking from my many years of experience as an accountant, I believe that most questions in this life come down to a calculus of profit and loss. That said, what we need is a way to reward individual members of the faculty for the numbers of students who remain in their courses and successfully complete them at the end of each term."

He clicked to a new screen and put up a formula. It was very simple. "If we calculate the typical rate of retention in each academic department," he went on, "we compare that to the average rate of retention for each course. And we pay the instructor a hundred fifty dollars for each student beyond the average. Thus, an instructor who retains four students more than the average for his department receives a check for six hundred dollars at the end of the term."

I stared wide-eyed at the concept and watched Wiley's jaw drop, although he stayed in character and said nothing.

"Are there any questions?" Sterling asked. "By the way, I might add that I have reviewed this proposal and it has my full endorsement. Dean Ransom, since this falls under the purview of your function, you will be asked to work out the logistics and implement it."

I sat stunned for a moment as Entwhistle turned off his projector. Then I exclaimed, "My God, that's the most outrageous idea I've ever heard of. You're going to hand out cash bonuses to professors for passing students—in an environment like this?"

Sterling asked, "You have some reservations?"

"Can you imagine where this might lead?" I sputtered on, "Students could demand kickbacks, all kinds of deals under the table. And what would happen to any sort of academic standards? Why, I've never heard of such a thing."

"And so, may I assume that you are unwilling to perform the task I have just assigned you?" Sterling asked. His voice was beginning to crackle.

"Your assumption is correct," I said.

"Well then," he replied, "It is my duty to inform you that your services will no longer be required at Ocotillo U. You can expect to receive a letter of termination in the morning." (He made it through most of that, though his voice cracked like an adolescent on "termination.")

As I rose from my seat and hoisted my satchel, my mind flashed forward to Trevor Cranshaw, my attorney, and I knew what I would do. I stopped for a moment and turned back at the door. It would have been a propitious time to stay silent and simply stare at Sterling. But I uttered six words that I would come to regret. I said, "And then we'll see what happens!"

I stumbled back into my office, picked up the phone, and called Cranshaw. His secretary put me through and I told him to send the cease-and-desist letter. "I hope it's not too late," I groaned. "He said I could expect a letter of termination in the morning."

The lawyer gave a malevolent laugh. "I'll send him an ominous email to expect my letter, overnight. It'll knock his socks off."

I glanced at my calendar and was relieved to see that I had no appointments for the rest of the day. I'd blocked out the time to schedule courses for the fall semester. So I picked up the first spreadsheet to reconnoiter classroom assignments.

And that was when my hands began shaking.

I went out and asked Arlene to hold all my calls. She gave me a sympathetic smile—news travels fast at OCU—and I commented that, in all other respects, my schedule would remain the same. Then I shut the door, shoved my work aside, and went into meditation.

It was a rhythm I'd repeat for the next several hours: grappling with the logistics of courses, time slots, classrooms, and instructors until my hands began to quiver—then turning from my desk to focus on some object in my office till my head cleared. At that point, it was a matter of watching and waiting to see if an idea or an image came to the fore.

About mid-day, I began to feel some clarity. It was from Kierkegaard, and the quote I'd come up with the other night: "To be a self and have a world..." And I knew in my bones that—for all its limitations and absurdities—Ocotillo U was my cosmos. It was the center of my life and all my significant relationships. OCU was where it all made sense for me.

And I had just thrown my world away.

Could I go back to Sterling and apologize, agree to administer his latest scheme, Peter Entwhistle's plan to pay bonuses to the faculty? Well, not and keep my head on straight. So I was stuck with the loss of my job, and the sole context for a life that made any sense to me.

At that point, I thought I should call Lisa and tell her what Sterling and I each had done. But I couldn't bring myself to do it. So I sent her an email and sat cringing for a half-hour till she wrote back. She sent a one word message—"Oh!"—and I could feel all of the pain in it.

I carried on my process without thought of lunch until, about three o'clock, I realized I had to get out of my office. So I picked up my satchel, turned out the lights, and told Arlene I'd see her in the morning. False bravado, but I had to maintain at least the appearance of a structured life, if for only another twenty-four hours.

When I got to my car, I realized I had a decision to make. Where the hell should I go: up on Tadpole Ridge, to Serena's, the Raven's Roost? As it turned out, I went to none of these places and, for reasons I could not name, I headed out of town due south toward Columbus.

22

When I reached Bayard, a mining town nestled in the low mountains, my hunger got the best of me. I spotted a Blake's Lota Burger and stopped for a grilled chicken sandwich with chiles and cheese, along with a cherry malt for the road. After bordering a big mesa that sheltered the smaller mining town of Hurley, the highway leveled out for an hour or so.

The prairie was bare ranchland, the color of parchment, with scattered clumps of green cactus. Now and then, a few black Angus huddled around some random tufts of grass. Once I thought I saw a herd of antelope and wondered if this land did not belong to them more than to the ranchers. Far off, here and there, low hills floated in the distance.

Deming, on the freeway, looked to be a town about half again the size of San Vicente, but with less of its historic appeal. I took time to drive around the residential sections: brick, Midwestern-style homes on one side of town and houses in stucco of many colors on the other. It seemed they'd settled into a pretty clear divide between the Hispanics and the Anglos. There were a number of restaurants in Deming, but I was still full from my chicken-chile-cheese delight, so I drove on toward Columbus.

Strangely, as I got closer to the border, the land turned more verdant. Now there were fields of crops growing in the shadow of the Florida Mountains. The hills were shimmering, glowing with golden poppies, as they did every spring.

It was a warm scene, except for an ominous sign on the far side of the road: "Border Patrol." It stood outside a trailer where three or four green and white patrol vehicles were parked at the ready. Several young men in hooded sweatshirts sat on a bench off to the side, their hands cuffed behind them. A half-dozen agents in brown uniforms stood around not doing much, except for one who was interrogating every car that paused at a stop sign, going north.

Columbus appeared as a wide place in the road. There was a small state park on the right, covered with many varieties of cactus, and a single, wide, main street in the opposite direction that ran off into nowhere. I drove down it slowly and located the town library, the site of Sterling's gig, along with a single café that seemed to be open only for breakfast and lunch.

By this time I was hungry again, so I went back on the highway and turned south. It was time to see what was to be found in Palomas. I parked in a dusty lot in front of a Family Dollar Store and followed a straggling line of people who filed through an open gate into what appeared to be Mexico. There was no welcoming sign, no uniformed officials, only a few teenage boys with their hands out. "Anything will help," one of them said in perfect English.

I walked down a somewhat spruced-up main drag that featured a farmacia on every block, along with signs for medical and dental services. Now and then there was a bar and café. I noticed a large one painted in fuchsia, the Pink Store, but walked on by to see a bit more of the town. Once off the main street, the road turned to dirt, with cavernous depressions. I was glad I'd left my car on the far side of the border.

I strolled over to a town square with a kind of band stand, a Catholic church on the far side. The houses I could see were squat and spare. A small group of Mexican men stood talking near the band stand, but as I approached they slowly disbanded.

By this time it was past six, and I headed back to the Pink Store. The place was not crowded, but something about the atmosphere was festive. It was a bar and restaurant on one side, and the rest of it was an emporium of Mexican crafts in every color one could imagine. There was a freshness about the paintings and plates and mugs and rugs that was captivating, and I knew I had to spend time with them. But first I had a thirst and hunger to take care of.

The waiter who seated me was a young guy who said he was Manuel, and he wanted to know my name. "Connor, can I interest you in a margarita?" he asked with scarcely a trace of an accent, and he didn't have to persuade me.

As one margarita led to another and I demolished a plate of beef enchiladas, I got to know Manuel a little. I wondered why his English was so good, and he told me he'd gone to school in the United States.

"And how was that?" I asked him.

"Well, as a matter of fact, I'm a U.S. citizen," he said, "born in Deming, the nearest hospital. There are lots of us like that. I went to grade school in Columbus and graduated from Deming High School, played basketball for the Wildcats."

"Is that very common?" I asked again.

"Come down here in the morning, you'll see maybe two hundred elementary school kids crossing over, two or three dozen high school students. Every one going through that check point where the feds look through their back packs."

"For drugs," I thought, but didn't ask. Then I did remark, "You're an American citizen, and yet you're working here," and immediately apologized for having said it.

He laughed. "No hay problema. It's natural to wonder. You have to understand Mexicans and la familia. In spite of all those who cross over for economic survival, we have ties. 'Most everyone who can make any kind of living comes back here."

"And if they don't do this," I observed, pointing to the store, "they do what?"

He said, "There are things we don't talk about."

I browsed the craft store and, on an impulse, picked out a beautiful blue bowl for Teresa. I stood there for a moment at the cash register wondering what I was doing—hadn't I just had a pretty intense weekend of it with Lisa?—when Manuel came up and spoke to me in a low voice. "Connor," he said, "it is getting late, time for you to cross over."

I shook his hand, picked up the bowl, and, head down, high-tailed it back to the border. Here, there was more formality with a customs official going over what I had bought—I'd been told that eventually they might require a passport—but in ten minutes I was back in Columbus.

I decided not to go right on into the library, but sat in the car across the street. I wasn't up for running into Sterling, for one thing, and I wanted to get a look at his audience.

They began to gather about seven, first some grizzled Hippies and ranchers: alumni from Columbus, I assumed. Then the cars with out of state license plates began to pull up—Arizona, Texas, Colorado, even one from California. The occupants were a mélange of races. There were some women but most were male and good-sized, as were the OCU faculty I recognized, stalwarts from Save Our Ocotillo U: SOCO. I didn't see the Jack Lofton, Bob Clifford, Pete Entwhistle GOCO contingent.

Then, about seven-thirty, as I was about to climb out of my car and go in, a dark blue BMW pulled up just ahead of me. The driver door opened, and a slim Hispanic woman with long black hair emerged. I recognized Linda Lucero. And from the passenger side came another brunette who came up next to Linda, touched hands affectionately, and walked with her lock step across the street and into the library. I knew her, too. It was Teresa.

There was a vestibule just inside the entrance to the library and I stayed in it, off to the side. Sterling was up at the podium, not far from the audience of thirty or forty. I surveyed them to see if I recognized anyone else. There was a tall, middle-aged African American man who I thought might have been Wiley, but I looked closer and it wasn't. Maybe a teammate from OCU. Then I noticed a somewhat rotund Anglo guy with a white beard and a sombrero pulled down over his eyes. Something about him seemed a little familiar, but I couldn't make a connection.

Sterling was attired in his best black suit, starched white shirt, and rep tie. He was into his stock speech: American education has a crisis of credibility. The public no longer believes in our rhetoric. We must have common standards of performance, measures of accountability, which is where Ocotillo U comes in. OCU: The Accountable University.

I was half listening, for I'd heard all of this before and, in fact, almost knew his speech by heart. But when he got to that last line, "The Accountable University," it was as though he'd pulled a trigger. For, from every side of the room, people began to complain. Not grousing or mumbling: shouts went up. "What do you mean, accountability? Is it accountable to promise us academic credit for what we've done in life and then cancel the Ex-travaganza?"

"That's nothing—you know what he did? He turned me in on my student loan, reported me to the feds!"

And, from an academic quarter: "He's actually going to pay professors to keep students in their classes." "Can you believe that? Pass 'em if everyone knows they ought to be failing."

The shouting mounted. I assumed that Sterling had provided for a question-and-answer time after his talk, but he would not get to it. In fact, the crowd was now rising to its feet and toward him. He looked aghast as they began to swirl around the podium, pushing him toward the exit. It was like a slow-moving mud slide, inexorable, and it took in almost everyone there, although I noticed that Linda and Teresa were still in their seats, and that they were smiling. Then I saw one other figure, the plump, white-bearded man in his sombrero. He got up quickly and bolted toward the side door.

At first I stood in the vestibule and felt an odd sense of inspiration at the mob bearing Sterling toward the door—black, white, brown, bronze—a vision of integration. But something else rose up in me and it led me to join them as they neared the front door. I moved in with the rest, shoving Sterling to the curb until, suddenly, as he was about to be thrown into the street, a shiny, black Lexus pulled up behind him. And the driver leaned over, throwing open the door.

The next moment would stay with me forever. Swaying on the edge of the sidewalk with the crowd surging toward him, the car behind him with its yawning door, Sterling peered at me, beseechingly. Did he not want to get inside? I reached out as if to pull him toward me. But then for an instant everything went dark. And when I saw us again it was from somewhere above. I watched us as I thrust out my arms and he tumbled in the car.

As the driver shot away and the door swung shut, I had two other sensations before I fell down and fainted. It was an image of the driver—I thought I might have known him—and then of something else. But neither would click into focus.

When I came to, I was in the arms of Teresa and she gave me some water. She said, "Where are your car keys? You're in no condition to drive back."

I'm not sure how I got in the passenger seat of my car, possibly with the assistance of Teresa and Linda, one on either side, but once there I zonked out pretty fast—overcome by the shock of my latest out-of-body experience. I was dozing for about ten miles until I felt the car slow to a stop and the driver's window roll down. Then Teresa was yelling: "No tengo que decirle a usted nada!"

I came to enough to see a brown-shirted Border Patrol agent stick his head in the car. He beamed me with a flashlight.

"Why don't you ask him if he's a U.S. citizen?" Teresa demanded. "Don't you understand the law? I'm not required to tell you anything, pendejo."

"Don't you call me that."

"Oh, so you do know Spanish. Well, okay. Here's my ID at the school where I teach, and a voter registration card. Will that satisfy you?"

He handed the cards back to her. "Have a nice night, ma'm."

"Damn racial profiling," Teresa muttered." I'll never get used to it, and shouldn't have to."

Twenty miles up the road, she pulled into a convenience store. We got some coffee, and I started talking. "It was the same kind of experience as years ago, back on the bridge with Ned," I began. I told her what had happened with Sterling in front of the open car door.

"And with your dad in the garage?"

"That, too."

"I remember telling you a term I learned in a psych course, 'dissociative reaction.' Does that still fit?"

"I think there's more to it," I said. "I went through the bridge episode with a psychiatrist once and he called it 'dissociative amnesia.' It's like, in the midst of that kind of trauma, you forget the main event. As in tonight: it was as though I was way up there above myself, taking a photo of Sterling and me, but then the picture was erased."

"And did the shrink know how to get it back?"

"Unfortunately, he had no clue. He said sometimes these situations resolve themselves, the memories return of their own accord."

We drove on in silence for a few miles. Then Teresa said, "I don't want to pry, but do you have any idea why that situation was so traumatic for you? Or, to put it another way: why the fuck you were down there in the first place?"

I told her what had happened with Sterling earlier in the day, how he had all but fired me. All that remained was receiving my written notice of termination. Also, I said, Jessica the reporter had told me something was likely to boil over that night in Columbus.

"And why were you and Linda there?" I asked her.

Teresa was silent.

Finally, we arrived at her townhouse. Linda's Beemer was parked in front. "I'd ask you in, but I already have company," she said.

"I understand that."

"Although, just because Linda is there, doesn't mean that we're..." she continued.

I said, "I get that, too...But, you know, Teresa. There's one other question I wanted to ask you. And, oh..." I reached into the back seat. "I was in Palomas and I got you something."

I handed her the package and she unwrapped the bowl. "It's beautiful!" she exclaimed.

"Yeah, well. I just wanted to ask you. Whatever happens, and whoever we're with—will you always be my friend?"

She wiped her eyes for a minute, then pulled me into an embrace and kissed me. She said, "I am as certain of this as of anything else in my life." Then she got out and went inside.

Driving back to my place, I felt a comforting sense of warmth and security, both of which I could use, in spades. But I did have one other thought about Teresa. There were very few things in her life of which she was certain.

23

I got to my office in the morning at the regular hour and launched into my schedule, while ever alert for a knock on the door or the phone to ring. There was a usual array of items on my agenda: disagreements over grades, races to meet requirements for graduation, plus the nuts and bolts of putting together the schedule for fall term. I tried to keep my mind off the fantastic events of the night before, and what on earth Sterling might do.

On the one hand, it would be difficult for him not to follow through and fire me, given the number of people who had witnessed his expressed intention to do so. But then there was the letter to cease and desist, which he must have received by now. I noted that I'd made no mention of it to Teresa, which might suggest that I didn't really give it much credence.

Then, too, there was the wild look in Sterling's eye as he'd teetered before the open car door last night. If he had any feeling for me at that moment, it was as some sort of Messianic figure who might pull his fat from the fire—not a recalcitrant subordinate to be terminated. But who knew? Hour after hour, one appointment to the next, I did my best to stay on task.

And then, about four thirty, the buzzer sounded. It was Arlene. She said Claire was in the outer office. She'd like to come in and speak with me. Oh, God: the letter of dismissal. I told Arlene to send her in.

Claire looked far more serious than I'd ever seen her, and she shut the door behind her. I asked her to sit down.

"Connor," she said, and I couldn't remember if I'd ever heard her call me that. "Connor, it's about the president..."

"Yes?"

"His wife called early this morning, about eight thirty. It seems he never came home last night. And then she called again just now. She said she's contacted the police. Doctor Holmes has gone missing."

"It might have been a little early for Daniela to have called the cops," Wiley yawned as he stretched out across a blood red booth at the Hanover Outpost. We were having beers along with a consultation that it seemed best to hold off campus. I took time to relate all the events of the night before, with the exception of my psychotic break.

"Well, then, maybe not," he reconsidered. "Could be he'd called and told her all the shit that had gone down. Do you have any idea who it was took him off in that car?"

I had to admit that I did not, although I sensed there was a trove of information buried somewhere in the depths of me.

Wiley waved to the bar. "Got time for one more round till dinner," he announced. "Been workin' late a lot this week and Barbara has been over me like hair on a gorilla. This business of bein' provost, you know it's basically running the school alone, aside from your job, of course."

The bartender brought over a couple of Coors and took away our empties.

"What I'm getting to, I guess," he continued, "is that if there's one dude around here who is highly expendable, that would be Sterling Holmes. Ask me what value that man has added to this institution, and you will hear a lo-o-o-ng pause in the conversation."

"His main pursuit seems to have been philosophical," I added.

"Exactly. So, I don't think there's much we need to cover in his absence. I've got commencement handled, except for the speaker: some dude named Doctor James Hargrove, vice president of something called the Shrub Foundation. That's where I need your help. Why don't you see what you can find out about him and the Foundation and prepare some remarks. I'd like you to introduce him."

"I'm on it. Was there any other, ah, pending business that Sterling left behind?"

"No, I checked with Claire, and...yeah, I see what you mean. Nope, right after that meeting, the man went home, got ready for his trip to Columbus. No time for correspondence: not your letter of termination, not the memo on bonuses to the faculty. He left her not-a-thing."

"Oh, and, Wiley. I know you have to go, but I wanted to tell you. Before that debacle last night, I went over and had dinner at the Pink Store in Palomas. I got to talking with the waiter and heard all about the elementary school in Columbus."

Wiley slapped his forehead. "I knew I left something out of that lecture. One of the seven wonders of the world, that little school. They take in all those indigent Mexican kids, hundreds of 'em, born over here. They not only speak no English—hell, they got no grasp of Spanish either. Next time we give out honorary degrees, we ought give 'em to our grads who teach at the elementary school in Columbus. They're heroes, every one.

"And I'll tell you one thing more, and you won't believe this. Last year the State of New Mexico institutes this new system of grading schools—part of the 'accountability' movement—an' guess what grade they give that school in Columbus, based on the students' test scores."

"I don't think I want to know."

"They awarded 'em an F. An F! Can you dig it? How's that for accountability?"

He chugged his beer in disgust, and headed for the door.

That night I called Lisa to tell her what had happened in Columbus. She was aghast—concerned in equal parts for Sterling and for me—plus increasingly uneasy over the situation she was entering. Perhaps Lisa was beginning to get it.

"Do you have any idea at all who it was who drove off with him?" she asked in an anxious voice and I told her that I had none—explained the crazed state I'd been in. Perhaps I'd get clearer about this episode than the last one with Ned, but I said I had no reason to assume so. It appeared that Sterling would have to turn up on his own.

Then I asked her to go back through Sterling's correspondence and try to find any other references to the Shrub Foundation and to search her memory, as well. I said I'd Google it, too, but we might as well plumb her resources.

She called back later in the evening. "The Shrub Foundation: they're big on education reform in the public schools—the Core Curriculum, and one other thing. Sterling was proud of this, an innovation just last year in New Mexico. They ranked the schools, and graded them."

Life without Sterling went on the next morning, very much as before. The San Vicente Herald had not yet picked up on the news of his absence. Claire seemed to occupy her time with social media, and I asked her to see if Wiley had some projects for her.

Mid-morning, Arlene buzzed me and said a police detective was out there. She sent him in: a middle-aged fellow in wrinkled pants and a sports coat with food spots who advised me that most missing persons showed up sooner or later, since they took off of their own accord.

He said, "It's too soon to look for a 'prepetrator'" but asked if I had any idea where Sterling had gone. I told him I hadn't and described in broad strokes what I had seen. If the guy couldn't pronounce 'perpetrator,' I wondered how many cases he himself had witnessed.

Now and then, I found myself beginning to relax in this new era. Perhaps my tormentor had hit the road for good.

But all of that changed at nine a.m. two days later, when the sheriff arrived. Arlene had buzzed and told me his title. As I strolled to the door, I found myself forming an image based on the detective I'd just met: cigar-smoking, paunchy, an over-the-hill guy straight out of TV.

Raul Escobedo was none of that. A tall, muscular man with slate black hair in his thirties, he wore a freshly-pressed olive green uniform and a badge that glistened in the sun. There was a pistol on his hip and he carried both a legal pad and a high-tech tape recorder. While there may have been occasions of joy in his life—his marriage, perhaps, or a graduation—I saw no hint of happiness right now. Indeed, the fellow seemed bound in a perpetual scowl.

"Doctor Ransom?" he confirmed.

I nodded, and motioned to a chair.

He switched on the tape recorder and got right to the point. "It seems, from witnesses at the scene, that you were present as President Sterling Holmes was driven away from the town library at Columbus. Is that correct?"

I nodded.

He said, "Please speak your answer."

I said, "Yes, I was."

He said, "Other witnesses have indicated that the last words you spoke to Doctor Holmes before he left campus, and just after he expressed his intention to fire you were..." he opened his legal pad. "'And then we'll see what happens.' Is that an accurate statement?"

I said, "I believe I have a right to confer with my attorney."

I sat and stared at the sheriff's business card for ten minutes after he'd left. Then I picked up the phone and called Trevor Cranshaw. His secretary said he had appointments all day but might be able to call me back during his lunch hour.

So I resumed my own schedule, but took time now and then to meditate— but on what, I wondered? If ever I needed a mantra... Then another line from Kierkegaard came to mind: "Purity of heart is to will one thing." And I set out to focus my thoughts on that much. What was it I'd been trying to accomplish at Ocotillo U? Well, surely not to do away with Sterling. Basically, it was to keep the school together, I decided. So I would center down on just that.

About eleven thirty, I went out and got myself a chicken-cheese-and-chile special from the Lota Burger along with a cherry malt and brought it back to my office. Then I sat and simply focused on the phone. Shortly after noon, it finally rang. Trevor Cranshaw cackled, "Well, the meter's on: client privileged communication, and all that. So, what's going on?"

I told him about the sheriff and what I'd shouted at Sterling.

He said, "Is that all?"

I said, "I wish it were," and told him the rest of what had happened.

He was enough of a professional not to comment, but I heard him groan.

For a moment he was silent, evidently making notes. Then...

"Well, point one: as far as the sheriff goes, what you're dealing with is a political maneuver. Someone's out to get you. Not to be technical, but any kind of legal case is what we'd call 'a long throw from third base.' Lots of people say things in anger. By the way, what action were you referring to—'And then we'll see what happens?'"

"Why, your letter to cease and desist. You did send it, didn't you?"

"Of course I did, and there's your alibi. Here's what you do: go see the sheriff and tell him the context of your threat. Suggest he go check Sterling's inbox at the president's office, and that should be the end of it. Then you might try to figure out who put him up to this.

"Now, as for the rest of it, of course, the best defense against being falsely accused of having done something is to find out who actually did it. But if you're hogtied by this, this..."

"Dissociative amnesia."

"Whatever, I'd suggest you try to get past it and find the son of a bitch who took off with that damn fool...aw, now I'm losing my objectivity. Well, you got your two hundred dollars worth?"

"And then some. Trevor, I'm indebted."

I settled in the rest of the afternoon and that evening called Lisa. She said she'd gone to see Trevor as well—"We're filling his coffers"—and that he'd put to rest any fears that Sterling might renege on her contract out of spite over having spilled his guts to her. 'Contracts are binding,' he'd said. 'When you made arrangements to pick up and move to San Vicente, he became obligated to honor his agreement.' So, then I felt relieved.

"And it freed up my head to do some research for you," she went on. "Scholarly stuff, finding research that might have been funded by that Shrub Foundation. It's a long process of tracking keywords and principal investigators and all. But you can't tell where it might lead. Oh, and by the way: we'll be there a bit earlier than

I'd thought, in time for commencement. So I'll be looking forward to seeing you all dolled up there in your regalia."

I got on task myself that night and looked into the commencement speaker, one Doctor James Hargrove. There wasn't much to learn. B.A. from Kansas, MBA Drake, doctorate from a school called Florida Historic University, which was where he was teaching. I'd never heard of the place and looked it up: a fairly new institution in Naples, Florida. It led me to track down Sterling's credentials, and found 'em. Wow. So that's where he went. I'd thought he'd gone to the University of Florida.

Hargrove had come from industry, a land developer outside Orlando and it didn't appear he'd taught anywhere before, but he had served on the board of an organization that supported education reform, also headquartered in Naples. I looked up the year of his college degree and it seemed he'd gone to work in higher education at retirement age. I wondered how we'd acquired him as our speaker and resolved to research him some more in the morning.

But that was not to be.

As I showed up at the office, Arlene passed me a copy of the San Vicente Herald. My picture was splayed across the front page: stumbling, bleary-eyed, between Teresa and Linda Lucero. Each of us was identified in the caption, dated: Columbus, New Mexico. The headline in large caps read: DAZED AND CONFUSED.

I suppose I might have expected that Jessica Madrid would have made the trip down to Columbus, inasmuch as she'd alerted me to the significance of Sterling's affair. And perhaps, in my stupor, the click of a cell phone might have made an impression. But none of that had. And so I began my day reflecting on the proposition that bad news is always good information.

The story had all the structural integrity of a Jambalaya stew. First, it was about the disappearance of Doctor Sterling Holmes, president of Ocotillo U. Then the focus shifted to me as some sort of prime suspect, hence my huge photo. There was a mug shot of Holmes and a small one of Sheriff Escobedo leaving my office. The source of information, it was noted, had requested anonymity.

Finally, we were reminded that commencement at OCU was coming up in a week, to be followed by an annual meeting of the board of trustees at which time the contracts of all the university administrators would be reviewed. Were there questions to be resolved? Readers were left to draw their own conclusions.

I retreated again to the inner sanctum of my office wherein I alternated attendance to my appointments and arranging the fall semester schedule, with periods of earnest meditation. I did go down to the sheriff's office in the early afternoon and follow my attorney's instructions.

I winced at things I overheard in town and even more at some people's expressions as they passed me on campus. And I realized how little weight legal conviction carries, compared to condemnation in the court of public opinion. Wherever I went, whatever I did, I saw the specter of Sterling Holmes.

There is social truth and visceral truth—the appearance of truth (as in Jessica's story) and another kind that is really so. Since the difference between them is sometimes difficult to negotiate, I quit trying to explain myself to others and gave myself over to something I could control: fitting bits of time into pieces of space called classrooms, and instructors into courses.

And so it was with almost a sense of relief when, two days later, I walked into the office and Arlene stared at me wide-eyed. "Connor," she exclaimed. "You'll never guess. It's the president. He's here!"

I closed the door and got on task, ready for whatever awaited me. I supposed it would come down to a couple of contesting letters: one for termination and the other to cease and desist. Essentially, the matter was out of my hands.

But I would not have long to agonize. About nine thirty, there was a rap on my door and, as it swung open, Wiley appeared and flopped down in my visitor's chair. At first he looked intent, then he broke into a grin.

"So, I was walking by the president's lair and there he was, head down, goin' through his desk drawers," he began. "I went in and said something like, 'Well, Sterling, so you decided to honor us with your presence. And the dude looks up like he never seen me before. An', truth be told, he hadn't!"

"Oh, my God, it was Stanley."

"Right. You knew about his twin brother?"

"Only since we've been down here," I said. "Sterling felt it was emblematic of how little I'd known or cared about him that I wasn't aware of his twin when we worked together before."

I went on to tell him about Stanley's role in Sterling's decision to leave the ministry, and that led me to the subject of his ex-parishioner, Lisa, and the research she was doing into the Shrub Foundation. I rambled on, trying to keep my mind off the weird sensations of hope and fear that were swirling inside me now that Sterling's return had evaporated.

I went on to share some of my thoughts on the education reform movement in general and its ties to our speaker for commencement specifically. And I wound up with a somewhat unconventional idea.

"Wiley, what would you say to giving out the diplomas first, with the speaker last? There are some things I'd like to say when I introduce him that, uh. Hmm...this might be my finale."

It did not lift my spirits when he nodded.

24

Old Lockhart Stadium is one of those archival places at Ocotillo U that sometimes seems to anchor it. Put up as a football field in the sixties, it was built for the ages, with hand-made, New Mexican stone seats embedded in the side of a hill. When the field was replaced by a new physical education complex, thirty years later, the bleachers on the far side came down in the course of an afternoon, but the stonework stayed in place.

Today, for commencement, it would accommodate a crowd of several hundred. The graduates, resplendent in purple robes, would sit before them on folding chairs at ground level, while the dignitaries, for the moment including me, were lined up on a dais in front. The few dozen faculty who'd cared to show up were seated behind us. A phalanx of brightly colored flags—for the United States, New Mexico, the university—would flutter above us.

As I trudged across the field about ten to three, it was only a few minutes till the scheduled time of the ceremony. But the crowd was still filing in and I knew I wasn't late. No event in the history of this state had ever begun on time. There were blankets spread out behind the dais and coolers for picnics that would follow. This summer day in early May was quintessential, with a soft breeze and temperatures in the seventies.

It was a day for celebration, and I might have let myself get into it, except for...what? Well, my get-up, for one thing. In a floor-length gown of midnight blue and canary yellow, the colors of my doctoral institution and academic discipline, I looked like some revenant from the Middle Ages. My silly blue tam didn't mitigate the effect: all of which, it seemed, was the point of it. Well, I'd never felt comfortable in academic gear, not even in the confines of a campus.

And then, of course, there was my other concern. How long was I even to be in these environs? Ah, well. I climbed up on the dais, walked over and introduced myself to the Honorable James Hargrove, our speaker, and to the chairman of the board, Manny Moreno, whom I'd never really met. Moreno was cordial but distant, which I might have expected. I picked up a program, fist-pumped Wiley Crane, and took a seat down at the end of the line.

"Ladies and gentlemen," said Manny, "Please rise for the singing of our national anthem." So he was President-for-a-Day. As I got to my feet, I wondered what on earth I should strive to be. Well, "Purity of heart is to will one thing." That was all that came to me.

My thoughts turned so far inward that I didn't pay attention to much of the proceedings. It seemed there were some eighty grads, maybe a dozen with honors. One of them was an Alicia Escobedo, and when her name was called I saw the sheriff pop up out of the stands. He not only grinned, but stuck two fingers in his teeth and gave a piercing whistle.

In time, I heard my name and Moreno turned my way. I got up and walked toward the podium. As I slowly faced the crowd, I stopped for a moment and gazed at the scene, for it seemed to seethe with a strange sort of potential. Part of it was the lambent sunlight of late afternoon, filtering over the fine arts building onto the remnants of the old stadium and the field, bathing us in a hallowed glow—infusing what we were doing with some sort of portent.

But the place was not placid. Just below me, the newly anointed graduates were restive in their chairs, high-fiving with grunts of exultation. Anything but a circumspect audience ready for instruction in the right ways of living, they were roiling like a purple stew, and I knew at once why commencement speakers were never put last in the program.

I suppose it was all of these elements, this living mosaic, that filled me with a sense of moment, a fleeting belief that something here might change me at the core. For I had a charge to fulfill on the one hand—no one knew about the Shrub Foundation and this speaker they had foisted upon us. That was one thing. And, I had nothing to lose on the other.

So I grabbed the microphone, whipped off my tam, and tossed it four feet in the air.

"Friends of OCU!" I shouted, "And our new grads. Hey, let's give them all a hand." I pumped my fist, and the crowd responded. "Isn't it great, the hope that education sows in our hearts, one generation to the next: the challenge, the sense of achievement?"

I pumped both fists, and they roared.

"Now, of course, we know that the profession of education is not perfect. Like health care in America, to take one example, we waste a lot of resources, and so we find ourselves looking to other industries such as business, for instance, for help and guidance. But in introducing our speaker who comes to us from a business-based organization, the Shrub Foundation, I want to make a few comments about the limits of business in education."

About then, I could feel Moreno beginning to rustle around behind me, and I might have got back on task. But I happened to glance into the crowd just as a ray of sunlight struck a certain glowing object. And I shivered as I saw that it was Lisa—her bright, blond hair—and a shock shot straight through the heart of me. Suddenly I was back up in the pulpit, above the podium and Moreno and the rest, and I rose to meet the message that was burning inside me.

"The Shrub Foundation is funded by a group of billionaires such as our speaker here, who made his fortune as a land developer outside Orlando, Florida. Nothing wrong with that, so long as the basic traits of entrepreneurs—the tendency to measure everything by the bottom line—are not applied to the profession of education.

"Which is what is going on today, and the reason, I believe, that Doctor Hargrove has been sent to address us. Now, there are two issues I want to raise with you before I introduce him. One is the Common Core: the movement to place a single curriculum in all the public schools in America. And why is that? So that the efforts of all our dedicated teachers can be measured by a single yardstick.

"And the second agenda, which I will describe in very specific terms, is to rank order our schools. I begin this point with a question." I could sense Moreno shuffling his feet again and, out of the corner of my eye, saw Wiley reach a long arm out and restrain him.

"How many of you folks have been to Columbus—you grads, family and friends? Let me see a show of hands." A lot of them went up.

"If you read the papers, I'll bet you know that I've been down a bit there myself." There was a smattering of laughter.

"And how many have crossed the border into Palomas? Again, hands up, everybody. Anyone ever sampled the margaritas at the Pink Store?" Again, lots of hands and laughter.

From behind me, a fellow from the faculty muttered, "This is most unprofessional."

"Can it, pendejo!" Teresa responded, in full voice. "It's a story that needs to be heard."

"All right," I continued, "A couple of days ago, I went back down to Palomas to the Pink Store, to buy a present for a dear friend who has come to join us on the faculty, and I timed my trip to coincide with the kids getting out of school in Columbus.

"Now, as I imagine some of you know, there are many children in Palomas who were born in Deming, site of the nearest hospital, and so they are American citizens and are eligible to attend elementary school in Columbus. Some two hundred of them cross the border every day to do so, and a few dozen others are bussed to high school in Deming.

"That elementary school in Columbus is one of the most amazing institutions in our country and do you know where the teachers come from? Do you?"

There were a few shouts from the stands.

"That's right. Almost the entire faculty of the Columbus Elementary School, teachers who work every day with Mexican kids, are graduates of Ocotillo U. Can we give them a hand for all they do?"

A rousing applause.

"So, one more anecdote, and I'm done. I was standing there in Palomas about three o'clock and the students were coming back across the border. And first it was the high school kids. A couple strolled by holding hands, and then a young guy came running up and swatted Pancho Villa's horse on the balls."

I let the laughter die down.

"And then came the dozens and dozens of kids from the elementary school, waves of them. One little girl caught my eye. She was running along, skipping, holding a sheet of construction paper with a drawing on it and some text—something in English, I guess, her lesson for the day—and she was so excited to show her parents what she had done, and her eyes were shining...."

And my eyes started brimming and I choked up and for a moment I had to stop.

"Well, I was just thinking again, of the work of that school and our graduates. But then a cloud came over me. I remembered the efforts of the Shrub Foundation, who have sent us our speaker, to convince the education authorities of the State of New Mexico to rank all of the schools in this state..."

I began to see two objects go in motion, from the periphery. James Hargrove had got up from his chair and was walking off the dais. And, far up in the stands of Old Lockhart Stadium, something white was moving toward a center aisle and rapidly descending the stairs.

"To rank the schools in the state and give them each a letter grade, based solely on their students' standardized test scores. So, one more point, friends, and then I'm out of your hair." (The object was a beard attached to a man who was now down the stairs and moving through the graduates in my direction.)

"Can you guess what grade the Shrub Foundation bureaucrats awarded the Elementary School in Columbus for the work they have been doing with those kids from Palomas? That's right, amigos. You've got it. They gave that school an F!"

And as I looked up, he was on the dais and staring me in the face. "Why, I know who you are," I exclaimed into the microphone. "You're Walter Driscoll! And I know what you did. You were driving that black Lexus. You turned south, toward the border. I remember it all!"

As my voice went echoing over the field, Driscoll tried to charge me, but Wiley jumped up and corralled him. I handed the mike to Manny Moreno and took my seat as he stepped back up to the podium without missing a beat, a public relations bank officer in his bones.

"Well, this concludes our commencement ceremony, as it seems our speaker has left the premises. But I have one more announcement. There will be a special meeting of the board of trustees in the president's conference room, to begin in fifteen minutes. All members of the faculty are invited, as well as Doctor Ransom and Doctor Crane. Doctor Driscoll, your attendance is required. (Wiley had him by the elbow.) And, Sheriff Escobedo, please join us, as well.

"Muy buenos tardes, one and all. Good afternoon."

But there was one thing more. At first, I'm not sure everyone up on the dais picked up on it as they shuffled to their feet. But I thought I'd heard something, and stayed in my chair. I glanced at Wiley and he had, too. It was a lowing sound with a beat, like a chant. Soft at first, it gathered strength, from the left side of the stands and then the right.

"Ocotillo...Ocotillo...

Ocotillo...Ocotillo...."

The antiphonal chant grew louder in the crowd, till it thundered in a climax: OCOTILLO U!

I walked along with Wiley to the admin building. "My God," I breathed, "what a mystical moment. Talk about transcendence, uplifted to another realm... that spontaneous chant."

He turned to me with a wry grin. "It was uplifting, all right. You got 'em outta their shoes. But, 'spontaneous?' Hell, you never been to a ball game? That's the Ocotillo shout."

I guess it should have come as no surprise that Walter Driscoll made for the head of the table when we walked into the presidential conference room. But Manny Moreno would have none of it. He put him on his left, with Wiley on the right hand side. Teresa sat at the far end and Driscoll peered down at her.

"And who might you be?" he asked, before the meeting had even begun.

She said, "You'll find out soon enough. Señor Moreno, I'd like to suggest that we invite a reporter, perhaps Jessica Madrid of the San Vicente Herald, or possibly record this session."

"I think that's a good suggestion, Ms. Ramirez," he said. "I've heard you're a journalist. And, Doctor Driscoll, this is Teresa Ramirez, who teaches here at OCU. Teresa, this is..."

"Doctor Walter Driscoll, president emeritus of this institution," Driscoll started, until Wiley cut him off.

"I've never heard anyone call you that. Matter of fact, I don't believe you ever officially resigned. Seems like you just cut and run one day, more or less like your successor..."

"Gentlemen, I believe we need to proceed on a more professional basis," Moreno intervened. "Now, Claire, will you please contact Ms. Madrid at the Herald. And, while you're at it, let's count noses, and call in an order for chimi-changas from the Raven's Roost. I have a feeling we're going to be here for some time."

I was sitting down at the far end, toward Teresa, and I didn't want to gawk, but I sensed the room was pretty full. I supposed there were a few of the SOCO faculty members from the Columbus debacle on hand, and the other trustees, though I didn't know any of them.

"Now, I want to suggest a way to proceed," Moreno continued. "I've had all of 15 minutes to come up with this format, so if anyone has any suggestions, fire away. But, first, I want to say that this is an open forum that has to do with...oh, good, welcome, Jessica from the paper, and here's the person to set up the sound equipment. I'll wait while you do that."

Five minutes later, he started again. "And so, we are here to begin to resolve the matter of our presidency, in the absence of our incumbent and the strange circumstances of his disappearance the other night in Columbus. While this is not at this point a legal proceeding, I have asked Sheriff Escobedo, an experienced investigator, to conduct this hearing, and I shall turn the meeting over to him at this point."

If the sheriff had let his hair down for a moment during the graduation exercises, it was back in place again, along with his funereal frown. "Not a legal proceeding, all right," he began, "but I will say this: if at any time, a question of criminal culpability arises—if I have any suspicion that a violation of law has taken place, I will stop this process faster than a bar fight at a baptism."

There was a bit of tittering, but not for long.

"Now, as for what went on in Columbus the other night, the first item on my agenda is to find a credible witness—someone who was present for all the events that transpired, but not directly involved."

He asked for the hands of those who were there, queried each of us, and quickly settled on the one person who appeared to meet his criteria. It was Teresa.

"And, so, you saw the person we now know to have been Walter Driscoll leave the library by a side door as the mob began to form. And then Connor Ransom, you say, became caught up in the crowd. And the black car pulled up in front of the building, with Driscoll at the wheel. And, then, did you see what happened?"

"I couldn't see clearly, from where I was standing," Teresa said. "You'll have to ask the two of them."

"I appreciate that response," the sheriff said. "It's always refreshing to find a candid witness, and rare. Oh, and by the way. What were you doing down there that night, Ms. Ramirez, in the first place?"

For one of the few times in my history with Teresa, I saw her stumble.

"Why, I came down with my partn...my friend, Linda Lucero, to see what might happen to Sterling Holmes."

"And why was that?"

She gave a wry smile and said, "Evidently you don't know very much about the tenure of Sterling Holmes."

As the recording would reflect, the proceedings were broken by a burst of laughter.

"And—Ms. Lucero, why was she there?"

"I believe you'll have to ask her. She is not a member of the faculty and, hence, is not at this meeting."

"Point, serve. And so, we are left with Doctor Driscoll at the wheel of the Lexus, the passenger door ajar, and Connor Ransom who was pushed to the head of the mob, confronting him. Is that what you saw, Ms. Ramirez?"

"That's accurate."

"So, we'll turn to the two parties involved. Doctor Driscoll, are you acquainted with Doctor Ransom?"

"Acquainted? Hell, I hired him to his position."

The sheriff's jaw dropped, along with his pen. "Time out!" he hollered. "Turn off the recorder."

For the next half-hour, Walter Driscoll and I were interrogated individually by Escobedo in the president's inner sanctum, to determine that, when Sterling Holmes flopped into the front seat of the Lexus, the two of us had not been in collusion.

It was an exhausting experience, and when I returned to the conference room, I grabbed the makings of a chimichanga and took my seat down near the end of the table.

The sheriff signaled for the recording to resume and actually flashed a smile. It seemed the questioning had not fatigued him. "Well, having got to know our esteemed academics here, I have concluded that, based on the quality of their relationship and the extent of their recent communication, the two of them couldn't mount a conspiracy to kidnap my cleaning lady."

Again, the recording was delayed considerably by laughter.

"And so, Doctor Driscoll, what were your reasons for ushering Doctor Holmes off from the library?"

"I wanted to preserve his safety, and get him out of that job."

"And did you feel that he wanted to go with you?"

"He was ambivalating."

"He was what?"

"It's a term from my profession, marital therapy. He both did and didn't want to go. He was going back and forth, ambivalent. The technical term is 'ambivalating.'"

"And as for you, Doctor Ransom, I remember hearing something about the condition with which you have been afflicted. What did you call it?"

"'Dissociative amnesia.' But, I'm over it, at least to some extent in this instance. I remember the pressure of the mob behind me, and seeing Sterling Holmes fall into the car."

"And, Doctor Driscoll, where, then, did you take Doctor Holmes? I believe we've established that Doctor Ransom saw you turn toward the border."

"I drove him several hours to the small Mexican city of Nuevo Casas Grandes, where he checked into a hotel. I heard him inquire about the local bus depot and receive directions to it. Then I turned around and drove back to San Vicente."

"And so the story has an ending," said Manny Moreno, as he got up and walked back toward the head of the table. "Sheriff Escobedo we are so…"

"Not through with you," I interrupted. "I believe there is a question or two still unresolved."

"Well, of course, there is the matter of your employment," Moreno said with an ominous smile.

I said, "Perhaps, but now that I've been doing such a good job of reminiscing, I'm going back to those presidential interviews at the start of fall term. There's something about the way you kept looking up at the audio visual booth, as the candidates were up on stage."

"I remember that, too," said Teresa. "It was like you were taking cues from somebody. And then the way this hokey finalist appeared. I never have been able to figure that out. How the hell does a university come up with a president like Sterling Holmes?"

The recording will reflect a pregnant pause. And then a clear voice rang out from the back of the room. "I believe I have the answer."

25

"And you are?" It was Sheriff Escobedo, back in charge.

"Doctor Lisa Nordeen, associate professor of sociology at Ocotillo U. Then she added, sotto voce, "Acting. I'm a newly appointed member of the faculty. My contract took effect last Friday, and I have it in my hand. I have taken an interest in this case for the past few weeks, and have some information that I'd like to share with you."

"Please do," the sheriff said, remarkably warm. "Come take a seat up here at the table. Welcome to San Vicente. And, as for your contract, why, we take you at your word."

Lisa sat beside me as Teresa took her in. Her face bore as many mixed emotions as I can recall on any human being—an apparent ally to her cause, but hardly at a personal level.

"I went on a database called Questia, which has something like nine million articles, and started searching for recent sources of grants. 'The Shrub Foundation' came up under the heading of 'incentivizing.'"

"What?" the sheriff asked. "I thought I was bilingual, but what sort of language is that?"

Lisa laughed. "I'm afraid it's a form of 'sociologese.' The grant turned out to be a study of human motivation oriented to educational policy—in other words, how to motivate teachers and students to behave in a desired direction. So that was part of what I found out."

"But there was more?"

"The 'principal investigator' who had been awarded the grant was a 'Walter Driscoll.' And one thing more. The subject of his study was the faculty of Ocotillo U."

"How much was the grant for?"

"About a quarter of a million dollars."

A whoosh went through the room.

The sheriff put his pen down and looked around. "Doctor Driscoll, I guess the floor is yours. And, Mr. Moreno, I doubt that you're excused."

There was a minute of silence.

Finally, Walter Driscoll spoke, in a low voice. "Nobody knows the kind of hell I went through in this institution, the way they brought me in to mediate between these factions—the SOCO and the GOCO—these guys that had been screwing each others' wives for all those years, didn't do any research, couldn't get jobs any other places. So they stuck me in the middle and sliced me up like a sausage.

"I couldn't get anybody to be dean, had to do that job as well as my own, till I found Connor here to take it over. And, of course, it cut into my first love, my consulting practice. So, one day I was leafing through the Chronicle of Higher Education and I saw this notice for the grant. Never heard of the Shrub Foundation, but there it was. I applied for the grant, and got it: had plenty of background in human motivation.

"And Ocotillo U was a ready-made lab. All the underhanded incentivization going on: McNulty's stratagem for culling his classes before the evaluations came out, then doing high-level stuff with the students who were left. And the professors who would sanitize their courses for the teenage students—the kind of thing where Connor got caught in the wringer."

"So you took a place that was basically a powder keg—a dysfunctional environment, a problem you couldn't solve, and you got a grant to study it? But why didn't you tell anybody what was going on?" asked Wiley. Then he answered his own question. "Oh, I get it. You would have ruined the experiment."

Driscoll nodded.

"And how did that lead to Sterling?" Teresa followed, sputtering. "Why did you have to make this tenuous situation twenty times more unstable?"

"Well, what I wanted to do was simply let life go on," Driscoll continued. "Study the issues that would evolve, SOCO versus GOCO, try to understand what was motivating the conflicts and whether, by modifying some incentives, that might be changed. I needed to take myself out of the equation at the outset, which I gladly did.

"The grant paid a lot more than being president, and I was more than ready to retire. But I needed to stabilize the environment: put someone at the top who would serve as an uncomplicated ideologue, represent the philosophy of the Shrub Foundation. I figured I could find someone like that at their Florida Historic University."

Wiley muttered, "Which you sho 'nuff did."

"And what was the payoff for OCU?" I asked, turning to Moreno.

He was a worm on the hook, wriggling. "There were financial considerations that it would not be appropriate to go into at this time. Let's just say, we were well compensated."

"As was Walter Driscoll," Teresa snorted.

"If you don't mind my asking," Lisa spoke up. "Isn't it unusual that a university this size could be manipulated this way for two hundred fifty thousand dollars?"

Moreno fell silent. Then finally he said, "With a gift of this kind, there is always the prospect of more—although I'm sure the good dean has probably settled that matter for us." He gave me a baleful glare.

Teresa exploded. "So you would tie us to an outfit like the Shrub Foundation because a guy like Walter Driscoll got you a grant like that! And all the while, you have a half-Hispanic institution, serving the fastest-growing minority in the nation. You don't think are other sources of funding out there for the kind of work we do? Why, do you even have a director of development? If not, I can sure enough tell you I have one in mind."

As my mind flashed on Linda Lucero, Wiley spoke up softly. "Hey, ease up on the brother, Mutha Teresa. You know, we all gotta live here in this town."

I saw her shrug and smile as the room relaxed in laughter. And I recognized at that moment who would be the next president of Ocotillo U.

"But something still bothers me," I said. "What really went on with Sterling Holmes? When you decided to go down to Columbus and confront him? And what's become of him?"

"What do you mean, Connor?" Teresa blurted out. "Why in the world would you care?"

I said, "I'm not sure I can answer that. But I worked with him twice, you know."

Driscoll paused for a moment. Then he said, "His notion of The Accountable University reflected the philosophy of the Shrub Foundation very well. We could track the motivations of certain players on campus under that rubric, and his vision never faltered. Although, as time went on, the innovations he tried to introduce seemed to exacerbate the conflicts on campus, fan the flames. I watched the growing controversies with interest, and some appreciation."

I shuddered, and saw Wiley shake his head. He said, "You really meant to see this place go up in flames."

Driscoll suddenly turned tense. "Do you think I was playing with Monopoly money? The people who funded me are serious. They want to see results in education, based on incentives. So I watched the rising rancor with some satisfaction and objectivity, now that I was out of the line of fire. I began to see it all more clearly. Until, one day, I had a kind of revelation."

There was a soft rap at the door and Claire came in. She said, "Sheriff, a call for you."

He scraped back his chair. "Hold that thought," he told Driscoll.

The room fell into a long, unsettling silence.

Finally, the door swung open and the sheriff went back in action. "Busting up the Hanover Outpost," he muttered, shaking his head. "Blowing off steam after commencement."

"Leave it to the students," someone scoffed and another snorted.

"I'm afraid not," the sheriff muttered, and frowned. "It was the faculty again. Some fool stood up to that behemoth of an athletic director, I guess over some fine point of educational philosophy. What's his name? Milo?"

"Aldo," I said. "Aldo Bruski."

"Size of a house," Wiley added.

"At any rate, they've called for an ambulance. My deputy's covering cleanup, waiting to see if anyone's filing charges."

He turned to Driscoll. "So, you said something about a revelation. Is that right?"

Driscoll was smiling faintly. He'd been gazing out the window. "It was a construct that came to me," he confided. "Suddenly I saw a new model of incentivization. Why, one could offer a McNulty approach for academic idealists: let them cut the dead wood from their classes and concentrate on the good students, but pay them less proportionately.

"And then there was Pete Entwhistle's idea of simply passing out cash bonuses to others for student retention. In effect, you could have two schools, two different systems of incentives under the same roof—such an energizing dynamic."

His eyes got bright. "Ocotillo U may become known. You know, the real role of a university isn't intellectual anymore. People can get all the information they want off the Internet— my God, those online courses."

"Not intellectual? What on earth do you mean?" Lisa demanded.

"No, the reason anyone comes to a campus nowadays is for the drama," Driscoll went on. "They want to taste the juices, butt up against others; they want action. And right here the teams are in place, the battle lines are drawn. You want conflict? Ocotillo's got it!"

At this, the whole room fell silent—stunned, I thought, by the enormity of this absurd idea, or else at the prospect that it could possibly be true. What if the school had finally found a niche in the higher education market?

Driscoll's eyes went wide, till he remembered the agenda.

"But back to the grant," he said with a sigh, "and President Holmes. So, the research environment became unstable as certain decisions at the university appeared ethically unsound. I suppose it was that tracking down of defaulters on student loans. Sterling couldn't maintain his upright image. The funders were on the phone."

"And so you cut him loose," I said, as I shook my head.

"And so I drove the car around the library and I opened the door, at which point..."

"You don't have to go on," I told him.

It was about then that the meeting broke up. As I got to my feet, I found myself between Lisa and Teresa in what had all the makings of a Mexican standoff. I introduced the two of them and was trying to think of something to say when Walter Driscoll walked up.

"Ah," he said, as he took in the three of us. "I believe I can see the dynamic here." He reached in his wallet and drew out a card. "Let me leave this with you, Connor, should you require the services of an experienced professional."

I looked at Lisa and Teresa and we broke into a grin.

I said, "Walter, I think we're going to work this out ourselves."

Readers Guide

Chapter 1

What do you think about the way Connor Ransom chose his profession? As the story goes on, do you think we can expect that his life's work will always seem meaningful? But given the traumatic way it began, might his career also turn out to be unstable?

The famed psychiatrist, Carl Jung, once wrote:

"I feel very strongly that I am under the influence of things or questions which were left incomplete and unanswered by my parents and grandparents and more distant ancestors. It often seems as if there were an impersonal karma within a family which is passed on from parent to children. It seemed to me that I had to answer a question which fate had posed to my forefathers, and which had not yet been answered, or as if I had to complete, or perhaps continue, things which previous ages had left unfinished." —C.G. Jung, *Memories, Dreams, Reflections*

Do you know of instances when individuals chose a line of work for the reason Jung describes? As far as you know, did these career decisions work well?

Chapter 2

How would you describe Connor's state of mind in his new profession? Does he appear confident, or insecure?

Does it seem appropriate for a new instructor at a university to be serving as dean of the faculty?

What do you suppose has happened to the president, Walter Driscoll?

Chapter 3

Have you ever known anyone in a support staff position, a la Alice Pendergast, who seemed more powerful than the person they worked for?

Did any of the Buddhist, Islamist, and Christian terms mentioned in this chapter resonate with you? Do you think you might look into one or two of them?

How would you characterize Walter Driscoll, from what you've seen of him so far? Do you think he might return to the story?

Chapter 4

Does Connor's plan to secretly access Alice Pendergast's files raise some ethical concerns? If so, do they seem to upset him?

How does Connor seem to feel about the various religious traditions he calls on when he's under stress? Is he serious about the traditions, or just using them as devices to settle down?

Chapter 5

Is it sometimes counter-productive to learn too much too soon in a new environment? Consider Connor's special dilemma, in that he's spying on the university.

If you're not employed in higher education, have you ever heard of the ploys Wiley is describing: TWI, the McNulty stratagem? If you are a teaching vet, do you know some other tricks of the trade?

Given Connor's voices in the night and other mystical episodes, does it seem that he has an unusually broad range of experience, and/or that he might in fact be suffering from symptoms of post-traumatic stress? How does he appear to regard these experiences?

Chapter 6

There are people who have an ability to go against the grain of any institution that employs them, and strike out on their own. Have you ever known an in-house rebel like Albert McNulty?

Teresa Ramirez seems to be another. As rich and complex as her background has been, what sorts of things might we have yet to learn about Teresa?

Chapter 7

Alice Pendergast suddenly seems to have warmed up to Connor. Do we have any inkling as to why?

Connor's young friend, Aaron, appears hyper-stressed from the pressures of his life and business. What do you think about Connor's take on self-transcendence and incarnation? Are those meaningful ideas today?

Chapter 8

According to William Faulkner, "The past is never dead. It's not even past." Connor
is shocked by the re-appearance of Sterling Holmes, and as his boss, once
again!Have you ever been surprised to discover how much you didn't know
about the personal life of someone older than you and in a position of authority?

What hints do we see that there's more to know about Teresa?

Chapter 9

Sterling's presidency is off to a flying start, with his inspiring quotations on higher
education, along with a few disconcerting thoughts about evaluating what goes
on in this field. Was it a good idea for him to include that stem-winding rhetoric
about acting on our passions? What might have been the significance of the
power outage?

Was Connor wise, as a new administrator, to have expressed his views in the
meeting on athletics?

Chapter 10

Deeper layers continue to unfold in some of Connor's current relationships, even as
he is forming new ones. Were you surprised to learn that: (A) Sterling had had
a hand in Connor's exit out of town, following Ned Nordeen's header off the
bridge and ambiguous note, and that (B) Teresa Ramirez and Linda Lucero have
a complex relationship?

Have you ever been in a job where you felt you were reduced to a "useful fool"? How
do you think Connor handled his assignment, and what were its apparent
consequences?

Chapter 11

Are you acquainted with conflicts in the field of education over "cultural literacy"—what an educated person in American culture ought to know? What do
you think of the argument that more than one culture needs to be taken into
account? Had you heard of the BITCH Test?

As some of the veteran staff members of OCU fall ill, Connor appears to take on the
role of parish minister, caring for them. Does that seem odd, since he has been
away from that line of work for several years? Or do our first callings never fully
leave us, no matter where we go?

Chapter 12

Pressed into constructing a spur-of-the-moment funeral service for Alice Pendergast, Connor deploys an unstructured, Quaker format in which everyone is invited to share their own memories and reflections about the person who has passed away. Have you ever experienced this kind of memorial service? If so, what were your feelings about it?

What do you make of the experiences Connor describes to Teresa in which he seems to transcend or step outside himself? Does it sound like a form of mental illness, as she suggests; or, as he implies, from a spiritual perspective, might there be more to it?

What, or who, do you think is the Source?

Chapter 13

Do some people in leadership roles feel a need to make changes in their institutions, whether or not they're needed? In the case of Sterling, what might be motivating him to do so?

What are the strengths and weaknesses of benchmarking—taking norms from other fields—in trying to effect change in one's own industry?

What are the characteristics of a mentoring relationship, such as Wiley offers Connor? Have you had a mentor?

Chapter 14

Consider the case of Margo Whitehead, recent PhD. Is Wiley correct that "easy" schools aren't easy to teach in, due to the range of skills and personal traits required? What do you think of his analysis of traditional craft trades as applied to education?

Sterling's ambition to transform Ocotillo U evidently knows no bounds, as he seems serious about adopting a medical model of screening faculty members for their competence to teach specific courses. Meanwhile, Teresa's students surreptitiously gather information by covering his speeches around town, while she and Connor learn the big picture of his intentions.

But how can Connor deal with Sterling first-hand, when the man has the power to fire him on the spot for insubordination? And how can he keep his head above water with Teresa? "Get over your 'SGS,'" she would advise. Unfortunately, that "Steady Girlfriend Syndrome" seems embedded in his genes.

Chapter 15

Connor invites his new assistant, Farley, to look into a somewhat dubious project: setting up a relational database to catalog all the skills within the faculty. But Farley is excited by the chance to engage his intellect, and so is Connor's new secretary, Arlene.

Still worried about Sterling's grandiose plans for OCU, Connor asks Wiley for a late afternoon consult on the notes Teresa has put together from his speeches. Apparently in the interests of time, Wiley takes Connor to the Rawhide Bar, an Hispanic hangout where the young dean has a bizarre, Tai Chi bar fight, and then a conference with his mentor on the history of violence in their community. Why did Wiley take him there?

Chapter 16

Connor, it seems, might be in trouble for a bar fight in which he demonstrated a classic Tai Chi move pretty well, but failed to land a punch. He does seem to have learned a little about the role of violence in the history and contemporary culture of San Vicente, and gained some sophistication about the local media.

Based on his response to Connor's encounter with the student's boyfriend, Black Bart Bencomo, does Sterling seem to have much empathy for the life of a college professor?

How do you think Teresa keeps coming up with so much inside data on Ocotillo U? Is it just from her investigative journalistic skills?

What might be the significance of a link between Claire, the president's secretary, and Linda Lucero?

Chapter 17

Now, also from Connor's past, arrives Lisa Nordeen. How does she strike you, in relation to Teresa Ramirez? Do you imagine she might have a different effect on Connor?

How did you respond to Lisa's description of the segments of a woman's life, and the need to stabilize one part of it? Did she give up too much of her professional life, in following Ned?

Why might Sterling have sounded pleased that Connor and Lisa had reconnected?

Chapter 18

Connor continues to behave like a transmogrified (someone whose outward appearance may have changed, but not his essence) minister on occasion, especially with Aaron. What do you think of his conception of faith in contrast to belief?

What do you think of Teresa's diatribe against people who get over-invested in concepts? Do our ideas sometimes get in the way of our experiences?

How do you imagine Connor feels, as Lisa prepares to enter the scene?

Chapter 19

Their relationship sinking to a new level, Connor starts to grasp the scam Sterling has in mind; it is one which, once again, promises to directly involve him. In sending Connor "out the door," does it seem that Sterling has taken the first step toward firing him?

But Connor finds a new arrow in his quiver in the person of Lisa's attorney, Trevor Cranshaw, and the adroit, last-ditch maneuver of the Garcetti Reservation.

Lisa is distraught at Connor's having contacted Cranshaw, lest it jeopardize her pending contract with OCU. (What was it Wiley had said about dealing with two women?) Then she recognizes that she has been falling into a state of "attention blindness" toward the new school, in her haste to get away from her old one. Have you ever suffered from that condition?

Chapter 20

Given the low graduation rate at OCU, the high rate of default on federal student loans among non-grads, and federal penalties on schools that have high rates of default, does looking up ex-students at Ocotillo U, a la Sterling's project, sound like a promising idea?

In recruiting a new group for an event, such as the Ex-travaganza, is there always a risk that the group may cohere and find an agenda of its own?

Once again, Connor assumes a pastoral role with Aaron Fell. What are your feelings about the choice he sets out between suicide and biocide?

Chapter 21

Connor finds himself transported, overnight, from the shadow of death in a hospital room to the heights of Lisa Nordeen's euphoria. As he accompanies her on a tour of prospective rental houses to a hike up Boston Hill, everything in Lisa's new world is glowing. Finally, he decides to bring her back to earth and address the realities of life in San Vicente. Have you ever found yourself, with a friend, in his position?

In a final showdown, Sterling and Connor have it out, and the young dean is fired. Given how the issues at hand had evolved, did Sterling have a choice in the matter? When Connor claims to have lost his world along with his job, does that feeling seem over-blown? Or do some people have that much of their lives tied up in their employment?

Chapter 22

It might be said of Connor that he has a nose for trouble. Have you noticed that every time he's in the presence of some crisis, he runs toward and not away from it? So it is with Sterling's speech in Columbus, New Mexico. Why do you think Connor wants to be there?

What happens when Sterling is pressed against the open car door and Connor reaches his arms out? Is it reminiscent of another incident in Connor's life? Who do you think is driving this car?

Why do you think Teresa and Linda attended Sterling's presentation? Do you have any idea why Connor keeps blacking out in critical situations? As Teresa cares for Connor, along with Linda, do you have a sense that these relationships could be ongoing?

Chapter 23

Connor's head is spinning, following the episode with Sterling, as he was driven off into the night. Had he been rescued from the mob of ex-students? Or kidnapped? Having blacked out, it was hard for him to tell. Connor hopes for his safe return. But would that mean he'll be fired? It's a choice from which there is no good outcome. Can you identify with a situation like that?

Wiley reminds him of a larger issue overhanging Ocotillo U. The elementary school in Columbus, which is providing remarkable bilingual education to hundreds of children crossing the border from Palomas every day, has been subjected to the State of New Mexico's annual evaluation based on standardized tests. And this landmark institution received a grade of F! So much for bi-cultural schools a la OCU, should this same, monolithic movement engulf higher education.

Everything at Ocotillo U comes to a head with a front page story in the paper featuring a photo of a bleary-eyed Connor from the night before, along with a suggestion that he might constitute a good suspect in the disappearance of Sterling Holmes. "There is social truth and visceral truth," Connor reflects, "the appearance of truth and another kind that is really so." How can he negotiate the two?

Chapter 24

Fresh from the crisis in Columbus, the unknown fate of Sterling Holmes, and a sense that his days at Ocotillo U may be few, Connor finds a routine commencement exercise transformed to a transcendent event. Have you ever found yourself suddenly moved to tears by a somewhat ordinary occasion?

The reappearance of Walter Driscoll begins to open the door on many mysterious circumstances of the past academic year, including his relationship with Sterling Holmes. What did you make of the term "ambivalating," which Walter used to characterize Sterling's feelings for his job as president of Ocotillo U? Have you ever felt this way?

What do you think Connor had to do with Sterling collapsing into the passenger seat of the Lexus? Was he more than a passive observer? What about another occasion when he blacked out in somewhat similar circumstances, with Ned Nordeen? What do you think might have happened back then?

Chapter 25

As Walter Driscoll describes his reasons for applying for the Shrub Foundation grant and the misery of his job, can you understand something of his motives? (A university president in the 1960s described his position as "a lone hydrant in a sea of dogs.")

Was there a point where both Walter and the entire school began to lose perspec- tive? OCU was mesmerized by the prospect of getting more funds like the Shrub grant, so anyone who might have known what was going on kept silent. Walter went over the edge with his plans to create more conflict on campus so that he could study it. And all the while, as Teresa notes, funding sources tied to the school's historic mission of Hispanic outreach were ignored. Have you ever seen this kind of situation?

As the story ends, what do you think the lives of the major characters will look like five years down the road? And how about Ocotillo U?